MICHAEL WILDING

Michael Wilding was born in Worcester, read English at Oxford, and has taught literature and creative writing at the University of Birmingham, the University of California at Santa Barbara, and the University of Sydney, where he is emeritus professor. He is author of a dozen volumes of fiction including *The Paraguayan Experiment* (Penguin), *Under Saturn* (Black Swan), *Great Climate* (Faber), *Wildest Dreams* (UQP), *Academia Nuts* (Wild & Woolley) and *Raising Spirits, Making Gold and Swapping Wives: the True Adventures of Dr John Dee and Sir Edward Kelly* (Shoestring), one of the *Economist's* Books of the Year. He is a former *Cosmopolitan* Bachelor of the Month and fellow of the Australian Academy of the Humanities.

ACCLAIM FOR MICHAEL WILDING

'Wilding's writing is rich in humour, fantasy and sharp social observation.' Bruce Bennett, *Contemporary Novelists*.

'Very funny. So funny that I had to stop reading it in bed in case my roars of laughter were disturbing the neighbours: so funny that it deserves to be the final great campus novel. It is unlikely to be challenged. For what Wilding's aged unreconstructed dons are playing with such absurd brio is unmistakably the last waltz.' Laurie Taylor, *THES* on *Academia Nuts*.

'The best of the talent emerging from down under.' *San Francisco Review of Books*

'The literature of challenge rather than the literature of escape.' Chris de Bono, *Melbourne Herald*.

'He is so exhilaratingly adept with narrative you cannot put the book down… Wilding's pen is sharp as a rapier.' Jan Meek, *Vogue Australia*.

'If, like most of us, you've begun to sense that life is not quite so simple, then maybe Wilding is exactly who you should be reading.' David English, *Weekend Australian*.

'Considerable entertainment.' *Times Literary Supplement* on *The Short Story Embassy*.

'Wilding has steadily produced, for over thirty years, work of high and lasting merit…To be a writer like Wilding is to be whole in a sense that should never be lost, not as long as the written word appears between the pages of a literary book.' Don Graham, *Antipodes*.

'A piece of esoterica designed to startle and delight the modern reader.' *The Economist* on *Raising Spirits, Making Gold & Swapping Wives*.

Wild Amazement

Also by Michael Wilding
Fiction
Aspects of the Dying Process
Living Together
The Short Story Embassy
The West Midland Underground
Scenic Drive
The Phallic Forest
Pacific Highway
Reading the Signs
The Paraguayan Experiment
The Man of Slow Feeling
Under Saturn
Great Climate
Her Most Bizarre Sexual Experience
This is for You
Book of the Reading
Somewhere New: New and Selected Stories
Wildest Dreams
Raising Spirits, Making Gold and Swapping Wives: The True Adventures of Dr John Dee and Sir Edward Kelly
Academia Nuts
Non-fiction
Milton's 'Paradise Lost'
Cultural Policy in Great Britain (with Michael Green)
Marcus Clarke
Political Fictions
Dragons Teeth: Literature in the English Revolution
The Radical Tradition (the Colin Roderick lectures)
Social Visions
Studies in Classic Australian Fiction
As editor
Australians Abroad (with Charles Higham)
Three Tales by Henry James
Marvell: Modern Judgements
We Took Their Orders and Are Dead (with David Malouf, Ros Cheney and Shirley Cass)
Marcus Clarke
The Radical Reader (with Stephen Knight)
The Tabloid Story Pocket Book
The Workingman's Paradise by William Lane
Stories by Marcus Clarke
Air Mail from Down Under (with Rudi Krausmann)
The Oxford Book of Australian Short Stories
History, Literature and Society (with Mabel Lee)
Best Stories Under the Sun (with David Myers)
Best Stories Under the Sun 2: Travellers' Tales (with David Myers)

Wild Amazement
Michael Wilding

Shoestring Press

Wild Amazement
© Michael Wilding 2005

This book is copyright. Apart from any fair dealing for the purpose of private study, research, criticism or review, as permitted under the Copyright Act of 1968, no part may be reproduced by any process without written permission. Enquiries should be made to the publisher.

First published in Australia in 2006 by
Central Queensland University Press (Outback Books)
PO Box 1615, Rockhampton, Queensland 4700
Phone: (07) 5552 4960: Fax: (07) 4923 2525
email: d.myers@cqu.edu.au
Web:www.outbackbooks.com

National Library of Australia
Cataloguing-in-Publication entry:
Wilding, Michael, 1942- .
Wild amazement.
ISBN 1 904886 35 3.
I. Title.
A823.3

Set in 11 on 13 pt Bembo by Frank Povah
at The Busy Boordy fpovah@bigpond.net.au

Published in the UK by Shoestring Press
19 Devonshire Avenue, Beeston, Nottingham, NG9 1BS
(0115) 925 1827
www.shoestringpress.co.uk

Printed by Q3 Print Project Management Ltd,
Loughborough, Leics
(01509) 213456

Cover portrait by Edgar Billingham, oil on board, 1968, photograph by Jo Billingham.

This book is generously supported by a grant from the Literature Board of the Australia Council.

All characters in this book are fictitious and any resemblance to persons living or dead is purely coincidental. Some episodes originally appeared in *Antipodes, Best Stories Under the Sun, Journal of Australasian Studies, Newswrite, Oasis, Overland, Quadrant, Social Alternatives, Southerly, Text, Westerly,* the festchrifts for Yasmine Gooneratne and Edwin Thumboo, and on ABC radio, and acknowledgment is gratefully made. *Wild Amazement* is a companion volume to *Wildest Dreams,* a part of *The Literary Pages* sequence.

To Brian & Suzanne Kiernan

Contents

1. Something Else 11
2. War and Pacifism 15
3. On the Road to Stratford 20
4. Early Days 25
5. Amazing Things 42
6. Mere Anarchy 61
7. Man of Letters 69
8. The Legend of Sam Samson 79
9. Asia Hand 86
10. Critical Distance 94
11. Some Dealers 100
12. An Australian Christmas 106
13. Arts Doco 118
14. Nephew's Story 132
15. Symposium 137
16. Somewhere Else 149
17. The Black Rocks 166
18. Not the Last of the Long Hot Summers .. 170
19. Fabled Cities 173

1
Something Else

'Something else,' the shopkeeper in the local delicatessen would say as he supplied each request. Cheese, marmalade, bread, olives, each transaction punctuated with its 'Something else'. There was no mark of interrogation.

It was a simple affirmation, or perhaps even an imperative. There would always be something else. Not all the gorgeous east would ever fill that aching desire. The shop could be emptied of its pastas and its patés, its smoked meats and smoked fish, its pickles and its peppers, its Leibniz biscuits and its Mozart chocolates, its Marvell dried milk powder, its Milton disinfectant, its Borges and its Dante olive oils, its Werther butterscotch and its Shelley's lemonade, but there would always be that yearning for something else.

It took me back. Now I have it, I would tell myself, buying my Stilton cheese and original Oxford marmalade in accord with the precepts of the best authors, now I ate as an English gentleman, albeit in exile.

Now the riches of those English gents' novels could be mine, together with those mysterious exoticisms my Oxford contemporaries had talked of so familiarly, terrines and quiches and frittatas and focaccia, croissants and camembert and brie and bagels, parmesan and pesto and lasagne and cannelloni, gnocchi and minestrone, dolmades and tzatziki, taramosalata and moussaka and melitzanes and pastitsio. Here it all was.

And every something else slid into somewhere else, enshrined the sites of desire, not just the tastes. The flavours of the other, whether the language schools of Italy or the holidays in Provence or the business trips to New York or the study tours of Greece. It wasn't the food. I hadn't starved. We had had egg and bacon pie and Yorkshire pudding, mint sauce and parsley sauce, shepherd's pie and suet pudding, bread and dripping and apple crumble, Blenheims and Bramleys, purple Pershores and yellow egg plums, raspberries and loganberries, rhubarb and gooseberries, all fresh from the garden or near by farms. But these were not the exotic. These were the everyday. And the unappreciated.

Now I appreciate them, but now is not then; now I admire and value and thank, all too belatedly, my parents' provision. But then it was the other I desired, something else, somewhere else.

That was the blight of the Midlands, the eternal yearning to be somewhere else. Landlocked, watching the sun stretch out behind the Malvern hills, or somewhere in that direction, mere topography fades before imaginative recollection, mere topography anyway was never the point of this, whatever was beyond those hills was unknown and purely imaginable.

Well, what lay beyond those hills was Ledbury and then Hereford and then Wales and then the St George's Sea and then Ireland and then the Atlantic and then America. That wasn't the point. There was no specific yearning for Ledbury or Hereford. Or Wales. Or America. Then, as now, America was not an object of desire. There might have been, indeed alas there was, a period in between when it offered its lures. But no longer. And not then. Facing westward, as the blaze of red sank towards the islands of the blest, it was not the islands of the blest we desired. We were not gazing in hopes of Arthur's re-emergence, Excalibur held aloft. We Midlanders had gazed westward well before Arthur took the plunge. He, like all political leaders, was merely capitalising on the legend. West was where everyone looked to, so that's where they rowed him off to and where he said he'd pop back from. The west. But he missed the point. It was not the west we yearned for. It was somewhere else, beyond the Malvern hills, beyond wild Wales, beyond Ireland, beyond the west. Beyond the west it became the east. We reached out with yearning to the further strand like Columbus, but unimpeded by the intrusive interposition of the Americas. Because we knew that in yearning for the setting western sun we yearned for the eastern dawn, and yearning for the rising east we passed beyond it and returned on ourselves, it was ourselves we yearned for, our incompletion, our unfulfilled potential, our unrealised hopes. There was no something else, no somewhere else; or rather the something else was all within. We didn't need something else, we didn't need somewhere else, we had it all *in potentia*. But before we realised that, or before I realised that, presuming to speak only for myself in this, before I realised that, I had sought out my somewhere else, tasting its black bread, its pilsener beers, its clarets and grenaches and shirazes, its moussakas and falafels and borschts and lakhsas and sambals and persimmons and peaches and figs and paw paws and melons, as if I had been starved.

Oh Sydney. It does not have the immediate ring of oh Athens, fair Greece, sad relic. It is not a matter of gender. Oh Paris, oh Georgetown, oh St Petersburg are no less masculine. Masculinist they might even write now. Later, when Sydney became gay centre of the world for ten minutes, the masculine nomination might have seemed apt. But that is the world of Joseph Wendel Holmes and his tales of male tenderness. Some of them, anyhow. Romance with visiting American GIs.

'They were not GIs,' he said, petulantly, pedantically, one of those words. No more they were. So to what service did those lithe young men in mufti belong? Joe never said. He never said so many things, despite his commitment to the word. And when I began to wonder we were no longer communicating. In those early days, those early stories, it was first remarked by Weil the bookseller. Loudly in the old Malaya restaurant, his hairy arms, that had carried so many boxes of remaindered books, spread all over the formica table, noodle strands from the lakhsa drooped from his revolutionary beard, and a heated over-excitement steamed in his porno-business eyes. 'You know who buys your fucking poofy stories, Joe? Fucking poofters, that's your market mate. They sidle up the back and lisp, "That Australian writer who writes short stories?" "Henry Lawson?" "No, that's not quite the name, more modern than that." They lap you up, if that's the right word. They think you're modern, you've got a profitable line there, mate.'

Weil sold Marxist classics and pornography, all part of the struggle. There was no doubt a camera concealed somewhere in his shop or in the upper window of the shop opposite that photographed your comings and goings, for in those days, like these days, there were not many shops that sold the Marxist classics nor, in those days, many shops that sold pornography, unlike these days. Joe seemed unamused. Not much less than total adulation amused him, nor was he alone in that, it was just part of the profession. And Weil's sneering, heckler's whine could never be interpreted as adulatory.

This was before Joe had come out, too, insofar as he ever did come out, before popping back in, like Mr and Mrs whatever their name is in the weatherhouse, one or the other coming out depending on the climate, never the two aspects in sight together.

So, oh Sydney. It might have had its homoerotic appeal to Joe's readers, like oh Jamestown, oh Williamsburg, oh Port Stevens, oh San Francisco, oh Isle of Man. A gazetteer could be compiled. But after sufficient iteration the sound mutates, the associations change, spin off or coagulate, recoalesce with new signification, signifying only itself now, its own icon, oh Sydney.

Other times I have chosen to think it was young Sir Philip himself who is commemorated so. That it was a later relative is immaterial. Same name, same family, the tradition carried on. The Sydney school of creative writing. That was the principle I followed, I would say, and still do, when asked, all too often. Look in your heart and write. What other way? What do you expect? Gaze into Weil's cash register and compute? Some took that path and where are they now? America. Some looked into their other organs. Joe, now, my old friend, ally I hesitate to say, enemy I sometimes feared, what bit is in his eye when he, with decreasing frequency, writes, dinner-jacketed in the Gothic splendours of the old college of buggers and spies?

'They must have read my books,' he said, 'that must be why they invited me.'

Poor Joe, he retains that touching belief that people read his books, that naive trust that the old world cares about the cultural production of the new. England, my England.

Well, he will find out. Anyway, that is safely in the fenny draughts of Cambridge. But Sidney was an Oxford man, however briefly. Our muse. Builder of our nest of singing birds. Only begetter of our epigraphic line, our work's motto, our shield's impresa.

I am not I, pity the tale of me.

2

War and Pacifism

Back in England back in time, a memory theatre of growing up there, all the struggles and resistances after the new world sense of freedom, back to accent, class, place.

How far back do you want to go? How much about childhood do you want to read? Running across the road in front of a convoy of tanks. A childhood of wartime: though not of war. It wasn't an episode I ever remembered myself, though I was told about it a few times. A few times: it didn't have the status of myth, nothing had the status of myth. My father's favourite book of the Bible was Ecclesiastes. It was not a good basis for parental support in the material world of capitalism red in tooth and claw. All is vanity. Myth a lie. Success unattainable, or if attained evanescent, corrupted. My father's favourite hymn was 'The day thou gavest, Lord, is ended, The darkness falls at thy behest.' We waited for the darkness. It always came.

'It was my gesture of opposing war,' I used to say, later, in my CND days. The war was remote. It hadn't impinged on us in its violence. I would hurtle down the garden path and scurry into the house when flights of aircraft came low overhead, off to bomb Coventry, or to intercept the bombers. Later I would hurtle out of the house to try and read the registration numbers on the wings or fuselage. But that was after the war. We used to get booklets that had lists of all the serial numbers of Midland Red buses, one after the other. When we saw a bus we would underline the serial number in the book. We tried collecting aircraft serial numbers too, but it wasn't often they flew low enough to read the registrations. I tried to compile my own master list, the registration of every aircraft that had ever flown. I had the letters, all I needed were the makes and marks of the aircraft themselves. Did it count if you saw the registration in a film or television? We didn't have television or often go to films. Sometimes I would see a serial number on the fuselage of an aircraft being taken by articulated lorry along the main road. Did a fragment count, a substantial fragment?

I would fly myself to bed at night, taking off from the dining room table in a twin-engine Dinky, vroom vroom, climb up the stairs, bank round the landing, land in the bathroom, refuelling stop while I cleaned my teeth, then take off again from the ceramic shelf beneath the mirror, off to bed.

For a while the prisoners of war had hoed in the fields at the back of the house, thin, stooped men in ill-matched clothes, hoeing away amidst the stones and crops.

My father had been too young for the First World War and too old for the Second. And he was working in a protected industry, old enough for that, leaving school at twelve. And there was a strong anti-militarist spirit in the family. My grandfather had refused to work Saturdays during the First World War because, at that point, he was a Seventh Day Adventist, which took some sticking out, my father said, not working on Saturday in the war. So there was a generally anti-war line. When it came to joining the school cadet force, one of the rites of puberty, I said I wasn't going to.

'Why not?' my father said.

'I'm a pacifist.'

There was a book in the house, *Vain Glory*, about the slaughter of the First World War, and I would read it to fuel my stand. It was a stand my parents were not very sympathetic to. This on top of trying to evade school games all the time. I was a bit torn. I would have liked to have gone into the air-force cadets and spotted aircraft. But you had to go through the army cadets first. Doing drill in the playground Friday afternoon, blancoing belts, brassoing buckles. There wasn't much pressure. 'I'm against militarism,' I explained to the commanding officer.

'Well, I'm not sure joining the corps is militarism.'

'I think it is,' I said.

I was drafted to the gardening squad, weeding the flowerbeds outside the headmaster's Georgian house. It was a predominantly lower-class crew. Not high-minded idealists there, I was sad to find out. Not the sensitive poets writing critiques of the system, but C-stream boys from working class families, not the aristocracy of labour but the resistant, sceptical, cynical non-collaborators, skivers, dodgers, idlers, those who refused to do a decent day's work, those who did not take on the school spirit, a work gang of the marginalised, the malingerers, the delinquent, not officer-material. Had I really thought it would have put me with the idealists given belated recognition and carved in marble and lain in shrines?

Then I was plucked out of the gardening squad and seconded to the school secretary. There were a couple of other boys from the year ahead in the same position. They worked the duplicating machine.

'The machine-gun of the revolution,' said Gordon.

They ran off documents the secretary gave them, put on stencils, loaded the ink tubes, wiped down the machine. They made inventories of the book store. Locked away in it, Gordon would take in hand my political education, his glasses dropping down his button nose and pushed back up again with his forefinger as he giggled at some administrative absurdity in the school.

I wasn't trying to be an outsider. I wanted to be loved, respected, accepted. I did the tasks efficiently. I proof-read the school prize-giving programme. First step into applied literary ability, first participation in the machinery of literary production. I found that the school's motto, sperno mutare, I spurn to change, had been printed spermo mutare, so I corrected it and felt proud of detecting error in an official document and of satisfactorily fixing it up for authority.

'Damn,' said Gordon, unpacking the bundles of prize-giving programmes. 'They noticed.'

'They couldn't have,' said John.

'Noticed what?' I asked.

'We changed the motto last year but they've gone and changed it back again. We thought we'd introduced a bit of obscenity for at least a decade. Spermo mutare is so much more suggestive, don't you think?'

I blushed.

'Oh, we didn't know you were so sensitive.'

I blushed easily. But I said nothing. I felt stupid. I tried to persuade myself I'd done the right thing, correcting error, minutely scrutinising for mistakes. But I felt stupid. I was not a natural anarchist though I was beginning to recognise the appeals of subversion. I felt negative, reactive, undoing the achievements of the creative imagination. And I felt guilty, not admitting that I was the one who had made the change. But I couldn't admit it, I would look so stupid and puritanical and conformist. I could imagine Gordon's reaction: 'You should apply for late admission into the army corps. You're missing your vocation here.'

The Midlands. 'O pastoral heart of England,' Quiller-Couch intoned on Eckington bridge. The dead centre, we intoned sardonically. We wanted to get away and if you couldn't get away you could imagine that there was somewhere else that existed and one day you might get to it.

A. E. Housman, for instance. *The Shropshire Lad*. He wasn't a Shropshire lad, old Bill, the English master told us, he was a Worcestershire lad. Shropshire was that somewhere else he could look across to. 'In summertime on Bredon my love and I would lie and see the coloured counties.' Counties. In the plural. Not just one, but others, there were others.

My father and grandfather had always read a lot. Grandfather had been liable to take days off work to read Walter Scott and Fennimore Cooper. That was deemed excessive. But reading was an approved activity. I wanted to be able to do something approved. So I read books to dream of other lives and got locked onto the idea of the books themselves as much as any lives they described; the lives I especially liked were the lives of books, the artist as a young man, the artist emergent, I would be a writer.

'If you were going to be a writer you'd have written books by now,' my mother said.

'There's no money in being a writer,' said my father.

I took no especial notice of them, it was no different from their reactions to anything else. It was depressing and demoralising but that was no different either. And having take up my position, I locked myself into it. That was it. A writer.

With the skills acquired at the duplicator we started a magazine, Ali and I, Ali another dissident who had refused to join the corps. We called it *Grendel*. A monster defeated by the first English epic hero could not be all bad. It wasn't utterly clear whether we were on the side of the defeated or the monsters. I suspect that Ali preferred the monsters. But already we had rejected the heroes along with the other leaders, warriors, sportsmen.

We designed it as an alternative to the official school magazine, undercutting it in price, offering more contentious and topical material. I wrote a story about the compulsory cross-country runs; somebody slipping on the icy towpath of the canal, breaking a limb and freezing to death. Tich, the master in charge of cross-country running said he was sympathetic to our endeavours but some things had to be done and this only made it more difficult. He was a socialist. As far as we knew the only socialist on staff, though that was not the sort of thing, being socialist, staff members would have publicised.

Tich told us about the architecture of banks. The reason banks had huge granite blocks facing the street and framing their doorways was to give the illusion of solidity in order to lure you to deposit your money with them. It was a revelation, that architecture was an ideology, that bricks and mortar and granite blocks were a rhetoric, that the concrete was an illusion. This was at the time that banks no longer built with granite blocks but projected a modern image of steel frames and glass curtain walling. Revelations are always about the old; the present ever awaits demystification. And in the Midlands we still lived in the past, amidst the provincial banks and the narrow workers' cottages. 'Look at the doorways of working peoples' houses, a slit in a wall to crawl home through, and compare that with the great porticos of the banks. What does that tell you about society?' Now my environment became fraught with significance, the social embedded in the visual. When I set my lonely protagonists in a story now, the rows of houses conveyed the message of social oppression, the proud porticoes the aggressions of power and money and status.

We sold *Grendel* along the morning bun queue when the school lined up to buy doughnuts or dripping cakes or buns to eat with their free milk. We financed a second issue by selling advertisements round shops in town. If some shops bought space under the illusion it was the official magazine they were supporting, it was not from explicit deception. But it helped the finances. After the second issue we liquidated the venture and spent the profits on buying a batch of Penguins and Pelicans and dividing them between us. I bought one on modern architecture and learned about modernism and functionalism and swallowed the claim that these styles were not only new but real, modern and true, honest. No more phoney granite blocks. All was now straight lines, Le Corbusier rectangles. The rest of the profits Ali spent on subscribing to the National Party, the British Union of Fascists. It was oppositional, like Grendel; and monstrous, like Le Corbusier. Since he was a boarder at the school, he used my address for his subscription. My father complained bitterly at what the mail delivered.

3

On the Road to Stratford

Membership of the Adam Lindsay Gordon Society was a step on the path of literary aspiration. We stayed back after school under the tutelage of the English master and read from our own work in a deserted classroom. But the invitation to the Shakespeare Reading Society was the mark of acceptance, reading from the works of Shakespeare on a Sunday evening in the Headmaster's house. This was the entrée to the higher world of culture and French words. French windows, too, opening out onto the croquet lawn from the long, low Georgian house, the trace of medieval monastic ruins beyond the grass at one end, the stand of horse chestnut trees at the other, and the Headmaster intoning Hamlet, Prince Hal, Lear, Macbeth, Othello. This was as the world would be, privilege, exclusivity: and the girls from the private school over the wall brought in to read the few girls' parts. Knees together on the long, low couch. The Headmaster opposite in his arm chair. We attendant lords from the sixth form on straight-backed, hard, auxiliary seating.

'It is his attempt to demonstrate that he is not a philistine,' said Gordon.

The attendant lords discuss the Head.

'In this, as in all else, he fails,' said John.

'A career built securely on the sure foundations of failure,' said Gordon.

Gordon was chubby, snub-nosed, cynical, beyond illusion, the son of refugee German Jews. John was local working-class, lived too near the back gate of the school so everyone could place him in his proletarian context. They were the outsiders who, no less than the Headmaster, were concerned to demonstrate that they were not philistines. Far from it. Not aesthetes, not like Kemp who wore his overcoat loose over his shoulders like a cloak and sported a carnation. They found Kemp as amusing as the Head. Non sporting, non members of the

Officer Training Corps, they controlled entry to outsiderdom. They transformed exclusion into exclusivity, and if you wanted to participate in that you had to knock on their door.

The Headmaster had been a runner. Not much else was known about him. Nothing said, anyway.

'He is certainly not known as a scholar,' said Gordon.

But he had run in the Berlin Olympics.

'We cannot blame the rise of the third Reich on his failure in the 440 yards,' said Gordon.

'But we will,' said John.

'Ah yes, we will,' said Gordon.

'I thought he won the race,' I said.

They looked at me wearily.

'How could you?' said Gordon. 'His capitulation to Nazi might prefigured the ignominy of appeasement.'

Under the banner of pacifism they refused to join the Officer Training Corps, but that did not prevent their decrying appeasement. I absorbed the contradictions silently. If they were contradictions. So many issues never seemed to become clear.

'Do we imply,' said Gordon, 'that he was suborned by Nazi gold to throw the race? And to assure Hitler that he had nothing to fear from Britain?'

'Or was he suborned by Churchill to throw the race, and to lure Germany into aggression, so Churchill could have his finest hour?' suggested John.

'Why not both?' suggested Gordon. 'Why should we imagine he was so scrupulous as to take money from only one side?'

'But where has the money gone?' asked John. 'Where are the evidences of wealth beyond Swiss dreams?'

'Blackmail?' suggested Gordon. His eyes twinkled. It was a delightful thought. Behind the Georgian façade, behind the drawn curtains, the Headmaster sits at his desk, his head in his hands, another letter of demand fallen to the carpet.

'Or the Rolls-Royce.'

'Oh, it must be the Rolls-Royce,' said Gordon.

It was the Headmaster's splendid assertion. That and playing the French horn in the school concerts. Badly, Gordon would insist, don't funk out on the adverb. And intoning Hamlet, Prince Hal, Lear, Macbeth, Othello, etc. The Rolls.

An old Rolls. It was still possible to pretend, at that time, that an old Rolls was the best Rolls.

But this 1924 model? No, the pretence was sad. All of a piece with the bad, balding Hamlet, the risible white-face Othello.

It stood on the gravel sweep before the Georgian façade.

'He gets his wife to push it out of the garage first thing in the morning,' the boarders claimed, or at least the dissident ones. 'The battery's flat and it won't start. So they push it. She got the milkman to help her last time.'

'Or is the Rolls the cover?' said Gordon. 'To conceal the fact of the blackmail? Indeed the blackmailers may have blackmailed him into buying the Rolls at a grossly inflated price as part of their scheme.'

It seemed not impossible.

Nothing seemed impossible. Not after an invitation to the Shakespeare Reading Society.

So there I sat. Waiting on my half-dozen lines. The anxiety of the debut. The agony of the straight-backed uncushioned chair. And around me polite manners, art and culture, private school girls. All that you could ever desire in England. There it all was encapsulated. Authority, status, art, sex, the inextricables, the future. And the Headmaster declaiming 'Oh that this too too solid flesh would melt' in his sensitive, strangulated vowels. To show us how to speak. Though there was no attempt at formal instruction, no lesson in elocution. It was as if he felt that we were what we were and it was best not to put a veneer of anything superior on this dull, resentful, provincial backwater. That way headmasterly superior distance was preserved.

For it was superiority he projected, the ruling class descending on this Midland outpost. And how could we see then, with no experience, no bearings, no points of comparison, that this was just the sad pretension of the under usher, the hired hand? He had taught at a minor public school before becoming our Headmaster. Just one of the lackeys of the system. That perhaps was why he was so cut off, so fractured, so neurotically unapproachable.

But he presented, and it was accepted, an image of the superior being, come to civilise this country bumpkin grammar school. He was not loved for it. Nor was there anything to respect. His Henry V was delivered to a room of Falstaff's cronies, young of heart and body but full of a resentment beyond their years. His Hamlet was assessed with the clear cold vision of the English master's gravedigger, Gordon and John's Rosencrantz and Guildenstern. Hearing his Othello our sympathies embraced Iago, admiring someone who could so effortlessly bring such an icon down. In Lear his ravings seemed typecast, despite a lack of grandeur or gravitas.

'The reason he invites in girls from next door to play the female parts is not only to discourage incipient transvestism,' said Gordon, 'but to prevent the enthusiasm with which we would play Goneril and Regan. Our contempt and loathing would be too apparent. What wouldn't you give for a shot at Lady Macbeth?'

Outside the French windows the midges and gnats spiralled in their dance of death. The hedgehogs snuffled for worms at the lawn's edge. Oh come into the garden Maud. But the girls sat in an unapproachable row. When the headmaster's wife brought in the execrable coffee in the minute English porcelain cups the Headmaster and the English master fraternised with the young ladies. We other ranks sat rigid on the upright chairs, all effort concentrated into not spilling, not dropping, not breaking the fragile cups rattling on their fragile saucers.

Oh art, oh culture. Oh literature. Was it better than crouching over the radio, listening to the Third Programme late at night, the sound turned down to its lowest so as not to keep my father awake who had to rise at six for his job, physical labour, filth and grime, real work, the cultural mission of the BBC, noble as it proclaimed itself, broadcast too late for such proletarian licence-payers to appreciate? One way or another culture, that liberation of the human spirit to which I aspired, into which I wished to soar and fly and be absorbed, involved a lot of discomfort. A discomfort inextricably linked with class, class perceptions, class roles, class possibilities. I might have learned from that. Or I might have suppressed it. Or I might have suppressed it and learned subconsciously. The slow incubation of an English disease. No wonder I followed Adam Lindsay Gordon to Australia.

It was on the road to Stratford that the Headmaster's Rolls broke down.

'Probably the very spot that Shakespeare stopped to have a piddle,' said Gordon.

The Forest of Arden, or the razed remnants of its perimeter, stretched out beneath us to one side. On the other traffic whizzed by. The headmaster's voice got higher and wheezier, choked with emotion and exhaust fumes.

'Maybe it's the carburettor, sir,' said John. 'Did these old models have carburettors, sir?'

The Headmaster walked away from our help.

'Maybe it's out of petrol,' said Gordon. 'Maybe the money he collected for petrol was to pay the blackmailers.'

Yes, the Headmaster had collected contributions for petrol from his impoverished proletarian and refugee charges. I found it unbelievable. No less unbelievable than my father found it. On that salary. But I paid up. We always paid up.

It was my first lesson in the household economics of the bourgeoisie. Until then I had believed impoverishment and penny-pinching were the unique preserve of the working class. That was their destiny, that was the doom I had to escape. It was a delusion I continued to hold despite this early evidence to the contrary.

The Headmaster fumed. He glared at his watch as he waited for the Royal Automobile Club patrolman to arrive.

'I'm sure we'll get there before the curtain rises, sir,' said Gordon, at his most oleaginously and least persuasively conciliatory.

'It's not the damn play, we'll miss the race,' snapped the Headmaster.

The play was the thing to get us to pay the petrol money. What the Headmaster wanted was to attend the regatta in the afternoon. Cheer on the school boat. Hobnob with other Headmasters from Headmasters' Conference Schools. Park his Rolls beside their Ford Consuls and Standard Vanguards and other such vulgarities of mass production. Before an evening at the Shakespeare Memorial Theatre.

'Maybe we should ask for a refund,' suggested Gordon. 'So we can catch the train back. To be sure of getting home.'

'Lucky we weren't taking the crew, sir,' said John.

The rowers had gone earlier in the rowing master's car and the deputy coach's car. They wouldn't be staying on for any play. We were just the rabble in the Rolls. Stage soldiers to walk round the back and out the front again. No wonder we had to pay for our petrol. We filed past the Rolls, peering in at its open bonnet, and round the back of it, like bad extras, over-acting our concern at the overheated, out of petrol, fallen piece of tragic hubris. The Headmaster glowered at us. We walked round again.

'A Ford, a Ford, my Headmastership for an Anglia,' said Gordon.

4

Early Days

'Often when we think we are writing one thing we are in fact writing something else,' Joe intoned, more than once. 'What you consciously devise is not where your unconscious is taking you,' he elaborated. For all his cultivation of the Lawson laconic mode of Australian demotic, he was often drawn to elaborate. Perhaps it was the potentiality for the exploitation of this that he envied in my academic employment, perhaps in his secret dreams he would have liked to have stood there, capped and gowned, elaborating in panelled halls. Well, now he has his opportunity in that college of buggers and spies. His words, I hasten to add. Though the teaching component of the fellowship, he told me, was something he had managed to have waived for his tenure. It was the teaching component that had made the fellowship so unattractive, certainly to me. That would have discouraged me from applying for it, had it ever been advertised. But apparently there was no advertisement. It was cosied up by invitation. Joe was never one to advocate public examinations and careers transparently open to talent. Competition, market forces, all that ideology that he proclaimed, was for the others. Indeed it was properly, precisely, an ideology: something that masked the true workings of society. Even its originators and progenitors could be heard to complain that it had never in fact been introduced into practice. It had remained a slogan to mystify the middle class masses, and Joe had been one of the happy advocates, though surely he must have known in the depths and shallows of his cynicism that things were never done like that, that society functioned on a system of deals and favours and controls and patronage, and the wise positioned themselves in order to benefit from the system.

So I am uncertain what it is that I am writing about Joe, uncertain indeed whether he is the subject or the pretext, and whether to plunge into recollection of times eating and drinking with him will result in my resurfacing in some other sea, or watercourse, carried by the current along one of those subterranean, even submarine, passages, rising up with surprise in the fountain Arethuse having submerged unawares in the sacred river Alf. Well, we shall see. Perhaps. In the meantime it is of Joe that I write.

Speaking to Joe recently by telephone – no longer do we meet, take lunch together, drink together; indeed rarely do we communicate telephonically, but I had rung to suggest lunch, which he declined – I suggested perhaps, if he were uncertain what now to write, if, as he was indicating, writing fiction became only harder, not easier, as one continued, that he might write his memoirs. He was appalled. Appalled silence and appalled expostulation struggled for simultaneous expression, enacting all the difficulties he confessed now to encounter with his writing. I had not realised I had made so lucky a hit, if lucky hits were the basis of our relationship, as in the past I felt he had seemed to imply, or as his actions had appeared to indicate. There were many memoirs poised ready for publication, or on the verge of being written, or at least postulated, held in suspense somewhere between thought and action, he told me. It came across as a kind of threat, but that may have been only his verbal mannerism, or my habitual interpretation of the mannerism. But that he should write a memoir, the idea rendered him speechless, incoherent. To find something that did that was always gratifying, and succumbing to gratification I failed to press my advantage. Was it because everything he had written to date was memoir and there was nothing left to exploit? I might have asked. Memoir disguised as fiction, of course, but that has always been the way of the best fiction. Or was it because his life story was so fraught with the inexpressible, the inadmissible? What was it that he was concealing, that produced such an excess of refusal? What secret life was he fearful of disclosing, beneath the multiple secret lives he had already presented pour épater les bourgeoises? Were there perhaps things that we who claimed proletarian origins and sympathies, even if we could hardly any longer claim identification, might find less delightful, things that we might find totally unacceptable? Would he care? Put like that I doubted it. Were there materials here that might reward a careful and comprehensive investigation? Or if not comprehensive, at least a pointed one?

It is not an investigation that I propose to undertake. I had enough exposure to the Joe psyche in those years when we were close. They were so long ago. Within the span of things they were so few, so brief. But they had an impact far outweighing mere chronological time, far beyond the mere measure of their days. Perhaps at that age one lives more intensely. Perhaps in the early years of one's discovery of the city, events and characters are imprinted more deeply, more vividly than in later stages. Perhaps it is merely a matter of first exposures making their mark on the unmarked sheet, gradually occupying the field until they have filled it, after which there is no white space remaining for later encounters.

There is enough, anyway, in those early impressions without resorting to investigative reportage. I have come to disbelieve in investigative reportage, anyway. I doubt that any journalist goes to that much trouble or takes that much risk. Joe had been a journalist. The revelations ascribed to the investigative all come, I have little doubt, from official leaks, from covert briefings, from unidentified sources who have an interest in manipulating events, or the account of events. No surprise that Deep Throat turned out to be in the FBI. The patient search along the paper trail, the brave and lonely vigil down the mean streets, these are just so much guff, like television crime show celebrations of police procedure. It is just a matter of informers. I suppose I could advertise, in a grapevine sort of way, that I am contemplating writing a memoir of Joe, even if not Joe's memoirs. This might send its vibrations along the sticky reticulations of the web he inhabits. Information might be forthcoming. But I am not sure it is that that arouses my interest. I have information enough. This is my answer when enthusiasts and others advocate using the net, the world wide web, accessing information electronically. I have never found myself short of information. That is not to say I have always known the truth. That is something else again. But I am not convinced that more information would make the truth any clearer. The problem has always been to read even a part of what is available, and to sort out what of that is likely to be relevant or useful. Or true. The problem is selecting and reading and absorbing and understanding, digesting and contemplating and coming to some satisfactory interpretation. There is much about Joe's life I do not know. He would remind and assure me of that constantly. I am not claiming or complaining of an information overload in relation to him. But I have quite enough stored and imprinted and recollected. I have quite enough written and published if it comes to that. But there is still much to be understood. Yet again it is a matter of that going over the same ground again and again until it speaks to us, to cite another of Joe's recurrent aphorisms. And after all, it may not be about Joe that ultimately I am to write.

I remember once saying of Joe that he was the reason for my returning to this city. And receiving what my father used to call an old-fashioned look. We were down in the basement of some gentrified terrace in East Sydney, an area of petrol fumes and prostitution and illegal gambling and dubious restaurants. My English agent had asked me about the prospects of establishing an office in Sydney. I had written a report enthusing on the possibilities. There were no agents practising in Sydney at that time. I received thanks, though no payment, and the office was established and here we were in it, the Australian agent and Joe and me. The agency thrived, though it never did me any good. It never placed anything of mine, though it did undo a couple of deals by demanding too much. One was an East German anthology. 'You should be relieved they kept you out of it,' said Joe. 'I am pleased,' he continued, 'not to have been invited.' I found that odd. In those days, probably in these days, little pleasure was to be found in not being invited into anthologies. It was one of the earlier of his declarations against the Communist world. Perhaps he had always been like that and I had never noticed. Or perhaps he did indeed undergo a development and this was one of its significant moments, an historic announcement.

What I meant, I think, was not so much that it was Joe that had attracted me back, but the world that Joe and I shared, the fact that there were two of us constituting a literary society, that we were not alone as we pursued our discoveries, our explorations through this dusty gentle city, its bars, its eating places, its pokey little offices in basements and up narrow flights of stairs. Sydney was still in its sleep in those years. It had not been drilled and shaken and demolished and rebuilt. There were lots of bars but not many restaurants. It was not a public city, it did not proclaim much. It was not much known to world travellers. Discoveries, once made, remained: it had not entered that ceaseless pace of change and transience, that endless process of demolition and massive growth. Discovering it was discovering ourselves, finding new sites for the new explorations of our own hopes and desires and partial realisations.

At this stage Joe was employed. Or perhaps not. Perhaps that was an earlier stage. When I first met him he was employed: though not for long. 'Writing is my employment,' he would state. Not explain, not argue. Writing was his employment and society was there to facilitate it. Eventually when society failed to deliver any more willing young partners to support him, federal funding of the arts took over. From being a drain on the national treasury he became a national treasure. Years later, many years later, he assured me it had not been a struggle. 'I have always lived well. I have always received above the basic wage.' 'And spent well beyond it,' his manager added. I would look at labourers digging up the roads, at hot, tired bus drivers driving through the hot tired summers, at truck drivers and office workers and builders on the girders of the high rise blocks rising up in the re-drawn city, and think of the sweat and toil and tedium with which they earned their far from generous incomes, and think of the percentage sliced off year after year to support Joe and the other national treasures. It was not something I expressed too often. Those same workers were taxed to provide the educational structure that paid for me. I could always have said, but I give in return, I teach, I mark, I assess, I attend meetings and I write on top of it, but I had doubts about it all. About education. Still, it in some way satisfied my conscience. Whereas with Joe I was affronted. I disapproved. It was of course the mode to affect an effortlessness. To produce but not to be seen to work. And Joe simulated that with an admirable ease. He was never seen to work. He wrote, if he wrote, when he wrote, with no public indication of production. Works would appear, but so would Joe, Joe with far more regularity than the works, a shining model of the leisured, the superstructural, in the bars, in the restaurants and in the other dives of that dusty, golden-morninged city.

When we first met he was employed. I inevitably hesitate to say worked. He was in a pokey little adult education office near the bottom of George Street where the old literary cultures of the city had once been sited, the weekly *Bulletin*, the publishing house of Anguish and Robbery, just out of sight of the quay where Conrad had once roamed and where Henry Lawson used to beg for the price of a drink. In such environs I think he felt he could safely be seen to walk a pavement and enter a staircase with the daily commuters, even if, especially if, he could on some pretext exit it shortly afterwards.

The idea of adult education had been a part of my childhood. My father, after the toil of the foundry, would study philosophy at adult education classes under one of the canons of the cathedral. It offered a vision, a taste, of the cultured life of the mind that the institutions denied to those who sustained their wealth. It was a socialist vision of access. It was a gesture of recompense, a way in which the blessed could help raise the unfortunate and excluded to some notion of the better life. And here, transported from its English origins, it flourished. I rhapsodised about it. Joe shuffled his hands uneasily on his uncluttered desk and suggested we went out for a drink, down the rickety staircase, down the sloping street, past the silent Brooklyn and along to the Newcastle.

How long was it before I began to realise he did not share my socialist visions? How long before I recognised that he paid no tribute to the dignity of labour. These were the mainstays of my commitment, how could I comprehend that he held them in contempt? Because they were phantasms based on so little experience, because they were touchstones of guilt-haunted affirmation rather than hard-won truths hewn from the mines of practical encounters, I had little by which to assess their role in Joe's pantheon. For me they were values I held to by the will. This privileged life of the university, from which I might have a morning free, indeed many mornings free, and afternoons and evenings too, in which I could stand at the Newcastle bar drinking beers at eleven or twelve or two or five, or all of them until closing time at ten, the canonical hours of Joe's foundation. His uncloistered, unconstrained Comusian rout, his community of one, was a life surrounded by a penumbra of anxieties for me, guilts that I should have it so easy while others, my father looming large in this, but countless others I might see or envisage or conceptualise all around, had it so hard. And even if they didn't have it hard, who else had it so easy? Well, Joe, Joe standing there with his beers, insisting in his somewhat taut and strangulated tones, in that tenor of anxiety he never totally shed, that we must be free of guilt, our first priority must always be to free ourselves of all restrictions and prescriptions.

That adult education had once been a socialist initiative there was no doubt. Indeed it may well have been targeted or penetrated by communists. Joe's mission, imperfectly understood by me, was perhaps to save it from such. If saving it from such might seem like undermining and destroying it, who was to say that was not a good thing? These were cold war days. Better raze an institution to the ground than let the enemy possess it. I did not understand these things then. But I think Joe did.

Certainly workers were not beings Joe held in respect. He showed no commitment to advancing their cause, removing their shackles, giving them voice. He held that giving some other person or group a voice was patronising: it was difficult enough to find your own authentic voice: though authentic was perhaps not a word he would have used. But finding his own voice, or finding organs through which to vocalise, was something with which he was concerned. On one of those early occasions when we met he produced his journal. Or perhaps not precisely his journal. The indeterminacy about the possessive indicates the problems that were to arise. It was a house journal, devoted to adult educational themes, and, who knows, to workers' advancement in its earliest days. Joe saw its potential. He took over the editorship and began to turn it into a literary journal, an intellectual review, like the Americana he so admired, *Partisan* and such like. There was a long way to go before those institutional products on bulky matt paper, funded and subscribed to and funded again, could be replicated. But he had his sights on them. Perhaps he envisioned international conferences of international editors in international centres. Almost certainly he did. And what we dream of with determination in some way we ultimately attain. In the end, in these days as I write, he has attained the international travel and the international conferences, without the demeaning worry of any editorial responsibilities, like a senior minister without portfolio, an editor without a magazine. It suits him.

Down in the Newcastle he unbuckled his briefcase. His briefcase was his protection, his insignia, his subterfuge. Walking out of the office with his briefcase he did not need to proclaim that he was off to a business engagement. The briefcase advertised business. It was his passport in and out of the office in those days before electromagnetic swipe cards.

He showed me the journal with a charming diffidence. He did have charm. Often when I write or think about him I neglect to acknowledge that. But it was one of his available qualities and he was able to deploy it. He did not ask, 'What do you think?' but that was implicit in handing it across. It seemed disappointingly slight. I had expected something more substantial, and this was thin and stapled and in a funny format, some 1950s institutional, educational format, a larger page size than the traditional quarterlies, but not large enough to be imposing, and because a larger page than the traditional quarterly and with more words per page, it had fewer pages, hence in part its thinness. It looked like a church parish magazine. I had indeed written for a parish magazine at least once. The neophyte writer: how to impress your parents and neighbours and vicar about the seriousness of your vocation. I was not eager to write for such again.

'Perhaps,' said Joe, 'you would like to review for us.'

What could I say but yes?

'Once in a while,' he added.

He was not going to offer me a regular feature. Perhaps that was a relief. But once in a while, well, why not?

'We thought you might like to review this.'

He produced the latest issue of *Meanjin*, that portentous, prosperous looking quarterly from Melbourne. I felt disappointment. Already. Reviewing the latest in international books, that was part of the literary apprenticeship I envisaged for myself. That was how you started a literary career. As long as you didn't end a literary career still reviewing there was nothing wrong with it, everything to be said for it. But reviewing another magazine. It did not seem to me the sort of thing that was done. I had never seen magazines reviewed in the review pages; the review pages reviewed books. But I did it. Later, when consistently *Meanjin* rejected everything I sent to them, I wondered if I had been set up. Had my demanding, high-minded, high-standarded, brisk, severe tone been resented? Almost certainly. And had Joe suspected that that would be the tone I would adopt? Almost certainly. He was astute, another quality, like charm, that I insufficiently acknowledge in him. Though, it must also be acknowledged, his astuteness had a certain short-sighted aspect to it. He did not always see the slightly larger picture. He may well have calculated, almost certainly would have, that for me to review *Meanjin* with the acerbity of youth would effectively exclude me from its pages for the future. What he failed to calculate was that he, too, would as a consequence be excluded. The Melbourne literary world was not without its paranoia: its members knew the editorial strategies by which editors select reviewers. They knew there was no such thing as a free hand: or rather, the hands might well be free, but the decisions about which free hands to employ would have been calculated, the workers would have had to be worthy of their hire, and the hirers would have known their business. So Joe, no less than I, found himself excluded from the pages of *Meanjin* for the next few decades. While not long afterwards Joe was removed from his editorial chair, on the grounds that under his direction the journal had lost its original focus, had become too literary. And not long after that it ceased publication altogether.

The poet Prickett phoned up one time to announce he would be in town and to arrange a meeting. He suggested the Newcastle, at about five. It had that sort of reputation for those out of town, the literary pub. Prickett too had a sort of reputation and I was, I suppose, flattered that he should want to meet me since he was not someone I knew well. I was flattered to meet anyone with some aura of literary status in those days. I wanted to insert myself into the international camaraderie of the literary. It was enough that someone should be a writer, no matter what sort, for me to believe in a natural, innate connection with them. It was early in the week that Prickett was visiting, but there was always somebody you knew at the Newcastle, whatever the day. Waiting for Prickett I encountered lots. It seemed remarkably full of literary folk. Indeed, he had phoned up all of them, making arrangements to meet them, minor poets, book reviewers, literary academics, to ensure that the pub would not be empty when he arrived. He acknowledged us, or most of us, regally, perfunctorily, and went off with some girl, leaving us to talk to each other.

He need not have done that. Friday was the big night at the Newcastle, but there were always people drinking there on a Thursday, preparing for Friday, and on a Wednesday, making an early start on the weekend, and on a Monday too, recovering from Sundays which in those days allowed no public drinking. Tuesday is traditionally the day no one goes anywhere much, restaurants do little business, so the Newcastle was the only place to go on a Tuesday, and you could be sure of finding somebody there you knew. There was always someone to drink with at the Newcastle. It had a reliability that nothing else has ever replaced. You might not be sure of always finding whatever you wanted, but there would always be somebody there. And generally Joe.

The Newcastle is photographed on the cover of one of my earliest books. I have taken it down from the shelf but it evokes few memories. Perhaps the angle of the photograph, from behind the bar, focussed on the customers, is wrong. It was not a view with which we were familiar. The photograph shows a high ceiling, open windows, something that looks like a street lantern on a post at the corner of the bar, of which I have no recollection. Joe is not in the photograph. Almost no one I remember drinking with is there. The faces are all unfamiliar. I think I see myself, partially obscured. Perhaps the people I knew were out on the footpath, or hiding behind the photographed figures. Stephen came up to me that evening remarking on the photographer. He had him marked down as special branch or one of the security services and had been ducking out of sight. These were the years of the Vietnam war and the protests against it. 'It's for the cover of my book,' I said, but he was unconvinced and made sure he kept out of shot. Perhaps that is why the cover evokes so little. Not even the poet Prickett. But then, we were not there for visual impressions. There were no views. The quay was a few hundred yards down the road, but out of sight. We were there to drink and talk. Though the talk has faded into the forgotten, as talk does. But we were there. Regularly. I can still visualise it, soundless wraiths packed in at the bar in the fading twilight. When the evenings became hot we would move out onto the pavement. This was strictly illegal and the paddy wagons would trawl by and we would retreat back inside. The publican tolerated our drinking outside as long as we returned inside when the police passed. But outside involved standing. No sitting on the pavement. Indeed inside generally meant standing unless you arrived early enough to find one of the dozen or so bar stools.

It was the poet Placket who decided to take a bar stool out onto the pavement. The landlord came out to expostulate, insofar as he could expostulate, having had his vocal cords removed in an operation for throat cancer. Perhaps he used his artificial voice box. Perhaps he gestured. Though a slightly built man, years of running that pub had given him a presence and authority. The stool was surrendered. The next evening Placket turned up with his own bar stool and sat on that. It must have been massively inconvenient bringing along a high, wooden bar stool by public transport each evening, or carrying it through the streets, but he did it. The success of his enterprise encouraged him to further poetic assertions.

After drinking for three hours it was the habit to go off somewhere to eat, to hail a taxi and take off whoever you wanted to eat with and evade whoever you wanted to avoid, waiting till they had gone to the bar or the urinal and then dodging away. Joe and I would often eat together, sometimes in a crowd, sometimes exclusively, avoiding some undesired company. Placket was undesired. He sought us out, but only to be scathing about our fictions and to aggrandise his own achievements, unlikely accounts of world-wide acceptances, alliances, kinships of poeticism. He would talk in a loud, mannered, penetrating voice, slowly, painfully, not very wittily. For all my belief in the fraternity of the creative, I accepted Joe's refusal of his company without question. But he pursued us. We sat one evening in the Greeks, overlooking Hyde Park, not in the privileged window seats where the *Bulletin* editorial staff held forth, but close, we were rising in status. We had our bottle of Demestica and our taramosalata and our tzatziki and were awaiting our main course when a voice called out our names, a loud, measured, honeyed, elocuted, theatrical voice, the voice of the poet Placket. 'Call yourselves writers,' it went on, 'you couldn't write yourselves out of a paper bag.' It was short on wit, but loud. 'You think you're editors. You couldn't edit a tram ticket,' it added. The trams had long since ceased to run and the tram terminal site had transmuted into the opera house, complete without car park. Urban planning. At least he hadn't called us architects. He sat there at one of the tables at the back, bar stool beside him, beaming in manic satisfaction. 'You think you're too good for me, is that it? But I can find you. I can follow you to the ends of the earth.'

Joe was ashen. 'Oh no, oh no,' he kept repeating, 'not this.' I thought he too was acting. But he was appalled at the invasion. My own reaction was more ambiguous. This, I thought, was the literary life. Recognition at last, even if in denunciation. But to Joe it was a sacrilege. Our names called out, for ever to be associated by the waiters and the *Bulletin* writers with madness, disruption, poetry.

The *Bulletin* writers were probably not there. They generally met at lunch, sitting in the window seat, the starched napkins tucked into their shirt collars. Seventy years earlier the *Bulletin* had had a fine literary reputation. Now it was transmuting into a business and finance magazine. But it was a part of the myth of the city. Joe still aspired to it. And succeeded. I had been there, done that, and been dropped. For a couple of years I had reviewed books for it regularly. And then my patron had taken leave, a mistake in the world of journalism as in the university, and on return found he no longer controlled the books pages. A new books editor brought in a new team and I was not on it. I was not especially distressed. Book reviewing was time consuming, tedious, productive of a factitious sense of achievement as my old tutor used to put it. Besides, it made you enemies. It was a small literary world, and touchy. Its members did not appreciate unappreciative reviews. Nor did I later. But in those early years I had all the acerbity of youth, all the vigour of determined judgement and considered appraisal. Joe, like many other writers, was smart enough not to review books. It was one of the many things about him of which I disapproved: he expected his own work to be reviewed, and favourably, but did not reciprocate. It was a wise choice. He avoided giving offence to other writers. He avoided displaying any inadequacies of taste or perception or analytic method. His refusal to review gave me offence but no other writers seemed to notice. No one remarked on it. His successful calculations in this gave me offence too. But that was Joe. No wonder he provoked the poet Placket to shout at him. At us.

So my days with the *Bulletin* were over, Joe's yet to come. Though soon. He aspired to a column, and he achieved it, and soon was sitting with the *Bulletin* editors at the window, gazing reflectively at the war memorial, his napkin tucked in above his tie.

'I used to watch you,' said Angelo, my publisher, my former publisher – as with the *Bulletin* I had my moment with Anguish and Robbery and then was dropped from their list. 'I would see you and Joe eating there and I would think how I would like to be there with you, to be sharing in literary conversation, to have been accepted as a writer.'

Angelo, against the back wall, slowly assembling his first book of stories, reaching from the undefined shadows to the literary life, watching us sitting there in the middle rows as we in turn watched the *Bulletin* editorial writers in their window seat in their success, loud, confident, resplendent in their achieved glory, their momentary splendour, before, inexorably, inevitably, they were sacked and replaced by the legendary Sir Frank, the owner, whom we never saw.

So we explored the city, discovering its eating and drinking places, its sites of memory, its signposts to the future. It was not discovery by any methodical survey. We did not work by grids and charts. But both Joe and I had come from elsewhere. Outsiders aspiring to get inside. In our warmer, happier, sentimental moods, we would draw out the parallels in our experience, country town upbringings, parental repressions, arrival in the city. The outline excluded much and made doubtful analogies. A country town on the New South Wales coast was not like a cathedral city in the English Midlands. Joe had experienced none of that surviving medievalism, those warrens of slums, those old stone cloisters, those memorials of martyrs and battles, defeats at the hands of invading Romans, defeat at the hands of invading Angles and Saxons and Jutes, temporary triumph over invading Vikings, defeat at the hands of Normans, self laceration in civil wars. The erasure of the coastal aboriginals was marked by no memorials.

The point anyway was not a shared past but a shared present, a shared discovery of the city we had settled in. And it was a discovery made in the course of other things. We did not have the time, or disposition, for formal exploration. We were not explorers of the old sort, with baggage and bearers and cartographers and botanists beside us. We were living in the city, working in the city, or at least employed in the city. What we discovered of it was in the course of work or, more frequently, of pleasure. So there always remained large areas of the unknown. We became familiar with this hotel, that restaurant, this bookshop. From these secured bases we would move out and find another pub, another eating house. There were not many bookshops. And the territory between these discovered sites would remain blank, or notional.

Or that may be merely my explanation for my lack of recollection. It may be that all I recall are places where we drank, places where we ate, places where we looked for books and magazines, all else in between an alcoholic haze of taxi rides, walks in which we talked and did not observe, bus rides in which we looked out of the windows, seeing but unable to touch what we passed. Not that Joe took too many bus rides. Nor did he drive. Taxis were his preferred mode. He would be endlessly impatient at my attempts at economy. 'A shared cab is more economical than a sequence of slow buses,' he would insist. It wasn't, not unless there were four of you sharing it. Sometimes there were four, sometimes just the two of us. Perhaps he had been told to economise as a child, as I had, but resisted the instruction as soon as he escaped from home. Or perhaps he had been brought up to a sense of his station. Or perhaps he had self-created his sense of his proper station, alone in this new city, from the beginning assembling and building the fabric that was to be his public presentation.

Near Central Railway was a great barn of an eating place, the Italian club, or, perhaps, more correctly, the Italo-Australian club. This, like the Greeks, was reached by a lift or a staircase. The restaurant was in a huge hall, used at other times for dances or meetings or social events, or so it appeared. The restaurant tables and chairs occupied only a small part of it. The rest as I remember was empty floor, perhaps partitioned off. There was an air of the temporary, the improvised, in eating there which Joe, naturally, did not appreciate. But I felt at ease in its ad hoc environment, perhaps because I still felt ill at ease in restaurant formality. And it evoked some memory of eating somewhere in Italy, some similarly improvised or sprawling eatery. The food was not especially good, but it had a predictable reliability, minestrone, lasagne, gnocchi, green beans cooked with onion and potatoes with a touch of oil. The waiters were utterly without pretension. They wore waiters' black trousers and white shirts, at least that survived from the old world. But they were free of the awful theatricality and supercilious intrusiveness that was later to develop as Sydney entered the age of eating out and the nouvelle. 'Bandits,' some woman exclaimed of them one evening, as she and her partner were deposited at my table where I was eating alone. 'This place is run by bandits.' I assumed from her accent and appearance she was Italian so I pursued the issue, the novelist on the information trail. 'Mafia?' I suggested. 'What is that? I do not know what that is.' 'Bandits,' I suggested. 'Bandits,' she said decisively, 'brigands.' My investigations remained unpursued.

Yet on one occasion that Joe and I lunched there the waiters were effusive, bowing, scraping, ingratiating it seemed at the time. It struck even Joe, who had begun to appreciate respect, as overdone, as approaching the parodic. We were eating there because it was a public holiday and our other haunts were closed. Anzac day, that celebration of defeat, Australia's Kosovo, the baptism of blood in the initiation of nationhood, the anniversary of the slaughter of Gallipoli. Its significance at this time was in transition. For decades it had been a symbol of the noble sacrifice of Empire, the expression of the colony's loyalty to its British sovereignty. Now, three score and ten years after Federation, nationalism was expressing itself. Now it was to become a symbol of resentment, the cynical butchery of Australian manhood, boyhood, by their exploitive British masters.

'That, of course, is a nonsense,' I expounded to Joe.

He glowered at me blankly, toying with his spinach and veal, young calf cut down in its prime.

'It's another case of nationalism being used to obscure a class analysis.'

He chewed.

'There were far more British troops killed than Australians. Eight thousand Australians, and forty thousand British. It wasn't a sacrifice of colonials. It was a sacrifice of rank and file by incompetent ruling class generals.'

'How can it have been both a deliberate sacrifice and incompetence?' Joe asked. 'Make up your mind.'

My mind was made up.

'Over the entire war,' Joe informed me, 'more Australians and Canadians were killed per capita than British.'

I stuck with the class analysis.

The waiter came up and asked how our meal was, was it satisfactory, how were we, what more could he do for us.

'Weren't the Italians on the British side in the First World War?' I asked Joe.

'The British side?' said Joe. 'Or the allies?'

'Perhaps he's Turkish,' I speculated. 'Perhaps he's conflating it with the second world war.'

Was it friendly solidarity as an ally, acknowledging sacrifice at the hands of the enemy: or a mocking parody of servility, taunting at defeat?

'Normally they leave you alone,' I said.

'And you like that,' said Joe. 'You get your own knife and fork from the cutlery box and ladle out your potatoes and gravy from the servery. Is that your preferred way? It reminds you of your English college?'

His irritation seemed in excess of the occasion. But nationalism was always a tricky topic.

The waiter reappeared.

'Signor,' he began.

'Coffee and the bill,' Joe snapped.

We sat in silence, alone. The restaurant was deserted. We might have been the only customers. Perhaps the waiter had merely been glad to have someone there.

'Even as you sit here,' said Joe, 'that girl is aborting her child.'

I could think of nothing to say. His statement had been delivered quite without preparation. There had been no establishment of tone, of mood. No context. No indication of the response expected.

Whenever I suggested the Italian club later, Joe refused. I don't think he ever ate there again.

The Journalists' Club on the other side of Central Railway was somewhere you could drink all night. I never did spend all night there, nor do I think did Joe. But we drank there when the pubs had shut and we wanted the evening to continue. I only ever went there with Joe, since you needed to be signed in by a member, if you were not a member, and I was not. This was a matter of continual comment by Joe. 'I cannot understand why you are not a member.' I offered various explanations. 'I am not a journalist,' I would sometimes say. 'You do not need to be a journalist.' That was true. Rarely did we see a journalist there on our nocturnal expeditions, hoping to spot some likely patron to advance our careers. The truth was you had to be nominated for membership, you could not just apply. 'We will nominate you,' said Joe. 'It will be a gift for Christmas.' It was variously promised for Christmas, Easter, my birthday, St Valentine's day, but it never happened. Perhaps I showed insufficient enthusiasm. It was a cheerless, soulless building, with a squalid utilitarian bar of 1950s style, and it offered no amenities that I could perceive except after hours drinking. I was drinking quite enough within hours. But Joe loved it as his own, or at least purported to. I do not think that this was because he had been a journalist. He was consistently unromantic and unenthusiastic about his journalist days, or about any employment. I do not think he had found fulfilment in that role, although he was always proposing to visit some war to be a war correspondent. Maybe not posted to the front but safely in the bars of Saigon with other international adventurers. That, anyway, was future projection. About his previous experiences he said little.

We would sit there in the ugly surrounds on the ugly furniture waiting for excitement to come to us and kick the evening along. It never did. Rarely indeed did we meet anyone there. These were generally lugubrious evenings, pouring down middy after middy of not especially appetising beer. The restaurant was always closed. There were framed front pages of old newspapers and honour boards on the wall. The poet of our city, Slessor, was rumoured to preside here, tossing salads, no longer writing poems. He had not written poems, or at least not published any, for twenty or more years. Instead he wrote hair-raisingly reactionary editorials for the hair-raisingly reactionary *Daily Telegraph*. Though since it was a tabloid that I never read, I repeat this only on hearsay. Similarly the salad-tossing bit. That was something Joe told me, a cameo he clearly treasured, repeating it more than once. It appealed to him, and I predicted in the silence of my heart, and probably enunciated in irritable or careless drunkenness in the tedium of the club, that I could see Joe fulfilling that very role in the fullness of time, Joe tossing salads and being pernickety about the table arrangements and placements, presiding over rather seedy, unappetising lunches and dinners, and writing no more. Like most of my predictions, it has not come true. Joe still writes, if only a little. And I doubt that in his high table dinners in damp, chilly Cambridge he as yet presides. I should not have told him my prediction. But then, would I have wanted him not to write? Not really. It was never his writing I found disagreeable or disagreed with. Much else I found disagreeable about him, primarily in those days his not writing enough. 'And what is enough?' he would ask. 'What constitutes sufficient Stakhanovite production in the collective farm of the commissar of creativity? Are we to write to order? Plant now, reap now? You would deny us the freedom of the body as well as the freedom of the imagination. What about volupté?' It was his new word, which he pronounced in a vulpine, rather Slavic way, devoid of any of the expected sinuousness and sensuality of its Romance roots. 'What about it? Tell me,' I would say as we sat in the Journalists' Club at three in the morning, no volupté in sight or likely to appear, but the atmosphere of the hair-raisingly reactionary all around us.

There is not much to recall for all those hours we spent there. But it was another of the myths of the city, like its presiding poet. One discreditable episode I do recall. We were joined by, or arrived with, Sled, some sort of acquaintance of Joe's; some sort of acquaintance of many people. He purported to some sort of literary identity. He may, indeed, once have written some poems. Who had not? Later he specialised in writing on intelligence, of the spookery variety, not mental attainment. At this time, like many of the previously occupationless drinkers at the Newcastle, he had some unspecified role in the new Labor party administration. Or he may even by this stage have left it and been surviving by contract work or committee sitting fees for some of the countless bureaucracies that had been established. I found him not especially inviting company, and somewhat sinister. He affected to know men in high places. Perhaps he did. How he survived financially was even more puzzling than how Joe managed.

I had always thought him a crony of Joe's, so that I was surprised when after he had gone, Joe indicated the briefcase he had left behind with some words or gestures of suggestive suspicion. It was not unlike the briefcase Joe used to carry with him and keep beside his desk in his role as an adult educationist. A standard issue briefcase, scruffy, scuffed, buckled and pleated.

It did not look inviting. Nor indeed did an investigation of Sled's secrets appeal. To open correspondence, rifle through purses, examine medicine cabinets were activities I felt improper. I still held to the proprieties. Joe did not; indeed, in the spirit of libertarianism he affected to despise them.

We downed two more middies and brooded, the shabby briefcase lying there flat on the chair, neglected, unwooed, unvalued. It was not locked.

'I have always wondered what he carries in it,' said Joe.

Did my presence their provide encouragement, complicity? We agreed it was an opportunity given to us. Like people giving you their stories. It would seem wanton to refuse.

We opened it.

Nothing. It was entirely empty. Not a sandwich, not an apple, not a dossier, not a document, not a recording device.

'I think he might be attempting to tell us something,' said Joe.

'You mean he left it deliberately?'

'Would he forget it?'

'If there was nothing in it to remember he might.'

'He takes it everywhere.'

'Perhaps it is always empty.'

Was it a desperate accessory, insignia of employment he no longer had but to whose loss he could not publicly admit? Or was it subterfuge, the proclamation of innocence, I am what you see, no secrets, nothing at all, the unconvincing decoy of internal security?

'I'll take it with me and return it to him,' said Joe, fastening the buckles.

'He'll probably suspect we looked into it,' I said.

'Of course,' said Joe.

I pondered on what he meant, why he meant it, whatever it was.

'But he will never know, only suspect,' he added.

'Like us,' I added.

Joe made no comment. A silence no less enigmatic than any previous utterance, a worthy allusion to of one of those unwritten poems of the salad-tossing poet of our city.

5

Amazing Things

Joe passed the typescript across. There was nothing said. No 'look on these words', no 'as when the sun breaks through the weltering clouds and pricks out characters of rare device'. Nothing but his blank expression, the expression he used when attempting lack of expression. 'Just be yourself,' I told him. 'That look gives it away, don't try, just act like you write, totally expressionless.' It made no difference. Somewhere, could it have been by correspondence course, he had learnt his expression degree zero, of how to achieve power over others, and he would never surrender it. That, you might think, boded well for the rest of us. A warning sign. But he used it so widely that what it warned could not be deduced. It did not necessarily indicate malice. It might be an attempt to conceal joy. Or desire. Envy. Despair. Anything but detachment or disinterest.

In this instance it could have been any of those qualities, as he handed over the half dozen sheets. Not, I could see from the typeface and margin width, something of his. We were not, at this stage, involved in any editorial ventures, no magazine, no anthology, neither jointly nor individually. So why did he have it? What, for that matter, was it? I tried to ask him but he waved the question away.

'Read it,' he said.

So I did.

With Joe looming over me there it was necessarily a double reading, for the piece itself and for the detection of his reading. In things like this, in many things, he was not easy to read. A piece of writing that was strikingly different might provoke his amazement or his disgust, enthusiasm or dismissal. There must have been an uncertainty within himself on which way to go, in this as in other things. The way of the new, the experimental, the avant-garde or the way of the common reader, of journalistic clarity, this complicated insofar as the avant-garde was so regularly far from new, quite over-familiar and dated, and the journalistic far from clear or communicative. These were times of uncertainty. We looked for a sign.

Is this what the piece offered? Was it the blazon of the new? Or was it re-run Anna Kavan and Anais Nin? Was this the age of Aquarius with its transcendent visions, or the usual load of old Cocteau? Joe was down on drugs. He had committed himself to an artistic model that involved learning how to mix cocktails. He was unwilling to surrender any acquired technique. He still wrote on those small slips of copy paper journalists in those days wrote on. A mark of professionalism. Similarly his two-fingered typing. And then the pub. This was the signposted route to celebrity, the wide, well-trodden track. '*Facilis descensus Averno*,' I would intone, knowing he had no Latin. That was about the extent of mine. But this, these six pages, were another world again, neither Latin nor cocktails, neither journalists' copy paper nor the great tradition.

His quizzical lack of expression hung above me like the full moon. 'Never go out in the full moon,' my mother warned me, 'it will turn you mad.' It beamed, it boomed down on me, but where was the light source it reflected? Those pages? I held them before me, a talisman to deflect his influence.

'Amazing,' I said.

He looked at me blankly. 'Amazing, you say.'

'Yes, amazing.'

He took the pages back and read through them again.

'Amazing,' he said.

It may not have been the first of Valda's writing I had seen. I may have glanced at a poem somewhere or other. But there was no end to poetry, poets were two a penny. This was the first prose piece of hers that I had seen. I hesitate to call it a story, I hesitated even then. And prose poem was a killer term. No one called anything that. When I got to know her I found she just called them 'things,' these things she wrote. Not dissimilar to the way I found myself referring to what I'd written, sometimes, as 'stuff.' 'You been writing anything?' 'Yes, I've been doing some good stuff.' It was that fear of hubris, of overrating your production and invoking disaster. Or was it a disdain for the pretensions of the culturati, those connoisseurs who laid claim to a world of privileged possession that had never been ours? By ours I mean Valda's and mine, a shared sense of exclusion that was perhaps one of our slender bonds; indeed, more than that, a self-denying refusal ever to partake of those privileges that made an even stronger bond. Something that Joe was too wise to share, set even then on the rights that he held to be his, and who was to blame him? Well, we did, Valda and I, in our shared resentment.

The thing, anyway, was amazing. And we were open to things. We being Joe and myself, and clearly Valda too. This was when we were attempting to dispense with narratives of the beginning, middle and end, to dispense indeed with narrative altogether. So this evocation of a directionless, unresolved, stoned world was, if not perfect, and we would have hesitated in ascribing perfection to any work of our contemporaries or indeed of each other's, was at least apposite.

What Joe was doing with it I never discovered. Had he positioned himself already as mentor to the young?

He was not so old himself. He had not published so much. But he was skilfully disseminating an image of achievement and authority. Hollow as that seemed to me, it may have fooled other people. Though it was hard to imagine Valda being fooled, her whole street-wise projection was one of nobody fools me. That, of course, could often be an invitation to foolery.

Nothing that I speculated made any sense. I could never understand why she might have given him that typescript. It became an itching sore, one of the anxieties, inexpressible, unacknowledgable, unanswerable, that irritated our relationship, and not one generating any pearl. Just an ugly suspicion, a fearful uncertainty, such as both Joe and she delighted to foster. So there was no point in inquiring the truth from either of them.

And what was truth anyway in this world of fiction?

I never felt it rated very highly with either of them. Both readily mocked my anxious search for it, or search for a version of it I might find acceptable, or tolerable, both readily categorised it as one of my obsessions, some personality disorder from which, in Joe's view, I would never recover, and in Valda's, I would recover only if I smoked more dope, listened to rock and roll, threw away my old tweed jacket and followed her advice, role model and life style, and even then it would be touch and go. 'You need to get your rocks off,' she would grin, that saurian, reptilian grin, such as Eve must have acquired from gazing so fixedly on the serpent. 'Have some of this,' passing across some apple she had crunched into with those pointed teeth, which would then turn to ashes in my mouth, or at least pour ash down the front of my sweater and leave it pitted with hash burns from my fumbling, uneasy inhalations. And then the world would be like that thing, no middle, beginning or end, but a recurring smoke ring of extended time, a Mobius strip returning back on itself as day turned into night and night turned back into day.

'See, that's better, isn't it?'

She was living in a rooming house on the water's edge in Balmain. The sea captains who built their splendid mansions on the Parramatta river and Snails' bay and Long Nose point had long since gone, their houses declining into subdivided and partitioned tenements. It was in one of these that she lived, sinister and decaying, the Maltese landlord suspicious and surly, rooms rented to decrepit pensioners and derelicts, survivors from the run-down ship-repair yards. The painters and writers were moving into the suburb, leasing and sharing the flimsy workingmen's cottages in the narrow streets that ran up from the water. But this was something different, desolate bare rooms, racking coughs, hawking, spitting sick old men and women, this was the indigence of decay and dissolution, not the temporary bohemianism of the upward mobile artist slumming before making it or coming into an inheritance. I felt uneasy there, and the landlord gave me looks of dark suspicion. The uneasiness it induced was without doubt part of its appeal for Valda. It provided some of the defences with which she always surrounded herself, that vulnerable fragility she projected encompassed round by this rusting barbed wire, these coils of protection surrounding her tiny boxes of jewels, her gypsy shawls and Indian bedspreads with their little reflecting disks of tin, all the tawdry gew-gaws of the exotic and impoverished.

And we fenced and feinted there, suspicious, mistrustful, sharing a joint but little else, as the old men coughed in their echoing rooms, and then Tina who shared the room with her arrived home from a party and we rolled another smoke in the deadlock and Tina went to bed and we dragged a mattress into the untenanted room next door, bare old wood floor, bare uncurtained windows, sagging ceiling and cracked plaster walls, and we shared the bed and blankets, but sharing bodies, could you call it that with such doubt and suspicion and wariness, the bitter wind howling up Long Nose point and chilling that cold gaunt house, the cold light of dawn waking us to the clatter of seagulls and the throbbing of tugs and barges and ferries.

She went off early to her job in the bookshop and Tina came in and sat on the mattress and rolled a cigarette or maybe even a joint and leaned across to offer it, her opportunity shop dressing gown falling open and her body offered there, but it didn't seem like a wise idea, and then the landlord came in and berated us about using the empty room without paying rent.

Then Sam got into the act, the very acme and avatar and epitome and embodiment, from my perspective and in this context and without prejudice, of untrustworthiness and treachery, and berated Valda about my untrustworthiness, the heart to heart or groin to groin of one poet to another.

'He'll just use you.'

Like many a poet of some facility, he was, I felt, limited in concepts. Using people was one of the well-worn counters of those times, probably of most times. I could no doubt think of others, phrases and times, but that would be a distraction from the thing in hand, welcome and alluring as such a distraction might be. So Sam would have given his wardress the slip and sidled round to the Maltese rooming house and spent the night spinning his poison, adducing a common bond of the outsiders and street-people and gaolbirds and hustlers and victims and the real, true and only authentic, endlessly exploited by those in tweed jackets and regular employment. And she always believed all that, not that she ever believed Sam, but for those things she had always believed and always did believe, then it was immaterial who repeated them to her, and Sam, who could spot a well-worn theme and snap it up in an instant and pass it across as new, Sam did his dirty work.

But wasn't there another beginning, in a rackety little weather-board cottage built right onto the pavement in one of those narrow lanes that ran down to the water at the bottom of Darling Street, a flimsy, two-storey, shaky structure that would have swayed in any wind but the streets were so narrow and pokey that it was protected there, propped up amidst old stone footings and old brick walls? Here she was sharing with two or three amiable desperadoes, burly, bearded men who wore football socks and worked on the council garbage trucks or who didn't work at all but sat around the shaky kitchen table in singlets, crushing beer cans in their palms, or crushing my shoulder in beery bear-hugs.

We were in her room there with its Indian bedspreads and gypsy shawls and mother-of-pearl hash boxes and beaded, mirrored purses and tasselled shoulder bags, while from a worn cardboard suitcase beneath the bed she produced her manuscripts, stacking the pages on the floor, 'Here they are, see what I mean, it's impossible, how do they think I'm going to do it, it's unreal, I can't be expected to do that, what do they know about anything, they can forget it, it'll never happen.'

The house rocked as the desperadoes opened and shut the fridge door in the kitchen and climbed up and down the stairs.

'It just can't be done so that's that, look at it all, it's ridiculous.'

She rolled a joint and after several hefty tokes passed it across.

'We can do it,' I said at last, passing it back.

'You reckon ?'

I nodded, waited for the joint to return. Before it did one of the burly men burst through the door with a massive monster joint like a small cigar.

'Here, have a suck on this.'

I did.

'Do you mind,' she said.

'I don't if you don't,' he said, all bearded geniality.

'We're busy in here.'

'Point taken.'

'How can I ever write without any privacy?' she said. 'Always the same. No one ever leaves you alone. Why do I ever bother? It's all impossible.'

She sat there amidst the colours of the shawls and drapes, her hair golden in the low light, her eyes shining sharp and clear and blue, complaining.

'It's not impossible,' I said.

'Go on then,' she said. 'How isn't it impossible? Show me.'

'First of all we'll look through them and put them in groups.'

'What do you mean, groups?'

'In categories. Like happy poems, sad poems, dope poems…'

'You can't do that,' she said. 'They're all dope poems. There aren't any happy poems. Happy poems, how should I ever write happy poems?'

'Any groups,' I said, 'it doesn't matter what.'

'You're just the same as them,' she said, '"it doesn't matter what".'

'Look,' I said, 'they said they'd do a book of fifty-two pages. So you've got about 250 pages here.'

'And the rest.'

'All right, and the rest. Now we can either just take the first fifty pages…'

'Don't be ridiculous.'

'Or we can select them. Now if we chose five groups and put them into those groups and then take the ten best poems out of each group…'

'We've got fifty.'

'Yes.'

For a moment she dissolved into a smile. The lights shone from the hash box, the tin disks in the shawl, the bangles on her wrist, her eyes.

'What categories?' she asked suspiciously.

'What are the poems about?'

'Read them and see. Poems are poems. What do you mean what are they about?'

'I was planning on reading them,' I said.

'What about ones that don't fit into any of your categories?'
'Then we make a category of ones that don't fit into categories.'
'Smart, eh?'
I nodded.
'I'll make a cup of tea while you read them,' she said.

I could hear her talking in the kitchen, voices, laughter, silence, whistling kettle, all the suspicions of the unseen, the overheard, what are they saying, what is going on, the child in bed excluded from the continuing words out there, her room full of doubts enfolding and taking me over. I forced myself back to the poems, skip-reading through them to get an overview, the publishers' way, the editors' way, refusing their request to stay, to dwell, to linger, to mull over, imploring, sad-eyed lonely poems passive there, immobile like barnacles on the rocks and ferry piers, imploring the sea to lap back over them again, read me, read me, love me, value me, cherish me, don't go away, don't move on, don't desert me, come back, come back, come back, remember me.

'There are no beautiful women in our world,' Joe pronounced.
I demurred. I often did with him. It was a feature of our relationship.
'Truly beautiful women,' he said. Did he add 'classically?' It was not normally part of his vocabulary. I don't think even he would have said all-American, even though he was heading toward heady support of the alliance. Most probably he left it there, reiterated but unclarified.
As I said, I demurred. There were lots of girls I found ceaselessly attractive.
'Beautiful, I said,' he said, 'not attractive.'
'Well, beautiful.'
'One or the other,' he said. 'They are not the same.'
'Beautiful,' I said.
'There are no beautiful women in our world.'
'Valda,' I said.
He gave his withering smile.
But she was, in those days she was remarkably beautiful. It was not that though that marked her out for me. There were other beautiful girls, striking girls, attractive girls. But there were other things that drew me. Her writing, undoubtedly. It is hard to say why. For one writer to be attracted to another writer is not an obvious formula for satisfaction. Competition, envy, resentment, yes, it could all too readily provide that. Criticism, distaste, contempt, all that too. That gamut was there to run through with Joe, if I needed it. I might

have thought it was something important, a subterfuge to mislead and inveigle myself. As for that awful component of pedagogic condescension, I can help you in your work, let me guide you, let me teach you, it was something I attempted to guard against. I had enough of the pedagogic at the university. Maybe I could fix up the full stops and semi-colons. I could even help edit. Certainly I derived a satisfaction from sifting through her suitcase of poems and making a fifty page selection that the publisher accepted. I was pleased with myself for that. And it was something she was absolutely unable to do herself. But that was hardly a teaching role. Whatever skills I had brought into play there were not the higher gifts of the muses. A practicality, a recognition of the contingent, a realism, a making of hard decisions, that sort of thing. Always easier to do with someone else's work or life than your own. A helping hand. But a helping hand because I felt, from the beginning, that there was little more that I could offer. I was not the one who would be the teacher. She held that pack, and played it very consciously.

'You don't know anything, do you?' she would say, not unkindly, smiling, her sharp little teeth bared. It was a line I was susceptible to. Joe pulled it all the time. And the naive, did I consciously play that in turn?

Or was I embarrassed with that role, was naivety something I had hoped by now to have lost, surrendered, transcended? It was not something I ever wanted to be, naive. I wanted to be knowing, informed, aware.

And that was of course what she offered, access to all that.

'I can teach you things you never knew, I can show you things you never suspected, I can introduce you to worlds you could never enter into except through me. All your life has been sheltered and limited, all your life you have been frightened and fearful of the real world, the secret world, the hidden world, but I will take your hand and guide you through it, something which no one else but me can ever do.'

And of course I responded to that. Responded cautiously, tentatively, fearfully. I could hardly say I was open to it. It was something I knew I did not know, it was an invitation to things I would liked to have known, experience to have had without the pain inevitable in acquiring it. It was a partially opened door. Look, I can take you through it, she said. And I wasn't certain. I wasn't certain that it was experience that I wanted, not certain that it wasn't something that would destroy rather than enhance. I stood nervously on the edge, that anxious indecision that for me characterised the writer's stance, fearful of that plunging in and total immersion that Valda espoused. What, after all, were you plunging into? Why, after all, was it any more real, why was it more real than this tortured indecision? It could as readily be the false step, the trap, the destruction as the entrance to enlightenment. This could be the door through to Rimbaud's gun-running and the end of writing. And maybe that was no bad thing, maybe that was the truth and writing the illusion to pass beyond. But I wanted to write a lot more before I came to recognise that. That, I knew already, would inevitably come. But why hasten things?

Winter in Sydney can be a time of clear skies, crisp air, gentle warming sun, the skies a cloudless blue, the air free of the humidity of summer, the sun no longer savage and scorching. Much like an English summer. But it can also be rainy, windswept, grey and chill, a cloud cover blanking out the sun and sky, blanking out distances to an omnipresent grey, rain-sodden haze. Again, much like an English summer. And because no one admitted that winters could be cold and wet and long, provision was not made for them. Indeed, such provisions that had once been made had been rejected. Fireplaces had been boarded over, chimney stacks demolished, doors removed from their hinges - whether for some ramshackle open-plan, high summer living, desperately to get the heavy air to circulate, or to burn for barbecues in the back yard, how would you ever know? The shops offered little help. 'Melbourne is the place for good winter clothes, stylish overcoats, swish raincoats,' people would say, the sort of people who affected to know, young ladies in publishing or public relations. But who would fly to Melbourne just to buy an overcoat or raincoat? 'Next time you're on leave in England bring me back a Marks and Spencers' sweater.' Here was the land of merino wool, of wool bales and wool stores and wool surplus and we sent back to England for woollen sweaters. While shivering through the winter, unsweatered, uncoated, wet without raincoats. It was just such a winter with Valda. Rain foaming down gutters and bursting back out of manhole covers, rain breaking up the surface of the roads, collecting in puddles in the backyards, dripping through the broken gutterings, breaking through the iron roof and trickling down the walls and through the ceilings.

I realise now that this is why my tweed jacket featured so much in her diatribes. To me it was just something I still fortunately preserved and wore in an attempt to keep warm. But to Valda it was a symbol, a portmanteau representation of everything that she resisted. It stood for class and authority and conservatism and repression and masculinity and colonial oppression and English superiority and solicitors and clergymen and doctors and private school masters and publishers and pipe-smoking intellectuals and cosiness and warmth and privilege and security and wealth and middle class suburbs and golf courses and afternoon teas and Agatha Christie detective stories and cricket matches and confidence and assurance, an immense thesaurus of the enemy. Later it would feature largely in the things she wrote: or it seemed to, in the things she from time to time showed me, amidst the Indian bedspreads and Indonesian batiks, sudden staccato diatribes stabbed out in a burst of machine gun fire from her Olivetti portable typewriter. And the leather patches to preserve its poor worn elbows, worn through with leaning on Bodley's desks, days and evenings in the upper reading room as the Oxford rain drizzled down over the stones and spires of privilege and the encrusted past, the patches I had found a migrant cobbler to sew on to extend the jacket's life, these particularly provoked her wrath. It was not my fault that in Melbourne they sold new jackets with leather patches already attached. If that was the world of the poet Prickett and other such self-satisfiedly self-proclaimed superior souls, it was no more loved or respected by me than by her. If it was an image from bad British movies, it was not one I had ever seen, my proletarian childhood being one in which going to the pictures was prohibited, and if that was the sort of thing she saw when sneaking off with boys to matinees, then that was her choice and her problem, not mine. But it became mine, as my poor old jacket attracted the rage of her heat-seeking missiles, along with socks the refusal of whose washing she loudly proclaimed, sock-washing, or rather its refusal, becoming another major icon in the catalogue of invective alongside the tweed jacket in the things she poured out. While the rain poured down, beating on the iron roof of the flimsy cottage, dripping ominously down the chimney behind the boarded up fireplace. 'A house without a fire is like a body without a soul,' Kim would say. Tramping along the rain swept beaches with him collecting driftwood to dry out and burn, the sea as leaden a grey as the sky, the line of their merger with each other indeterminate, imperceptible. 'Why do you mess around with people like that, you can do better than that, surely?' he would say. He was like Joe on the lack of feminine beauty in our world. Was it a matter of concern, of aesthetics, of class, you deserve a higher class of partner, richer and more beautiful? Or was it a disgust with womankind altogether, why do you mess around with such, why do you need women? The answer, in part, of course, was class. It was all there in her rage at the tweed jacket, though monstrously distorted and confused. But it was a matter of class identification. That was what I thought we shared. Or what I projected.

And so we come to class, the English disease. And though obscured in Australia, it was nonetheless present. Not strident. The democratic veneer was such that you did not feel endlessly judged in every restaurant, at every bar, with every purchase. No doubt judging went on, but it was more covert. It was not like the offensiveness and insolence of England where every phoneme of your accent, every thread of your garment was being pored over, microscopic examination of education, region, blood line, family, connections.

But to believe that this brave new world was free of all that was to be deeply in error. The girls whose alleged lack of beauty so distressed Joe down at the pub had for the most part all been to expensive private schools. I hesitate to write 'the best schools' because that would be to surrender to their value system, but that was how they saw it. Bohemia, as ever, recruited from the privileged bourgeois. The girls especially. It was their rebellion, their seeking out of rough trade. Valda was acutely aware of this. She stood to one side in disdain, sniffing sardonically at their slumming. She could drape her room in shawls and batiks, but those were all cheap, found at stray stalls in the markets, at opportunity shops, amidst the second hand discards sold at St Vincent de Paul's. Whereas the strapping private school girls wore their worn and threadbare slumming clothes with all the confidence of their expensive labels, bought their rounds like a man because they could always go back to mummy or daddy and get cashed up again.

So though she might be drinking down at the Forth and Clyde on a Saturday afternoon, standing out on the pavement across from the old, disused dry dock, she would more likely be talking to one of the bikies who drank there, or one of the daughters of one of the unemployed dock-workers still in the suburb. From the libertarians she felt excluded. And was. And this was the sense of exclusion I was drawn to, something known and lived with for a lifetime. Nurtured even. That in the end was the danger, it was your familiar so you fed it, it became the rationale of your everyday behaviour, your style, your ideology. By coming to Australia I had given myself a choice, a new possibility. Here, unknown, without background, unplaced except for that comfortable, privileged job, I could live as if the world were mine, or at least open to me. I did not have to cultivate exclusion.

I could slip into it readily enough. It was always available in the dark hours, waking up hung-over, dehydrated, depressed, and surveying the wasteland of it all, how have I got to this hopeless point, by ostracism, by exclusion, by my fate as a proletarian? And waking to cold, wet, English-style mornings could readily encourage the mood. But in practice it was optional. It was an indulgence to slide back into, and a sunny day and a clear sky and an acceptance by a literary quarterly could disperse all that, so easily. But for Valda it became less an option, it became a recurrent condition.

Then, though, in those early years, that windy, watery winter, it was a position I could latch onto. It was what we had in common. Literary ambitions, sexual adventures, shared joints, everybody had that, offered that, participated in that. Occasionally movie-making rather than literary ambitions, less often painting or music in the world we knew, sometimes just sensitive connoisseurship or docile groupiedom. But class resentment, that was not part of the notation, that was what we could uniquely share.

So I would take off the tweed jacket, this is not me, here is the real me, shivering in my sweater before the inadequate single bar of the electric radiator.

'So get into bed if you're cold.'

So we would get into bed and shiver between the sheets as the rain poured through the rusted guttering and slid down the walls and drip drip dripped down the blocked drain pipes. And I would try to excavate the details of her life, layer upon layer, prizing out the shards and shattered fragments, for wasn't that what all these encounters and engagements, these couplings and conjunctions were about, vicariously experiencing other lives, the frissons of fear and fascination, discovery and disbelief, the pursuit of the mystery of how to be, what else there was, what you had missed, what the other had known, until it all became too painful.

It all, or a lot of it, depends on point of view. To Valda I was initially, if not always, a representative of the other with that tweed jacket and a university lectureship. For a while she was working in a bookshop in town, not just any bookshop but the shop that at that moment was the foremost literary bookshop, run by a former ship's captain and his wife. The captain used to run cargoes of cane down the Queensland coast, sugar cane, not the beating sort, and his shop was stacked with similarly enticing allurements, recent remainders from the Americas, direct imports from the United Kingdom of the rarer literary titles. It was a cargo culture in those days, perhaps still is though less explicitly so, now there is less variety of cargo anywhere but it has all penetrated everywhere, the same ten publishing conglomerates, the same five car manufacturers, the same three basic food suppliers. Amidst the inadequate sameness of the old colonial bookstores, Abbeys was a place of excitement and discovery. It attracted the poets like wasps to a sugar press, not something the coastal captain always appreciated. One time he rang up the books editor of the old daily paper, flagship of a fading provincial empire, to complain that one of their reviewers had been stealing books and had run out of the shop when they tried to apprehend him. That was Martin, in dispute with his publisher, stealing copies of his own book of poems to present to friends, or maybe to supply to reviewers. Had Valda been working there that day without doubt she would have encouraged him. 'Hey, Martin, here, take these too, stick them up your jumper, go on.' Maybe she was, maybe she did. But when some wretched academic approached her and asked did they give a discount on purchases to university teachers, she fixed him with a contemptuous eye and a scathing tongue. 'I think lecturers get away with enough already without giving them discounts as well,' she snarled. Maybe it was the sea captain's policy, no discounts, though at that time most shops offered this privilege, this enticement.

But it was just such privileges that she resented and rejected. I came in for a lot of resentment and rejection. For Joe privilege had always been an attraction. He found it endlessly fascinating, noted it with an anthropological enthusiasm and approved it without any worries about lack of academic objectivity. After all, he was not an academic, and his anthropologicalism was something I felt he had acquired less from disinterested study than for the targeting of privilege and status. There was never any need with Joe to justify my job, its lack of defined hours, its lack of defined objectives, its generous and trusting provision of time and facilities in which to think and write, features of an age now passed. But with Valda, as she left on an early morning bus to go and sell stupid romances and idiotic thrillers to stupid and idiotic people, I was ever on the defensive. And when she announced, 'I reckon you've got it easy' I had difficulty in succinct denial before she had left, all sniffs and tight lips.

And to say, I too am a child of the proletariat, I knew deprivation, I have experienced struggle, I suffered exclusions, found no responsive warmth in her. Who likes to be labelled a proletarian anyway?

It is something one may admit to grandly, when free of it. But to have someone insisting that they like you are the lowest of the low, the oppressed of the earth, the underprivileged, rejected and despised of humankind, does not warm you to them. She was not responsive to these appeals of class solidarity. She had only contempt for the political. She took no sides on any of the issues. To her they were all a vast irrelevance, the unappetising cold porridge served up by the daily press, the *Sydney Morning Sickness* as she called it, and not worth consideration. She had no wish to fly a banner of proletarian art, she found all that stuff, insofar as it could ever be found in those cold war years, uninteresting. She had no commitment to a world of solid, stolid workers.

She had slipped through that, found it unimaginative, unexciting, and had run off to a lumpen world of bikies and causeless rebels, down and out musicians, junkies, prostitutes, pimps, dealers. Or so her stories proclaimed.

The stories were of course less stories than things, they had that indeterminacy of things, they floated there with an undoubted specificity but unanchored in consequence or cause, never located that minutely in time or space as a realist treatment might have required. I could read the mood but the detail, the why, how did it happen, was it true, what did you do next, none of this was provided. Nor was it in any later inquiries. Inquisitions. 'What's this then, an inquisition?' she would say, sitting on the bed, painting her toenails, while the rain crashed down on the iron roof and sheet lightning illuminated the sodden yard. And realism, after all, was something we had all given up, Joe on political grounds because of its distasteful association with the left rather than from any especial attraction to the new, the avant-garde, the experimental that had seduced me, and Valda, Valda had never been at all interested in it. Her things were expressions of emotions, of states of mind, and if they touched on the materials and settings of the realist tradition, that was simply because that had been a life she had lived, not an aesthetic or political choice.

But what had she lived? The rape by bikies, was that felt life or empathetic evocation? The pimp with his feet up sharing a joint with his girl before sending her out onto the street, was that drawn from the life, and from a life lived, or observed?

The cocaine dealer in his chill, white, high-rise apartment, the girl he has picked up for a week, was that the girl I spent my nights with?

It could have seemed archetypically literary, one of those English novels of exotica, the sensitive literary young chap, posted abroad, falling in love with some girl from a seedy cabaret, or seen on her evening beat round the red-light district, memories of old Berlin or Athens or Alexandria or Shanghai. But that had already been written, written over and over again. And that was not a world I was lovingly in pursuit of, avidly recording in notebooks of the time, savouring to write up in the convenient cottage of some further exile. It might have appealed more to Joe, whose ideology of all transactions as cash transactions had encouraged, or rationalised, exploration of the local brothels. But I wanted none of it. 'If you want some squeaky clean virgin fresh off the shelf, why don't you go out and buy one?' Valda would say. 'She'll wash your socks for you. She'll sew your leather patches on. Go on, piss off, don't hang around here asking me all those stupid questions, go out and buy yourself one.'

And the things would be packed away in their worn and battered cardboard suitcase and stuffed back beneath the bed, ticking away all too audibly, in syncopation with the dripping down-pipes and broken guttering, waiting through the cold black night for their next detonation.

'You want to get out there and live. How're you ever going to write anything if you don't live? Look at you, what do you know? Nothing but books. Books isn't what it's about. You've got to get down there in the gutter and experience things.'

'The gutter isn't the only place to experience things.'

'You reckon? You reckon that? Is that what you reckon?'

'Yes.'

'We'll see then, won't we? Or perhaps we won't. Perhaps we won't ever see anything at all, will we?'

'Perhaps not.'

' "Perhaps not," he says. "Perhaps not." They ought to put that on your tombstone. That would be perfect. That would say it all. "Perhaps not".'

It was not all rain and recrimination. There were good times. How easy it is to forget them in recollecting the others. But there were sunny days when we ventured out, stood on the pavement outside the Forth and Clyde and sunned ourselves. We would live. I would live. Real life, a life of literature. Enough of this mouldering away in the academy, enough of these laborious studies, enough of criticism and analysis, enough of history and the past, we would live now in the present, throw in the job and go to South America. I had always wanted to go to South America. Ozzie Cambridge, our man of letters, was horrified. He came up to me as I went to order more drinks, and took me aside to a darkened corner.

'You're not really going to do that?' he asked.

'Live,' I said, 'live, I'm going to live.'

'But you need something to live on. You're not going to give up the university? Are you?'

'Why not?' I asked.

Did I hear a note of eagerness in his question? He probably had intimations of his own imminent and involuntary departure. Not long after the university gave him up and he was out there if not on the street certainly grubbing a living in Grub Street. The issue may have been sensitive to him, he may have begun to suspect that three years on a research scholarship and not a word of research to show for it might have brought him to the end of a good thing. There was no doubt he saw it as a good thing. His concern at my talking of giving it up was genuine. Joe likewise never suggested it was something to give up, though Joe might have believed or hoped it was damaging to the creative imagination. But neither of them believed that institutions were to be rejected: they always valued them as one of the means to survival. Survival was not one of Valda's terms. Survival sounded like calculation and calculation like compromise and compromise like defeat and defeat was the death of the spirit. For her life was the grand gesture of rejection, refuse life before it refused you.

There were other grand gestures, likewise unfulfilled.

'I nearly came by the other night,' said Joe. He was on his own. The bars were all shut. His women had all rejected him. His boys too.

'I put a bottle of bourbon in my pocket and set off to beat on your door.'

'You should have,' I said, always one for company.

'I thought I might not have been welcome.'

'You'd have been welcome.'

'Oh,' he said.

'That makes it less appealing?'

'In a way,' he agreed. 'I was not looking for welcome. I was in a state of rejection.'

'We could have rejected you.'

'I wanted to beat on your door and demand you come out and drink with me.'

'In the gutter?'

'I had other places than the gutter in mind. I felt your new friend already had you in the gutter. I wanted to retrieve you from it.'

'But in the end you decided to leave me there.'

'As it turned out I didn't know where your house was.'

'It's not my house.'

'That could be why I didn't know where it was.'

I suppose I could have given him the address then, but didn't. There were already enough blows beating against our fragile walls, from within as much as without.

'Some other time,' I suggested.

'There is only ever one time,' he said sententiously. 'And if we miss that time we miss it forever.'

'So that's why you didn't come?'

'I felt the drunken writer beating on the door was too much a literary cliché.'

'That's never stopped you before,' I said. 'Certainly not in your writing.'

I cannot recall his reply. Perhaps there was no reply. Perhaps I did not say that. Already too much had been said between Valda and me. Perhaps I was learning discretion. Though I doubt that.

As for Joe's projected visit, I was rather saddened he had not come. It might have cheered up a winter evening, diverted us momentarily from our destructive dissections of each other. Or was that idiocy?

Wouldn't Joe's presence only have added to the tensions? Almost certainly yes. But in absence, in its fortunate unfulfilment, I regretted his non-arrival. I would have liked that mark of his interest, an incident for our memoirs, an incident, indeed, for our fictions. Well, nothing to stop you writing it, he would no doubt say. But it is not only a matter of truth, a matter of not commemorating what never occurred. It is also a matter of judgement, of discrimination. As Joe himself saw in aborting the incident, it belonged too much to literary cliché. So he left us undisturbed to wallow in our no less overfamiliar clichés of fear and suspicion and jealousies and resentments, of life and what it was and what it wasn't and what one knew or never could know about what it really was.

One memory of the tortures we inflicted on each other will suffice as representative. Nothing is to be gained from a loving, languid, leisured recollection of them all. And they were perhaps not consciously designed as tortures. Who knows what we intended, who knows what drove us on? Desires supposedly, but desires for what? 'We walk over the same ground again and again until it speaks to us,' said Joe. He claimed to have been reading Freud. Perhaps.

As well as the Maltese rooming house and the rickety smugglers' cottage, there was another place, single storeyed, set back in a block somewhere in Balmain, constructed of some man-made substance, some carcinogenic asbestos compound or some by-product of sugar-cane, masonite or some such. It was cold and it tilted and when I went round Balmain to indicate the literary associations of streets and houses to Kirkpatrick the antiquary, not so long ago, it had gone. I could not remember precisely where it had been, its site now buried beneath post-modern mews and millennial townhouses. It is this cold, unfeeling house I remember, in its sea of clay and puddles and unkempt grass, and one of the football-jersey-wearing heavies she shared it with meeting me outside. Valda wasn't there. She might have been in the bookshop, she might have stormed off. 'We had a bit of trouble last night,' he said. She had gone down to the Mandarin club, a gambling joint in Chinatown. Gambling was not characteristic of her. Money had never been a goal. She had learned to get by, with infinite complaints, and never showed any desire to acquire great riches. That was all part of those worlds she despised. But the Mandarin club, with whatever tawdry exoticism it might have been associated, offered the lure of some seedy exploration. And I, where had I been, off somewhere with some well-bred young lady in publishing, screwing in some expensive apartment on one of the smarter reaches of the harbour. This was reprisal time, clearly, and who began it, what began it, when it began I do not remember. Such a blank might suggest my own responsibility. But then responsibility was something Valda despised, wasn't it, all that middle class moralising business. Had I taken here at her word, I think not, I think I knew enough not to believe her word. Was I, for all my proletarian bonding, one-sided as it was, registering a chill fear of the gutter, was I reaching out to check the competing demands of wealth and status and privilege?

And was I so immersed in such a cocoon of questions, was that the literary appeal, that indecision and qualification and minute dissection of motive learned from the world of George Eliot and Henry James that had once seemed so central, so necessary, so absolute? The one surety, or near surety, is that Valda had no such preoccupations. She went down to the Mandarin club and picked up someone who turned out to be trouble.

'He wouldn't leave. Couldn't take a hint. We had to see him off. Fortunately there were a few of us having a drink out the back. Playing cards. After the pub.'

We sat in the kitchen and drank instant coffee. No one had any dope. The sun tried a few feeble yellow rays across the trampled grass and treacherous slides of clay. And Valda, Valda, Valda was not there, nor did I know where to go to look for her, like a cat she had her secret hiding places that she never revealed to anyone.

We had no word for the sort of writing we were producing in those days. We did not call ourselves postmodern because the term had yet to become current. In the end we were categorised as 'new' writers. Like Valda's use of 'things,' there was a certain lack of imaginative creativity in the categorising. But if asked we would probably have said the creativity went into the writing, not the labelling. And did we, anyway, want to be labelled together, Valda and Joe and Sam and Martin and myself? Did we have anything in common beyond being contemporaries? Valda would have been suspicious of any such grouping, of any attempt at self-aggrandisement by the formation of a school. Neither she nor Joe nor Sam were of a co-operative nature, though only Joe was explicitly to celebrate American individualism and the market economy.

But though unlabelled, without manifestoes, the spirit of the times had imposed certain aesthetic preferences on us. We were not much into plot. We stood aside from the ravellings and unravellings of genre fiction. We were less concerned with narrative than with lack of narrative. Metaphor, maybe, or setting, image, mood, the encapsulation of character and moment. Some self-consciousness of formal strategies, some self-reflexive moments in which the fiction demonstrated an awareness of its own structuring. The fag end of a dying modernism still offered an intermittent beacon. So we tended to avoid simple progression. And that after all was concomitant with our lives. This was a summer playground, even if a rainy one. We had escaped from childhood and were now enjoying ourselves. Careers would be made from our talents, not from any further laborious years of training and strategy. Joe may have had a strategy. But the only world view I heard him utter in those days was his advocacy of *volupté*. We lacked *volupté*, he would announce. He would pursue *volupté*. Other times he would go bushwalking. From my perspective, as I no doubt announced to him, it was all an indulgence. There was no sense of heading anywhere. We were where we wanted to be. Bushwalking was not something you did in those days for a destination. The exploring had been done, the route across the Blue Mountains discovered over a century earlier. Bushwalking was a matter of going into the bush and back again, maybe going round in a circle. Working off the hangovers of a heady *volupté*. So progress, development, linear narrative was absent. Things just were and then they ended. And that's how it was with Valda and me. Undoubtedly there were recriminations, resentments. But I have no recollection of things working up to a climax, I have no recollection of the slow, or rapid, unravellings of plot. Probably the ending was already implicit in the beginning. Our sense of inevitability may have led to our comparative lack of concern, or expertise, with narrative. I don't remember. It is tempting to write that it was just one of those things, and to succumb to the temptation in no way undercuts the painfulness of it all. Those things were often very painful.

6

Mere Anarchy

Even to have imagined that the push, the world of the Libertarians, as they called themselves, was a site of the exotic seems, from this distance, something in which the search for the appropriate word can only fail. Absurd, bizarre, comic, daft, extraordinary, an alphabet of possibilities begins to assemble, though with no decision, no certainty, just indication of, if not firm deprecation, amused equivocation. And yet within the possibilities known to me, within what was perceived as available, at the time, and entirely without reflection, neither forethought nor foreboding, it was new, sensual, exciting. If it now looks different what can I remark except to remove that 'if.' Certainly it now looks different. But at the time it provided its allures, pursued as they were in a haze of unconsciousness, unawareness, oblivion. How else could allures prove effective?

It was an imperative, an unthought thrust, a drive. There could have been better worlds. Possibly there were. Certainly there were worse. Some of those last I had experienced. This I had not. So there I was. Amongst it, amidst it, or at the least on the periphery. Regretting nothing.

The appeal of course was sexuality. The push was a meeting ground at the end of an era when such meetings had had to be performed more circumspectly. But within the push there was a proclaimed openness. Women could come up to men and ask for a fuck. This was not normative in those times, but it was part of the idiom of the push. Sexual exchange was what it was about and jealousy was, though not unknown, frowned upon. Although in theory, of course, nothing was frowned upon. And in theory, of course, sexual exchange was not what it was all about, it was about other things too. Anarchism. It was about Anarchism. There were discussions. There were meetings, which I did not go to. Perhaps you had to be invited: there was a strong sense of an inner elite corps about the whole operation. Perhaps I found the idea of meetings and discussion groups unappealing. I had enough meetings and discussion groups in my daily employment at the university. Discussions in the pub, preparatory to going to a party, were fine. Totally acceptable. You couldn't just stand all evening at the bar saying nothing. Well, you could. Ozzie Cambridge often did, unable to commit himself to some aesthetic preference, perhaps, Lowell or Olsen, which was it to be, or just sozzled. And there would be Dreadful Jiri, one of the theorists of anarchism, one of the leaders of this ostensibly leaderless sect, always ready to belabour anyone unwary enough to engage with him. 'No, that is plainly ridiculous. No, that is quite impossible. Why? It would take far too long to explain why, there are a thousand and one reasons why, namely –' and he would begin to enumerate them. Dreadful Jiri, who the time I passed out passing a bladder stone took the opportunity to make his own pass at my girl-friend. But that was the point about the push, there were no taboos, do what you want was the whole name of the law, as long as what you wanted was not Socialism or Communism or religion.

It would be tedious to describe the endless push parties. Tedious, anyway, to attempt to recall them. Standing in kitchens and hallways, drinking beer or flagon wine from chipped cups, old glasses, newspaper wrapped bottles. With some enforced colonial gentility, bottles of beer bought from bottle shops always crossed the counter wrapped in newspaper, and wine bottles in long narrow brown paper bags. It concealed the nature of your purchases from the wrath of the godly. Or perhaps the abstemious had insisted on such coverings so that women and children would not be led astray by the sight of naked bottles carried down the street. Or perhaps it was simply that newspaper absorbed the dampness from the bottles kept in the fridge, the condensation that developed as they encountered the hot summers. No doubt it was assumed that the bottles would be unwrapped before their contents were drunk. But push parties favoured the practice of derelicts and winos in the parks, leaving the newspaper and bags in place.

Predictably I have followed the practice of Dreadful Jiri, enunciating what I have announced would not be enunciated. Perhaps now I should proclaim the pairings and copulations that the drinking prepared the ground for, so that I can leave them as read.

'Why is it?' asked no less dreadful George, 'that we have no novels about the push, why has it not been written about?' He was a philosopher, his questions were not for you to answer. 'I have thought about this,' he would continue, 'and I have concluded that we are too critical, too incisive, the intellectual tone is too sharp for writers to capture.' Word had it that he had written a novel himself. Perhaps that captured that uncapturable, incised, felt life.

It was not all drinking and sex and parties. There was politics. Perhaps I missed this for a while, wallowing around in the Circean sty. But Circe had her agenda. Those the Congress for Cultural Freedom failed, or chose not, to embrace were seduced by the sexual congress so readily offered by the push. Some, indeed, participated in both worlds. The agenda became clear to me at the election night party the night Labor finally won after twenty-three years in opposition. Opposition had been assured them when they split and the Catholic anti-communist faction formed what they called the Democratic Labor Party. It was a strategy successful in various countries in those Cold War days.

Election night parties were a tradition for the political intelligentsia. Contemptuous of politicians, the push nonetheless held its party after the pub shut. It was not unfascinated with what it derided. We gathered in some old sea-captain's mansion on the Balmain waterfront, the sea-captain long consigned to the deep, the house decaying and awaiting renovation when the suburb became gentrified. Meanwhile a group of Libertarians rented it. It was never clear who owned these splendid old houses, nor how the people who rented them heard about them. It was as if they were safe houses operated by some deep cover agency. Perhaps they were.

Was it this party or the party to watch the American moon-landing on television at which some girl newly come to the push danced on a table and began to remove her clothes? Watching the American moon-landing seems an unlikely site of celebration for anarchists, the assassination of an American president would surely have been more appropriate, but they did indeed watch the moon landing. There was only one television – they had not yet achieved an American profligacy of television sets in every room – so the girl soon acquired her own audience surrounding her, drinks in hand. Perhaps they were the less political or the less moon gazing of the party goers. She danced around with naked breasts for a while then, when incited to remove the remainder of her gear, refused, and collapsed into hysteria or epilepsy. But parties were not usually like that. Such displays were frowned upon as vulgar, suburban. If you wanted sex you went off and had sex. Titillation, theatricalism, performance was, though not prohibited since nothing was prohibited, looked down upon with a chill disdain. It was in many ways a strongly puritan society.

Having announced politics I see that I have diverged into byways of sexuality and drinking. So it was. But it is the political that lodges in the memory. Not in image: it is attached to no detail, no place, no individuals even. If Joe was there, and I am sure he was, I do not see him. Nor do I see the television with its prediction of Labor victory extrapolated from the early counting by computers and panels of psephologists. But it was that predicted victory that got the push pundits going, got them calculating their strategies, how they must straightway expose the falsities and contradictions in the Labor programme. They knew the authoritarian legislation that socialism would bring.

'They've not even taken office yet and you're already planning to attack them,' I said to someone. Joe, Gwen, dreadful Jiri.

'Of course.'

'How do you know they'll break their promises? How do you know they will fail?'

'They're politicians. They always do.'

I was appalled, I was outraged. Which perhaps only shows how unpolitical and innocent I was, not only about the company I had been drinking with and having sex with all these years, but also about the so-called Labor party. But at that time it all seemed like the beginning of a brave new world.

And unsocialist as it proved to be, that Labor administration nonetheless worried some forces enough to provoke its destruction. I don't think the sort of dark deeds that led to its removal were being hatched at that Libertarian party on election night. Surely not. Yet elsewhere without doubt they were. And there was a homology, a unity about the conception of those hydra-headed plans. Presumably in some basement room in Virginia, and Whitehall, as the results came in via the satellite, and bottles were opened less in celebration or even resignation than in the spirit of invoking inspiration, have a snort to get started, things were thought, plans initiated.

But the ideologues of the push, were they inspired by any more than a spontaneous bourgeois spoilt kids' anarchism, an inherited fear of the working class, an intuition to mobilise immediately against the repressed, like their forebears in those mythic general strikes, pouring champagne from the bank windows on the heads of marching workers? Or was it the secret services organising immediately, calling their shock troops out to combat the slightest risk of social change? Or can such distinctions between class interest and internal security be drawn anyway?

And so Australia emerged from its chrysalis into the late modern world. It had safely slumbered for half a century, comfortable, prosperous, introverted, ignorant. Now it was to emerge as a vain, resplendent butterfly, ready to be crushed on the wheel. But we did not know that. We had not sufficiently read history. We responded to the blandishments of the new, the modern, the American way of life, and it would destroy us. Subsonic, supersonic tones were transmitted and we stirred inside the carapace, tugging at its structures, like Samson. For a few years we wore our hair long.

It was the era of the underground press. Sometimes it was referred to as the alternative press. But underground sounded much more exciting, combative: a world of partisans and hidden caves, presses assembled and dissembled, inflammatory manifestoes. For decades the Libertarians had issued a foolscap, duplicated publication, magnificently if misleadingly called the Broadsheet. Here the headier deliberations of the high-level meetings of the inner caucus were published, analyses of the arcana of anarchism. It was taken very seriously. I believe at one point Joe published a study paper in it, if appearance in such an organ can be called being published.

I was not alone in believing publication involved something rather more substantial than this typewritten duplicated effort. Gwen, a Libertarian who was a postgraduate student, mounted an editorial bid for a university student newspaper and succeeded in gaining control. I was not convinced that hijacking a student paper was a worthy aim or a suitable venue for publication, either. But then she and her group lost control of the paper and set up their own independent version of it, which they pitched at the entire city. Somewhere along the line Joe became the literary editor, possibly even a part of the editorial collective, though ideologically he opposed such things as collectives, and the Libertarians themselves claimed to despise structures in any way formalised, so that it was never clear who was in effect running the paper. And now Joe began his career as a columnist, first lucubrating on the female orgasm, a hot topic for public intellectuals in those years and one to which he devoted his deepest investigations, and after the success of this piece he initiated a regular space for himself, holding forth on the issues of the day, or the month. I remember none of it. No doubt it was the collective intention to deflect attention from the serious and restore the margins to the centre. Meanwhile the official student paper resumed its opposition to Australian participation in America's Vietnam war, to conscription, and other such topics, deemed distasteful and engagé and leftist by most of the Libertarians and their columnist.

 Joe asked me for a story.
 'Are you the editor now?'

'No, no, I am just asking you for a story.'
'Are you literary editor or something?'
'You worry so much about roles and designations.'
'I think we both do,' I said. I didn't. I thought he did. I thought I held no respect for such things. But I was worried about what might happen to my contribution. I worried it might disappear for ever, that the inner conclave of anarchists might dismiss it as unacceptable and lose it altogether. But it appeared.

'I liked your little story,' said Gwen.

Maybe as a sociologist specialising in media she was uninformed on the technical terms of our trade and would have said, had she known the usual phrase, short story. Or maybe it was just the ruling class note of those Libertarian girls, smiling down on the writer, *de haut en bas*, to appropriate one of the French phrases that Joe had not learned at that time but was later massively to affect.

I confess I was pleased with the appearance of my piece, spread magnificently over a full page, tabloid rather than broadsheet, alas, but still splendid. Publication was not easy in those days. And what literary quarterly could give you such a display? I handed Joe a second offering down at the Newcastle one evening.

'What is this?' he asked, holding it by the corner of its pages, then raising it to such light as came into that gloomy front bar.

'A story.'
'A story?'
'A story for your underground paper.'
'I will hold onto it until it's your turn,' he said.
'My turn?' I said. 'Is it a matter of turns?'
'Yes,' he said, unbuckling his briefcase and putting the typescript away.
'What sort of way is that to run a paper?' I asked.
'By rota,' he said.

At some time it was Valda's turn. I don't know how her typescript was acquired. Not through me. I felt resentful, proprietorial. We had spent so many hours squatting on the floor of that cold cottage before the single bar of the inadequate radiator, planning strategies, targeting this magazine, that magazine for her work. It was always more easy to direct someone else's career than your own. I could see opportunities for Valda when nothing was apparent for myself.

Perhaps Joe had acquired this piece, though I did not know that they were seeing each other. Perhaps Gwen had obtained it. Valda's work was perfect for their needs, sex and drugs and written by a woman. The absence of the political was ideal. The war raged on, the bombing escalated, and the Libertarians fought the fight to print four letter words. They would have liked to appropriate Valda. Perhaps that was a temptation for all of us. But Valda would not be appropriated. She held them in contempt, their intellectualism, their theorised sexuality, their unstylishness, their straightness. She held pretty much all of us in contempt. Perhaps there was a component of envy, their moneyed backgrounds, their university scholarships and grants and salaries. To Valda they were people playing at bohemianism, with an escape route always on hand. For her, for the authentic existence she espoused, there could be no escape. She began to slide away from us, or we from her. Increasingly it was the world of the Cross, of hard drugs, of opiates, dependency, the twilight demi-monde that claimed her, or that she claimed. Her story appeared in its turn. But nothing further. For a start they didn't pay, the Libertarians. This was an alternative press insofar as it did not pay contributors. Normally that would have been against Joe's principles, but his principles were always open to negotiation and he had longer term interests in play. Not so Valda. Vain she might have been in some ways, about her appearance, her image: she was not an unkempt, spontaneous natural. But vanity publishing had no appeals to her. 'Typical,' she snorted. She smiled wryly, with a certain satisfaction, at the double page spread, folded the paper away, stashed it in her scuffed and battered cardboard suitcase beneath the bed along with other things in manuscript and print. And that was it. No more. No more from me, either, not my turn. But Joe continued productive.

'How come you appear every issue but I have to wait my so-called turn?' I asked him.

'Because my contributions are a column, whereas yours are an occasional literary feature.'

'A column?'

'It is the nature of a column to appear regularly.'

'And that is why you write a column?'

'There are things to be said in a column and things to be said in fiction.'

'And the column appears in every issue.'

'I sincerely hope so,' he said.

When the paper finally died, and how it survived so long and who financed its printing were mysteries beyond my knowledge, the column transmigrated. It made a unique transition from anarchic opposition to reactionary establishment and appeared each week in the *Bulletin*. Such were the contradictions, or conjunctions, of our city. And Joe, Joe too drifted away from me. But whereas Valda sank down beneath the surface into the sad and seedy worlds beneath the Cross, Joe rose to the raised row of tables in the window of the Greeks, lunch with the *Bulletin* editors, chewing dead sheep, admiring the view of the war memorial and praising the American effort in Vietnam, no doubt. I don't know. I cannot imagine what they would have talked about, I wasn't there. Nor did I know what he wrote about in his column, since like everyone else I ever knew, I no longer read the *Bulletin*.

But before Joe was translated to the window tables of the Greeks, beginning his inexorable rise to honours and orders and ribbons, the vice squad moved and indicted the paper for obscenity. Here was the theatre of fame and glory, ready to house a Libertarian spectacle. Dreadful Jiri rose to the occasion, convened meetings, planned rallies of solidarity with mass readings of obscenity on the university lawns, proposed we all announced our complicity and presented ourselves en bloc before the magistrate. It seemed an insane strategy. Perhaps I had more fear of authority than heady Libertarian contempt for it. I had no wish to stand in the dock. Even then I sensed the power of the state. I chose not to attend the hearings and acknowledge my role in exhuming a nineteenth century celebration of hashish. My contextualizing note to its reprint was little more than bibliographic. I could see little glory accruing to me from admitting responsibility: nor was this a scholarly publication I might claim in the university's annual publication report. If the drug or vice squad wanted to act, let them find me. I declined Gwen and Jiri's invitation to come to court. In the event the magistrate remarked of the hashish reprint, that it was a transparent and specious attempt to give the paper a veneer of literary respectability. Joe's role in all this fades on the memory. Perhaps it faded even at the time. As literary editor he might have been expected to have been charged. Perhaps he was not literary editor and only told me he was to obtain and suppress my second story, or to solicit a thing or two from Valda. Certainly it was only Gwen who was gaoled. It got her a lot of publicity and launched her on a subsequent high profile though short lived media career. Perhaps the notoriety of the case helped Joe in his, inducing the *Bulletin* editors to take over his column. No good came of it to me. In solidarity I joined a couple of other Libertarians in handing out copies of the next issue of the paper while Gwen was in gaol. On her release she thanked me graciously for having done so. 'It meant a lot,' she said. But what the meaning was I never did discover, nor cared to ask.

7

Man of Letters

Ozzie Cambridge certainly had a lot of books. Even when he first appeared on the scene. Later he would call it his obsession, this collecting. But when he first appeared it was more a young man's hurry to be an authority, to acquire the weight and bulk necessary to occupy the role. How he got the role was not at all clear to me. This was another of the eternal mysteries never revealed. In a general sense an explanation could be offered, but the specifics were shrouded, as always. In previous eras you had a patron who placed you in position. And in Ozzie's case there was a university person who had spotted him as a student, not that the university person was of much weight himself nor that the position was much of a position, a little magazine, one rift with plots and coups, and Ozzie was brought along. Not that he wrote anything, neither stories nor poems. But he came into that world of the editors, the review editors, deciding what went in or more important, what didn't, and assembling the beginnings of a magnificent library of hard backed review copies. It was part of a network, these people who were around the magazine and around the university and around the pub, all comparatively young, few of them, looking back on it, actually producing very much, but getting themselves onto committees and editorial boards and film funds and adult education programmes, yes, these were the early years of networking before the term was coined, the actuality achieved before the word.

So, it was a scene to be around in, intersecting circles that offered a world, an environment, a theatre. It looked like all you really had to do was stand at the bar with a glass in your hand and adopt the stance of holding forth. You didn't necessarily have to utter, just look as if you had uttered or were about to. To be the possessor of a lot of books was an excellent qualification. That baggage was stacked there in the background like a wall of sandbags, the security of substance, the penumbra of a library. Nobody was going to demand you take a book off the shelf and read from it, much less read from it without taking it off the shelf. No one was going to require a sustained assessment. At the most a few hanging phrases, an allusion or an insinuation. And considered silences. They were always an impressive qualification. And everybody was eager to hold forth, offer opinions, deliver judgements. People, people in pubs, literary people, film people, university people, adult education people, poets; people prefer, generally, to speak rather than to listen. Don't you think? Wise, nodding silence. Sometimes it seemed Ozzie was blind drunk, still standing in that authoritative way, still holding his glass, raising it, drinking from it, all the while becoming that much more static, that much more fixedly and substantially standing there, that much more glazed, like the doors of a glass-fronted bookcase, locked.

I suppose what he specialized in was arcane bibliographical knowledge. Fugitive issues. Elusive imprints. When you are young it is flattering to have someone know of some piece you wrote in an obscure, defunct magazine which you had thought was lot to view for ever. Flattering, no you don't think it is flattering, satisfying rather. I found it so. Reassuring. That the words were not eternally lost.

'I'm glad somebody's read it,' I said.

'I didn't say I'd read it, I said I had a copy of it,' said Ozzie.

For every satisfying exchange there was the price of deflation. That was the idiom of that world.

'There's still time,' I said.

'I probably have a fuller collection of your ephemera than anyone else in the continent.'

And in any other continent, was the inevitable implication.

'Really,' I would have said.

You hope maybe, years ahead, people may begin to collect your work. But already, at this stage, before there was even that much of it in print, when most of it was ephemera anyway, to have someone collecting it, you can come to no conclusion about it; the satisfaction is uneasy, there is something unsatisfying about flattery and you are not sure it is flattery anyway, you find it strange, your confidence in your future is strong, though not without its deep trepidations, its trembling doubts, but that anyone else should have such a commitment to it as to have invested in it, already to have opened a collection on you, this is something obscurely disturbing, this is something not so reassuring after all.

It is one thing to collect books, another to read them, and yet something else again to have anything to say about them. The bookseller Weil used to chortle at his customers.

'How many of these books you buy do you actually read? Come on, level with me. Ten percent?'

'Well, you have them there for when you might want to read them.'

'I'm not knocking it,' he would say, 'don't get me wrong, if it wasn't for loonies like you I'd be out of business. I'm all in favour of it. It's only you and the sex trade keeps me off the dole.'

And Ozzie was one of the foremost purchasers. Collecting contemporary American writing as it came in, in the erratic way it came in, made him inevitably the expert. The book trade was dominated by English publishers and American writing was routed through English imprints. A lot of American writing, consequently, was unavailable. But there were a few fringe operators in the business who could see which way the wind was blowing. They brought in container loads of American remainders and found there was a ready market of readers starved for this recondite material, the regular pabulum of the American campus bookstore, the beats, Black Mountain, Black Panthers, college paperbacks, CIA subsidized overstocks.

It all seemed new and radical. It was certainly different from the traditional English product. And there was a cunning in it. This was the hard to get, the esoteric, the for so long repressed and denied, and it was arriving as if smuggled in, sold not through the decaying old and established bookshops, that now seemed so boring, but in the ramshackle bargain hunters' outlets, mixed in with the old Left standards and the pornography. The old Left standards challenged the conservative society, the so-called pornography challenged censorship, the American imports challenged the publishers' cartels. These were the days of challenge. Later, when American values had saturated Australian society, it seemed less challenging: but by then the taste had been formed. Marketed like illegal drugs, the American imprints had created their addiction. In the end they were everywhere.

But this was the beginning. And Ozzie was right there at the start. His thesis suffered, never quite begun. He was so busy buying books and buying beer it was hard to find time actually to write. These were the heady days of the Newcastle, where every night people talked about books or film or magazines or poems they had in mind, and in the mornings the determined worked on them; pretty well every night after the pub there was a party, or if there wasn't you created your own, you went off with a few bottles and drank on with someone or had a smoke. Ozzie had immense stamina. He could sit there drinking on and cataloguing the names of books until the fruit bats flew back to their roost in the Moreton Bay figs at dawn. They were good days, good nights. In the end his scholarship was cut off.

His girl-friend was in tears. 'It's terrible what they've done to him, what's going to happen to him, can't you do something, get it changed?'

Ozzie stood at the bar amazingly unscathed, a bit ashen perhaps, the termination had launched him on a day and night bender so he was probably short of sleep. Or maybe now he no longer had his university room there was nowhere he could sleep, the evenings being too full of pubs and parties to waste, what has night to do with sleep?

'It's so unfair,' she said, 'he's got such a potential and he really loves books and look what they do to him. English departments.'

She sniffed, blew her nose, red like the rims of her eyes. 'It's all there,' she said, 'he's got all the material for his thesis, he's only got to write it.'

But he never did.

There were a few weeks of drinking with the condolences of friends and acquaintances and then he resurfaced as a regular book-reviewer for one of the dailies. It augmented his library and gave him a role, an identity: and by now he had established the weight of authority, the calories of the beer had given him the bulk, the hours of practice at the bar had confirmed him in that pulpit stance of public utterance. Now he was a man to be wooed, instead of the wooer. The writers came to him rather than he to the writers. It probably meant more free drinks, more invitations, the regular by-line his open sesame to irregular occasions. Joe added Ozzie's name to the chart of literary power, the tapes and coloured pins coding the interconnections of editorial boards and advisers and publishers and reviewers. This was in the days before the arts bureaucracies, before there was only one game in town and all the tapes seemed to lead to the same source of central control.

'Now he's a powerful man,' said Joe. 'A man of power. A man of war. A man of letters.'

'I might write a piece on you,' Ozzie said.

'You want another drink?' I offered. It was a purely rhetorical question, everyone always wanting another drink. We were in the beer garden of one of the pubs near the university. Even though his connections with the university had been formally severed, Ozzie still drank there in the weekday afternoons.

I came back from the bar with a couple of beers.
'What sort of piece?'
'Oh, you know,' said Ozzie.
'I'm not sure I do.'
'Getting anxious?' Ozzie asked. 'Nothing personal. Purely lit. crit.'
How pure was lit. crit. anyway? It was that illusion of 'purely literary values' I was spending my academic hours assaulting.
'You've no objections.'
'No, not at all,' I assured him.
'I didn't think you would have.'
'No, I'd be pleased.'
'Nobody's written on you, have they?'
'Well, reviews.'
'Apart from reviews. No, I didn't think they had.'
These were the early days, the beginning days.
'Nothing like getting in first,' said Ozzie.

I probably would rather, if I'd thought about it, and after this I did think about it, have had some distinguished critic not personally known to me write something in some international forum. Eventually I came to realize that wasn't how it was done. Eventually I realized it was a tissue of networks, certainly in the early stages, till the logs were rolling.

'We probably need to have a few sessions to talk about it,' Ozzie said. 'Not that I just want to parrot what you think you intended.'

Intention was deemed to be a fallacy in those days. So that you ceased to inquire what anyone's intentions were. Which looking back on it was rather a mistake.

'We can talk now,' I said, always one for getting things over with, no time like the present, make hay while the sun shines in the garden of the Forest Lodge hotel. But what hay, what garden, what forest? It was very much a conceptual garden, a concrete triangle with brick walls, definitely postlapsarian.

'No need to rush things,' said Ozzie. 'Now I know you're happy with the idea I'll draw up a list.'

'A list?'

'Of points. Make sure we don't miss out anything obvious.'

He got up with the empty glasses and headed for the bar.

'Good. Now that's all settled we can relax.'

The hay was left to rot unmade. At the edge of the garden the wolves stretched in the afternoon sun, and the bears sharpened their claws on the trees in the forest.

Ozzie was going to write the piece for a left-liberal review, a struggling fortnightly version of London's *New Statesman* and New York's *Nation*, but thinner. In the end it got so thin it ceased publication altogether before Ozzie had actually got the piece written. That in itself provided its own subject for jocular discussion, as the weeks and months and years passed in this infinite deferral of literary assessment. Occasionally I would remember the project and get irritated and offer Ozzie no more than a terse nod at the bar and seek out someone else to talk to. But most of the time I forgot it and we carried on talking much as ever, without any list of points or arranged meetings. We met naturally at the pubs and parties anyway, and I would readily enough outline various current plans and intentions, it was a perpetual afternoon of good intentions, the novels to be written tomorrow, the stories, the film scripts, the critical essays, the new magazines that would provide their own equivalent of *New American Review* reoriented to the Southern Hemisphere in its entirety, or *Village Voice* re-jigged from New York for Sydney, any number of imitative adaptations, imitations of imitations, as we learned to speak and write and find our own voices.

Ozzie assumed the manner and mantle of literary authority. As his library grew, so did his girth, which gave an air of solidity, though it might have been puncturable, and without the heavy hand made shoes he wore he might have floated to the ceiling. But he impressed visitors. When an English editor came out and decided to do a special issue of his international journal, he asked Ozzie to do a survey of the new writing. And of course Ozzie failed to deliver. The deadline was extended, but to no avail. 'Tell him,' the English editor wrote to me, 'we are very disappointed in him.' I told him. He chuckled. In fact in the end he did write the piece and it appeared in a later issue of the magazine but that rather missed the point of the special issue and it didn't help focus the international readers onto our new writing, which would have been valuable: at least, I thought it would have been, for me. And then the other longer promised article appeared, but in the interim it had changed, it no longer focused on me alone but on others too, which satisfied none of us. Still, you could perhaps say that Ozzie had been applying his critical attention; though it was more than a bit laggardly, and less that earth-shattering. I suppose in a way it was ground-breaking since who else was writing anything about any of us? But there again, it didn't seem to say an awful lot. I went through the piece looking for some bits I could excerpt to quote on the jacket of my new book, but there was nothing sharp or concise enough. I went through it again, but there was nothing I could use. I mentioned this in the pub one weekend. 'No,' said Ozzie, 'I make sure there isn't.'

'You don't want to be quoted on the jackets of books?'

'Absolutely not,' said Ozzie.

I didn't believe him. But it was odd that there was nothing that could be taken out and used.

For all his inadequacies he was still one of the few critics we could hope for anything from. None of the others could be relied upon at all. They all tried to display independence and integrity and, even more than Ozzie, had their gaze fixed on other shores, American shores, delivering servile accolades to those already established overseas. The people they drank with were too close, had no international stamp of approval, if they wrote about them, us, they might be proved wrong sometime. So Ozzie it was. And he could simulate an interest, a concern with literature in the making. This was how he borrowed and lost the manuscript of my new novel.

'Someone stole my briefcase in the pub. Sorry, cobber.'

This was in the days before word processors, personal computers, information storage, the days when even photocopying wasn't that omnipresent. The copy I still had was a carbon copy. But I had it. I was aware enough not to trust anyone with an only copy. As for comment, Ozzie had nothing to say about the book. I had been very excited with it, for me it was a breakthrough, a new voice, a new vision, I was exhilarated by it. But Ozzie had nothing to say.

In the protest movements of those years a number of skills had been acquired. In protesting against the war we had learned the technologies of poster making and pamphlet printing, we had produced alternative papers, organized meetings, held readings against the war, made contacts with the media. We carried on these activities afterwards with magazines and small presses. Ozzie was around too, helping us pack and dispatch books, suggesting printers, helping out with some of the systems, mailing lists, review lists. It began again with purely literary values, a relief from the earnest engagement of the anti-war campaigns, but I soon found myself tugged back into commitment, purpose.

As well as publishing the new writing, we began collecting the uncollected, leftovers from the old left, anything that the mainstream publishers wouldn't do was worth taking seriously. We had break-ins. One time a fire was started but Ozzie discovered it before much damage was done. We put it down to vandalism at the time, at the time we weren't inclined to conspiracy theories and paranoia. That was gradually to evolve. The political was only a tendency on our list anyway, most of it remained literary, alternative, oppositional perhaps but hardly hard left. The boxes of radical lit. crit. that caught fire were surely not deemed such as would shake the foundations of the state.

These were politicized years but not paranoid. This was the Indian summer of radical protest, before the paranoid realizations froze the very sap of opposition, leaving bare ruined cells. This was before the big silent purges. Mass market paperback houses were happily issuing Marx and Engels, Christopher Hill, E. P. Thompson and Jack Lindsay. You could build up a good library in those years. You could talk freely about left initiatives and I did, about what I was working on, the political novels I wanted to write after I'd finished my book on political fictions, it was that oh so idyllic world in which you could formulate your ideas in dialogue and discussion, in endless conversations in the pub and on the telephone, in long discursive letters to friends overseas, unreal world, to be paid for ever after.

I had found some part-time work for Ozzie, editorial work on a collection of essays we were publishing. I wanted the quotations and references checked, I still believed you needed to quote accurately and I knew this was where error crept in and the essayist in question wrote prolifically and quickly and was liable, I suspected, to those sort of slips. Ozzie changed a few 's's to 'z's or vice versa and sent the collection back, late of course. I went through the manuscript myself and found, as I knew there would be, the predictable quotations with their quote marks lost so the passage ran into the text and to a hostile reviewer could look like plagiarism; lines dropped from quotations; names misspelled; all the usual errors of transmission as the essays had gone from typescript into magazines run by people like Ozzie. I don't think I was being obsessive. When you published this sort of thing, selections from the old left, you needed to ensure that there were no easy targets for attack. That was the point of paying someone to copy-edit it, so you wouldn't be vulnerable, discredited. I was furious and told Ozzie so. He was suitably contrite and this time even wrote a confession. A confession, that is, of error. 'I know I have let you down,' he wrote. It was a long letter, abject, with no address so I could not respond, even had I wanted to. It seemed to have been posted in America. These were the years when people began going to America rather than Britain, though you never quite knew where or why.

On his return Ozzie landed a job in publishing. He was vague as to what sort of job it was, as with so much else. In his new suit he looked like an editorial director and the writers round the pub looked forward to good things, one of their drinking mates had penetrated the walls, now the days of contracts and advances and glory were on hand, even just being published was on hand. But it never turned out like that. Perhaps it wasn't such a splendid job, just a matter of changing 'z's to 's's or vice versa rather than commissioning titles.

'Look,' I told him, late one evening it must have been, the time for straight talk, candid advice, 'you're going to get sacked anyway so you might as well publish some good stuff before you go. Everyone always gets sacked in publishing. There's no point playing it safe and doing nothing just to hang in there because you won't hang in there.'

And he didn't hang there, inevitably he was sacked. But, like everybody in publishing, he turned up in a job somewhere else with some other imprint. He was on the merry-go-round now. But it didn't do any good for any of the writers in the pub.

He would phone up, though. Now he had an office he would spend his time phoning up. In those days I liked to use the mornings to write, before the day got to me, before I looked at the papers or talked to anybody except maybe a brief exchange at the corner shop to buy fresh bread or milk, but no sustained or intrusive conversation, I liked the fresh, crisp feel of the mornings, blue sky, blue harbour, fresh clear winds, the uncontaminated breath of inspiration. And then Ozzie would phone up. Sometimes it wouldn't matter, I would have written my quota of words for the day; other times I would say call back later, I'm writing now; but too often it would break into the mood and fragment it. I always answered the phone, who knew, it might be Hollywood calling, girls, adventures, publishers, editors, fame and success beyond the power of the imagination, but generally it was just Ozzie.

We must have been drinking one night, maybe we'd been out at the pub or a party or a book launch, something lost in the amnesia of time, and Ozzie just stayed on. Usually I would drive him home, or he would ring for a cab, but this time he said he'd just sleep on the couch, no problem. In the middle of the night I got up to have a piss or get a drink of water. Ozzie was sitting up in the living room, reading through the folders on my desk. We exchanged a few muttered words and I went back to bed. Insofar as I thought about it at the time I was obscurely flattered. Here was somebody interested enough in my writing to want to look at work in progress. A couple of days later Ozzie went on one of his benders, downing a bottle of whisky and ending up in hospital. The usual malign pub gossip was that it was a suicide attempt, conscious or unconscious. I rather doubted it. I had never detected any underlying self-doubt, any troubling unease in Ozzie. But then I felt a sudden anxiety, a twinge of guilt. In my current committed mode I had written a diatribe about the literary scene, the evasive critics, the refusal not only of engagement but of even saying anything, and I had cited Ozzie in a dismissive aside. Could that have been something he had read that night, something that had plunged him into self doubt and self hate? I was appalled. Had I all but killed the only critic who had ever written on me? I tried to remember which folders had been on the desk, which ones Ozzie had been sifting through. Was it that diatribe, or new fiction, or unanswered correspondence he had been going through?

'You should keep copies of your correspondence,' I remembered him telling me.

'I do,' I had said, 'I keep the letters, I don't need copies.'

'No, copies of your end of the correspondence,' he answered.

'Why would I do that? I'm swamped by paper.'

'For the record,' Ozzie had said.

Maybe he hadn't come across the diatribe, maybe he had just been reading the correspondence. I never asked him.

He soon recovered and was back in the pub. He continued to appear in the reviews pages, for a while. I bumped into the literary editor of one of the papers in the Malaya one night. We shared a table.

'I don't know about Ozzie any more,' he said. 'I start to wonder if he ever actually reads the books. He reviewed this novel the other week and I looked through the book and it was a collection of short stories, it wasn't a novel at all.'

'Ah well,' I said, not so much charitably as thinking, as I often did, of my own work. 'Times are changing. The old genre distinctions are fading. Sometimes it can be hard to tell the difference.'

He dug his chopsticks into the sambal.

'I still think he should have noticed,' he said. 'I don't think it's unreasonable to expect him to have noticed that, do you?'

8

The Legend of Sam Samson

Joe was convinced, or claimed to be convinced, which was far from necessarily the same thing, that Sam Samson was much older than he said he was. Twenty years older. What Sam claimed was to be younger by a few years than us. Joe was not having it. Whether he was threatened, or annoyed, by Sam's rapid acceptance and success in the literary world or just perceptive, I could not tell. Certainly it was not a journalistic desire of setting the record straight and getting to the truth that motivated Joe's insistence. Such alleged desires were one of the lies about journalism we were fed in those years. But Joe had not been a journalist for nothing. He had no more commitment to the unvarnished truth than any other journalist still in the business. Nor, for that matter, did Sam.

    Certainly Sam had been readily accepted. There was a sentimental love for an old con, an eager romanticising of gaol and crime and social delinquency. The older Libertarians had always maintained associates in the criminal fringe, and were not especially romantic about it. They saw it all as reality, social organisation a crime anyway committed by self-styled authority, and in the world of whatever you want, get it, the existence of crim contacts was useful. But the new wave of Libertarians like Gwen came from their bourgeois bowers very dewy-eyed about it all. St Genet and such like shit. Now they had their own jennet. His needle aubades and psalms of smash and grab, songs of statutory rape and anthems of amnesia sat well in the underground paper alongside the full and unexpurgated text of 'Eskimo Nell' and whatever that ballad was that James Joyce allegedly wrote.

    Joe pursed his lips. Possibly Joe was fiction editor and columnist but not overall literary editor, not in command of poetry. Possibly Ozzie Cambridge had acquired that role. Possibly neither of them had handled Sam's manuscript, but the poet himself had thrust it on Gwen in the pub one night with a suitably ingratiating lisp, shirt tail hanging out of his trousers over his buttocks like a French maid in a theatrical farce or a specialist brothel such as Joe claimed familiarity with. Though Gwen was equally capable of soliciting it herself, coyly complicit in their campaign, less clearly against society than scrambling up its façades to some convenient roosts on the higher window ledges, ready to pop in at the top. A shock for Joe admiring the view of the war memorial from his window table at the Greeks, chewing casserolled lamb with Cultural Freedom's greediest and grossest, to have Sam and Gwen scaling up from outside. Joe had managed to slip into the *Bulletin*'s pages without having them slide in behind him, but he failed totally to confine them to the smudgy columns of the underground and alternative. They pressed on his heels.

Sometimes you suspected, we all suspected, that Sam's alleged life of crime was more a fictional construct than a matter of record. Always with Sam there was an awful lot of talk and an absence of substance, characteristic of his verse, as of many of his contemporaries. Post-modernism suited him. He came into his own, or everybody else's. The poems were full of a life of crime and literary borrowings. Allusion it was called rather than theft. Creativity rather than a lie. He found it a paradise and in the tired, genteel, official literary world of that era, he made an impact. This was the era in which Ozzie Cambridge and his cohorts would go on about debilitating gentility in literature, and write, or fail to write, their theses on the shock of the new in American poetry. It, this new tough stuff, had the impact of the new but was safely approved on other shores. Whether they bought the colonial rights or simply helped themselves to them, who was there to ask? In such a world of appropriation, Sam was what they wanted. Made to order. He suited them, they suited him. How true any of it was, how would you ever know? Was it any less true than Ozzie's reviews of unread books? A world of illusion, spectacle, lie.

Then there were times in more anxious or resentful moments when you suspected, I suspected, that Sam was some irredeemably criminal plant inserted into our society by some equally irredeemably malign covert operation, a Charles Manson, perhaps, or a beyond-ideology urban terrorist, a product and puppet anyway rather than a self-created child of the streets. But perhaps it was from children of the streets that the brightest and best recruited their materials. His women tended to have the characteristics of prison warders or spy mistresses if you let your mind drift in that direction. Perhaps this indeed was his authentic criminality, this aura of menace and complicity he inhabited, complicity not with you, indeed a complicity that could never be defined or demonstrated. There were those who liked this notation of danger. Valda for instance. For a while they were close. Then as Sam gradually rose from the underworld to compete with Joe for a place as a national treasure, Valda steadily sank down to that lumpen and sordid demi-monde of sex workers and drug dealers that Sam apparently so successfully put behind him.

Having a real crim around in the little world of our unreal city undoubtedly had its appeal for some. Romantic, menacing, exciting, apprehensive. Joe again was unimpressed. 'He's not a real crim,' he remarked, scornfully, looking across at the city skyline from the room where he wrote, towers of Mammon, hotels of Sodom and Gomorrah, masts of mass distraction. 'The real crims don't go to gaol, real criminals don't get caught.' Later I discovered it was one of Sam's own lines. At the time I had not read it and I was impressed at the insight, not so much as an insight, after all in itself not a remarkable one or even that original, but for the radical critique of the social order that, uttered by Joe, it might be taken to imply. Perhaps within the *Bulletin* columnist and the incipient national treasure there remained a social conscience. Even until the end I looked for signs of the progressive in Joe. In the later depths of my disillusion with the self-proclaimed left, my sense that it was all suborned and collaborative and fraudulent and objectively reactionary, I still held out hope for the public intelligentsia of the right. Their right wing proclamations, after all, could be as false as those of the left, and in their case a masquerade for a secret subversion, infiltrators of the establishment in order to corrode it from within. It was my last remaining fragment of the dialectic of hope. So Joe, dining in his Cambridge college of buggers and spies might, along with the entire high table, embody the possibility of revolutionary change, a last supper of establishment traitors, could it be? Inauthenticity might well have been the distinguishing characteristic of one so able to detect inauthenticity in others. And Sam Samson's inauthenticity as a criminal was one of Joe's firm convictions. Along with the falsity of Sam's proclaimed age. So amidst the warm welcomes Sam received in the pub, Joe alone held back with a chilly distance. But then Joe was never that welcoming to new arrivals. The scene was quite crowded enough. The market was already over-supplied, and to a believer in market forces the arrival of a new supplier could only be unwelcome if you were a supplier too. And poets, anyway, were not sound. Unprincipled, unpublishable in any legitimate commercial context, they drove prices down by their readiness to appear anywhere, do anything. Writing short bits and pieces that could be used as fillers, they enabled the media to fake a literary concern, slipping in an ode here and a lyric there when an advertisement failed to materialise or a columnist delivered short measure: and that would be the literary token, while those of us, Joe and myself, writing longer prose pieces, remained with stock unsold. Joe would never have spelled it out like that: that would have looked like an admission of defeat, a failure properly to judge the market. There were many things Joe preferred not to spell out.

But if Joe was unenthusiastic about Sam's arrival, others were full of welcome. Ozzie Cambridge saw in him a useful force, something to direct from behind or to attach himself to, and Sam was conscripted as editor of a poetry review which Ozzie and his cohorts seized in some poetic coup. And with Sam as the front runner, Ozzie was able to secure his position as reviews editor, and spend the brief winter months writing requests to publishers, throughout the globe, to obtain review copies, in his ambition to have the largest contemporary literary collection in the southern hemisphere. The books poured in. Occasionally he would let Sam have one or two. It is doubtful that he trusted Sam with the key to the post office box. Ozzie had a patrician sense of responsibility: never let servants or ex-cons have keys. And Sam had no wish for the responsibility of going to the mail and collecting submissions. He scattered papers around him like St André the thresher. It was his way of avoiding responsibility. Such devices I recognised, familiar from the university. He was happy for Ozzie to control all that paperwork, and Ozzie did.

There is a story of someone at a party opening the fridge for a beer and encountering Sam curled up inside it.

'Aw, thanks mate, glad you came, I'd hidden my heroin and I was trying to find it and the door closed on me.'

The story was told me by a film producer and has that visual quality a film producer might value. But like most of the stories about Sam, it is lacking in resolved narrative. In that it befits a poet. Image, composition of place, but not much else.

Not even the necessary truth of fiction. Effect, affect, and that is it. I never saw Sam using heroin, never saw any indication that he did. It was one of those stories he put out, or allowed to be put out, like driving smash and grab getaway cars and being raped in gaol. They may have been true. Or they may have been movie ideas, recycled episodes and impressions from day time television re-runs.

But there were the bloodstains. Some times then were times of disruption that affected us all, some larger cosmic upheaval to which we were all subject.

I had broken up with my girlfriend and was living temporarily in East Sydney. I missed a stop sign and collided with a tow-truck and was taken to hospital shedding blood everywhere. The cuts were all superficial, though for months afterwards pieces of windscreen would work themselves out of my skin. I moved back to Balmain and took a room in a cold, ramshackle wooden house Sam's girlfriend had rented. She and Sam too were breaking up. I came home one day to find blood everywhere, Sam having severed an artery smashing in through a window. He survived. But it was adduced as evidence of an underlying neurological problem by one of the eminent doctor poets of the city.

Brain surgery was recommended. Sam and his girlfriend were back together, I had moved on, settled in a house on my own. One morning the doctor poet called me. Would I, asked the doctor poet, persuade Sam to have surgery? Get him to visit this specialist. It would only be a quick snip. Sever some cortex. Whip out the enlarged pineal gland. Something simple. It will stop his headaches. This is why he gets recurrent headaches. He cannot continue using pain killers. He will have kidney failure. This is why he used heroin. To deaden the pain. But he cannot continue doing that. One quick snip of the surgeon's knife and the pain will be gone. He will be calm. Content. No longer a trouble to his friends. And acquaintances. No more rage. No more erraticism. No more blood on the hallway floor.

I think I may have been persuaded it was a good thing.

'He will listen to you. He needs sound advice.'

I could have passed on the advice. On the other hand I could have easily not. These were the days when doubts were being voiced about lobotomies and leucotomies and other simple little strokes of the specialist's knife.

Blood, knives, they were part of the imagery of the time, poets' imagery, menacing potential, fearful associations, romantic suggestions, rhetorical excess, well-worn associations. Perhaps it was to avoid the surgeon's scalpel that Sam announced 'Gone Fishing' and moved up the coast. He settled on the swampy alluvial deposit of a muddy river with his minder. Maybe it was her idea to keep him out of trouble, trouble being synonymous with the city. He sat up in the swamps and sang the songs the bullfrogs sang, occasionally visiting town for a few days of excitement, less drink or dope than sitting up all night playing Leonard Cohen and raving on with whoever was unwise enough to let him in.

Then a girl was found murdered up the river. The carpet of leaves and bark, the body by the creek, the chill mists of sex and death. The police parked their command unit caravan in front of the house Sam rented. The prison record, the alleged penchant for under-age girls, the blood-stained knife on the kitchen table all told a story, but whether it was any truer than Sam's stories hung there in doubt.

His alibi was a party in town. He had escaped his minder and driven into Balmain.

'A party?'

'A party.'

'And whose party was it?'

'My lawyer's.'

'Your lawyer's. Very convenient.'

'Yes.'

'And is your lawyer prepared to testify you were there?'

'Yes.'

And he did. He was a useful lawyer to have around. Not long earlier he had been arrested for setting off a smoke-bomb at an anti-war demonstration. He gave his name to the arresting officer as Richard Milhouse Nixon, a name with its own legal associations, and defended himself by phone under his own name. At one point the police became suspicious.

'You're pretending to be your solicitor. You're Richard Milhouse Nixon.'

'Certainly not,' he said in firm legal tones. He got away with it. Maybe that was the celebratory party Sam said he was at. 'You remember.' Some people remembered, some didn't. It was hard to distinguish one party from another, there were parties after the pub most nights, it was hard to remember where they were held let alone who was at them, the shifting pattern of the same faces, the shuffling partnerships. He might have been there. He might have been there some of the time. He might have been and gone. He might have been and gone and come back. It was a fruitful theme for speculation. Even critics like Ozzie Cambridge became creative, weaving possibilities and speculation and suggestions into unpersuasive narratives.

'It was my fishing knife,' said Sam. 'It's covered with fish scales. It's fish blood.'

Did fish have blood? we asked. We did not know. We lived lives of blithe alienation in the city, how should we know where food came from, how it was killed, whether it bled or screamed or flailed in agonies unknown to us.

Did the doctor poet call again? 'Even if he didn't do it, it would be safer for everyone if he had the operation.' Snip, snip, a deft flourish and the knife withdrawn, bits of brain tissue and blood adhering.

It all came to nothing, like an elusive modernist poem. Some poor disturbed youth confessed. The police were satisfied. The command caravan was towed away.

Not so many years later the doctor poet was found dead, suffocated in plastic sheeting. It looked like murder, but the forensic doctors at the morgue decided it was suicide designed to look like murder.

And the party-giving lawyer became Joe's business manager. They would tour the brothels of the inner city together, sharing young girls.

'We're doing it for you,' Joe said to me, 'we're looking for Valda for you.'

As for Sam, his reputation in no way suffered. These were the years when the older north American writers were seeking out murderers on death row to write their stories. This was the forefront of literary development, the sort of thing Ozzie Cambridge's ill fated thesis had been poised to examine. Sam's legend grew. He was now as unstoppable as Joe.

9

Asia Hand

At this time I was editing a series of Asian writing. I had seen Ripley's translations in literary journals in England. Or in one journal, anyway. Did I get in touch with him? I don't think I did since I had no idea how to contact him. I think he must have seen or heard of the first volumes and approached the publisher with a proposal.

It was an impossible proposal. Something like the complete works in twelve volumes of a modernist Japanese poet. Something massive, something mammoth. But the proposal was forwarded to me and I wrote back saying how about a single volume to begin with?

At some point he replied and said he would be visiting Sydney and perhaps we could meet to discuss his proposal. I replied, By all means, come and have lunch at the university. Fair enough, he turned that invitation down, he had probably had enough lunches in universities. The very mention of such a possibility makes me shudder now. But this was years ago when I could eat anything in any ambience, or thought I could. No, he wrote back, he had a busy schedule, could I meet him in his hotel for a coffee?

He was staying in the Menzies. There weren't many hotels in Sydney in those days. This was the posh one. International visitors and graziers. This was before Sydney had become a tourist city.

The Menzies was not a place I'd ever had cause to enter. I remember it as gloomy and forbidding in those days. But I went down there, somehow located him in the lobby. How did we do that? Was he carrying a folded copy of *The Times*, sporting a carnation in his buttonhole, reading the stories of Osamu Dazai? My lack of memory only underlines my lack of observation, the naivety of my lack of suspicion. I blundered in, eyes wide open, eyes closed, either way it didn't matter, those happy years of innocence and unawareness, when the city was always bathed in early morning sun, even in the endless evenings drinking down at the Newcastle, nothing clouding the horizon, nothing darkening the vision, if vision it could be called that seems to have perceived nothing. Those were the happy days. Bliss was it in that dawn, etc.

I probably suggested we went down to the Newcastle. It was a home from home in those days, where you would always find someone there to talk to, writer, journalist, painter, academic, political hanger-on. The literary life. It was the thread of continuity with a hundred years of bohemia. Half a dozen years later it was closed down and demolished, and after years of being an empty lot the site became the empty forecourt of some post-modern high-rise. And radical, anarchic, political, literary bohemia never found itself another home, all that talent and no ability to agree on a new meeting place. Whatever calculating, repressive force that engineered its closure had calculated well on the inability of that world to re-create itself.

He declined.

'It's only round the corner,' I said.

But he preferred to stay where he was. Not exactly where he was, in the lobby, but down a level to an even gloomier site, the coffee shop. It was not a place I felt easy in. Was that something he calculated?

We sat in that bunker till mid afternoon. Four hours is the figure I remember, which suggests we must have eaten something at some point. But again nothing that I remember. Maybe toasted sandwiches. He was not a person I associate with eating. Or drinking. Coffee, endless coffee. *Kaffee, Kaffee muss ich haben.*

It seemed to me extraordinary that someone should have flown into a city like Sydney, any city, and not have wanted to look around. In those days I always wanted to look around. Even while failing to look directly in front of me. He was older, though, and now I realise he had probably done enough looking around. But to sit for hours in the gloomy underground coffee shop of a stuffy hotel, while outside the sun danced on the harbour, and the wind rippled the hair and clothes of the girls, and no doubt the boys too, and the peaches and oranges and nectarines glowed on the fruit barrows at the street corner, it seemed to me very odd indeed.

But there he sat in his business suit as the morning sunk into the afternoon. I told him about the series. He told me about his poet. We didn't come to any clear resolution about the publication of the twelve volumes.

He talked about a recent experience that had impressed him. In some formal garden, was it in China, how had he been in China at that time?

perhaps it was in Singapore or Hong Kong or Taiwan or even Japan, but in some formal garden were placed these boulders. What are they? he had asked. Stones, they had said. And what do they symbolise? he had asked. 'Nothing,' they had said. They represent nothing. Emptiness. Absence.

He was much taken by the concept. It is the one detail I remember from our four hours in the coffee lounge.

He worked for the British Foreign Office looking after airline landing rights. If the Japanese wanted to land in London then the British would want to land in Tokyo. 'Gets all very high level as you might imagine. High level enough for HMG to think it worthwhile keeping me in Hong Kong.'

I must have expressed surprise that there was enough negotiation to keep him occupied full time in the far east. But then, the Pacific was soon to become the fastest growing area for air travel. Though I don't know that it was then.

I'm not sure that I ever totally believed him, even from the beginning. Not when I thought about it. Perhaps I did. But not for long.

We kept in some sort of correspondence. But he remained intransigent about his twelve volume project. There seemed no way he would agree to a selection, or a representative single volume. But we kept in touch.

The next visit was as the first. Sitting in the shadows of the Menzies coffee lounge, hour after hour. I wondered if he were waiting there to be on call. But no call came.

He quizzed me about the literary scene. What magazines, what quarterlies, what about radio? He took out a little pocket notebook and wrote it all down, addresses, names of editors, frequency of publication. '*Southerly*, that's purely Australian, that wouldn't publish translations. *Quadrant*, that's the CIA one, Cultural Freedom, I wouldn't write for that.'

But he did. And for various others. His translations from the region began to appear regularly. He made contact with ABC radio and soon they were broadcasting half hour features of his translations. How did he ever manage that without leaving the Menzies for their equally gloomy dull brown studios at the Cross? For years afterwards his translations cropped up. I was amazed at the steely efficiency of the way he had gone about it, eliciting the information from me, writing down the names and targeting them so effectively. I don't remember that he ever thanked me.

He had one of those crisp, glass-cutting accents of the ruling class. Public school, Oxford and Royal Navy. He had been a naval pilot. I think he went to Oxford after the Navy. It emerged that we had been at the same college as each other, but it formed no bond. It was not something he ever talked about, except in some exchange of credentials. It was a long way away from him. It was a long way away from me, too.

'How long have you been here?' he asked.

I told him.

'Detribalised,' he said, that voice like a cracking whip. It implied the unreliable, the unsound. With that accent it was like the Headmaster's assessment on my last school report: 'No house spirit.'

And then to my amazement he included himself in the same category.

'We'll never fit back in now,' he said. 'Once you leave the tribe you're out for ever.'

And you could see it in his eyes. I should have realised that before. The business suit, the short back and sides haircut, the carefully knotted tie, all bespoke the archetypal ruling class Englishman, conformist, public school, all the unshakeable certainties of rank and caste. But the eyes, the eyes were no longer the steely blue of the naval pilot. They had the opaque cloudiness of the seer, the psychic, that milky sheen of the increasingly inner-directed, of the inner-directed who has seen enough of the world to know it without having to look any more, but who nonetheless knows and continues to know.

After Oxford he had joined the Foreign Office. 'Suez,' he said. 'Half the FO wearing black arm-bands to work. Of course Eden was totally mad. Like his father. Had to lock the old chap up. Used to fire his shotgun at visitors to the estate. Can't get away with that sort of thing any more.'

Though he rarely talked about the past. Most of his stories were scenarios of the present or future.

'Take Japan. The Japanese economy continues to boom. Why? Because they have no military spending. The USA is threatened, it decides to cut back their rate of growth, says they should contribute to their own defence. Japan re-arms. Then one day they announce they're making a film about the Japanese invasion of Singapore. The director hires a battalion of the Japanese army as extras. They fly into Singapore and occupy it. What do you do? Can't blast the whole island away. All that valuable real estate.

'Or terrorism,' he said. 'But on a large scale. Take some maverick military division. Some disaffected South Korean general. Same story. They say they're making a film, re-enacting the Japanese invasion of Singapore. Fly them in. Then they take the whole place hostage.

'That aircraft that went down over Malaysia. Probably terrorists. A shoot out with the air-marshal. Bullets ripped through the fuselage. Lost pressurisation.

'That Korean airliner that was forced down over the Soviet Union.' This was before KAL 007 was shot down, an earlier version. 'Lost its way. How did it lose its way? Somebody put the wrong flight programme in the computer.' He did not elaborate on whether by accident or design.

'Met this most beautiful woman,' he said. 'Miss Philippines. Brilliant. Gifted. Half a dozen languages. Then she went into the hills. Joined the guerillas. Your sort of chaps got to her. Filled her full of all this revolutionary stuff.'

My sort of chaps. I'd not disguised my politics, confused as they were, nor my background. No point in disguising your background with his sort of chaps. They could always tell, place your accent in one. But Maoist guerillas, I didn't feel I was quite in that league. Maybe I felt a heady glow of romance, these were the Che Guevara years after all, Che, tracked down by the CIA and murdered. But his 'your sort of chaps' inspired a dim sense of unease as much as any glow of romance.

His son was learning martial arts. He was in trouble at school for throwing his teacher to the ground. Ripley had been delighted. 'Tough little chap.' The whole family wrestled at night, practicing holds and throws on each other. He was preparing them for the cataclysm.

'When the urban hordes start sweeping across Europe,' he said, 'it will be every man for himself. They'll cut great swathes through the populated centres, looting and pillaging, murder and mayhem.'

He had located a place to retire to, away from the route the scavengers and dispossessed would be taking. He had bought a house in the far south-west of England, in the promontory of Devon and Cornwall. The hordes would be on a track from Glasgow and Newcastle through Birmingham, Oxford, London and onto Paris and Frankfurt. Or vice versa.

'It has to be a place you can defend,' he explained. 'On a rise. Clear line of fire. Stockpile it with bows and arrows. Firearms will be useless. Ammunition doesn't keep. And when the crisis comes you won't be able to buy any. Bows and arrows are the only thing.'

He was a man of culture. Or perhaps more accurately, a man who recognised the role of culture. And I think valued it. When he did business in Japan, he would always recite a poem at the beginning of proceedings. The people he did business with recognised the role of culture. It was how they all did business. Sing the plangent folk song. Intone a vision of falling cherry blossoms. And then in for the kill.

But there was also a high-handedness in his cultural doings. Some of the poetry he translated was traditionally unspecific about number, quantity. He valued precision. He replaced the many and the few by specific figures. It wasn't arbitrary, he assured me. He had studied numerology. He selected the appropriate number. He felt it rather improved the poems. He was known in the circles in which he moved for his numerological studies. He had advised the Anglican archbishop of Seoul on the appropriate date for his marriage.

His mother had been a psychic. 'Rather a good one. Terrible when you're a young naval pilot to find your mother knew everything you were up to.'

It is hard to remember how often I saw him, how often he visited. In those days so much seemed to be happening, there was such a surface flurry of activity, those naive and happy days when we knew nothing. When I knew nothing, anyway. The learning was to come. And very soon.

I was summoned to meet him one day at a hotel in the Cross. He had moved from his haunt downtown. It was November 11, 1975. Once again he refused to leave the hotel. Once again it was as if he had to be there on call. So we sat in the rather unattractive, chintzy lounge of this small hotel for the usual span of hours. I would have met him at twelve or twelve thirty. It was about four or four thirty when I drove back through the gates of the university. Again I remember nothing about what we talked about. Some uneasy memory of something involving 'your sort of chaps' lurks, but I cannot fish it out, it prefers to sink down into deeper waters, just the silvery impression of the scales of its back to let me know it was there, or something like it. Driving back through the gates of the university there was a news flash on the car radio. The Governor-General had dismissed the Labor government, the Governor-General with his lines through to the British establishment by virtue of his position and, as we later learned, to the CIA by virtue of his one time presidency of Law Asia and other Congress for Cultural Freedom connections.

If I hadn't wondered before, I wondered then why Ripley spent those long hours just sitting in hotel foyers on his visits, why he kept me bailed up there. And I wondered what he was doing in town on that auspicious day.

But the events of that day created so much else to think about. That was the crack in the democratic consensus, that was the invitation to conspiracy theory, that was the prompting to read the books that were already around about the secret state, Philip Agee's *Inside the Company: a CIA Diary*, John Marks' *The Search for the Manchurian Candidate: the CIA & Mind Control*, Victor Marchetti and John Marks' *The CIA and the Cult of Intelligence*. They were all about United States operations, of course. There weren't the same revelations about Britain's MI5 and MI6. That all remained blandly impenetrable behind the conservative suit, the short back and sides, the public school accents.

At some stage a typescript arrived. Not the twelve volumes of the Japanese modernist, but a selection of haiku or sijo, translated into rhyming couplets. In those years I was still thinking in modernist terms. But even when I began to doubt modernism I never turned back to Augustanism. How could we publish heroic couplets two hundred and fifty years after their moment? This was the sort of issue that agonised me at that time, despite what he might have thought 'your sort of chaps' were engaged with. I was torn between the archaism of the mode, and a recognition of the work that had gone into the project. Could he, I suggested, write an introduction explaining why he had chosen to translate into rhyming couplets rather than free verse. It didn't have to be a long piece: just something to indicate there was a thought out and defensible reason for what might otherwise appear bizarre.

He never wrote it. No doubt I should have realised he never would, that to ask him to explain, to ask for reasons behind his decisions, was to ask for the impossible, the unacceptable, the inadmissible.

He turned up one evening. It is the only time I remember him outside the confines of a hotel. We had been watching the television news, a bus load of pensioners had crashed over a cliff. I was telling Lily my father's theory, that they deliberately used old buses with faulty brakes for pensioners' outings in order to get rid of them. And then there was a knock at the door and Ripley had arrived.

'Ah, you're here,' he said. 'Thought you might be out blowing up bus loads of old ladies. Going to be an increasing drain on the welfare system unless there's some decisive direct action.'

We asked where he would like to eat.

He didn't really want to go anywhere, Greek, Italian, Chinese.

'What I'd really like is just a fried egg.'

Later I realised this had been his ploy not to go anywhere. He must have thought that even my sort of chaps could produce a fried egg. But we insisted in hustling him out across the city to the Viennese Gelato bar at Bondi. Maybe we thought that was the only place that would fry an egg. Or was it some intuitive attraction to the Third Man associations? It was a long drive and when we got there it was crowded. 'Maybe we should try somewhere else,' I suggested. 'The Balkan up the road. . .'

'Don't worry,' he said, 'I'll clear a table.'

'What, psych them out?' said Lily.

He nodded and did it.

I don't remember if he ordered a fried egg. Someone at another table ordered a banana split to be sent across to our daughter. She was delighted. I wonder now if he had psychically induced that.

It was crowded and hot. Lily developed a migraine.

'I'll give you a pill,' he said.

'What sort?' she asked.

'Something to fix it.'

'What is it, though?'

'I don't know what they call them here,' he said. 'Get them in Hong Kong. Absolutely guaranteed. Knock you right out.'

We took him back to his hotel and he produced the pill and Lily took it with a glass of water and we left him there.

The next day was her graduation day. She slept through till midday and missed the ceremony.

I think that was the last time I saw him. Not long afterwards he retired and went back to England. His translations continued to appear in the journals. He wrote to me that he was taking up a security consultancy to one of the sultanates for a couple of years. And then we lost contact. The series of Asian writing closed down. Indeed a lot of things closed down, those sunny, hopeful years, those days of hope and aspiration. I sometimes thought of visiting him when I was in England, calling in on his fortified stronghold. But it didn't seem like a good idea by then. The days of repression had unmistakably begun. There seemed no point in voluntarily bearding lions in their den, even amiable lions, even if you might not have been their prey. Even if you individually weren't, and it wasn't clear whether you were or not, your sort of chaps pretty clearly were by now, and no doubt always had been.

10

Critical Distance

It was probably in one of the corridors that the thing came up. Most treacherous business was done in the university corridors. Most business, indeed. Indeed most university business was probably treacherous. You would be walking along, blinking in the gloom, the memory of the bright sun still imprinted on your retina, and somebody would sidle out of a room and catch you off guard. I should have been on guard, it happened so often. But I wasn't. These were still the innocent years, the naive years, the sun shone brightly outside, no one worried about skin cancer, the gloomy corridors were just the price you paid to pay your way, they were not something you thought about.

As always, I forget who the messenger was, professor, head of department, postgraduate co-ordinator, I have no recollection, what self-erasing skills, what amnesiac projection did those lackeys of destruction deploy?

'There's this character wants to write a thesis on your stories.'

Flattery, was it flattery that was supposed to suck me in? But youthful naivety was well supplemented by unproblematical youthful confidence in those sun drenched years. So someone proposed to write a thesis on my fiction. So it was only natural, only to be expected, only my due, so what?

'Oh yes,' I said.

As well as naivety and confidence, I had a low cunning. A thesis meant supervision. Supervision meant a nuisance at the least and decades of tedium and trouble at the worst and it was usually at the worst.

'Maybe you should talk to him.'

I should have played it by the rules and said no, I think it best he talk to someone else, I don't think the subject of the thesis is the appropriate person to be a supervisor. But we didn't have any rules. I made the rules up later. At the time curiosity, vanity, laziness, the wish to be well thought of, all the personality defects and social virtues triumphed over the protective low cunning. The hardest lesson to learn is how to say no. You only learn it from episodes like this.

Of course it wasn't a thesis on my writing. Not on mine alone. It was on me and some others. The usual others. The unnamables. But he named them. Joseph Wendel Holmes and Sam Samson.

'I thought it would be a good combination,' he said. He was like a dog wagging his tail and bringing you a stick all covered with saliva. A big dog, somewhat battle scarred but in good condition if a bit hungry, a hunting dog, kept at that hungry edge.

I could have said it was a terrible idea, just deal with one writer, just deal with me. But I didn't know how to say it without sounding egomaniacal.

'They're mates of yours, aren't they?' The tail thumping the floor.

'Well,' I said. How did you put it? 'I haven't seen too much of them for a while.' Least said soonest mended. I must already have been wary.

'I'm not sure about supervision arrangements,' he said. 'I'm only out a day a week at the moment.'

'Out?' I said.

'Didn't they tell you?' he grinned. Maybe it was a nervous reaction, a grin of anxiety, not the slavering satisfaction of a hungry dog eyeing a meal. 'I'm in prison.'

'Oh,' I said, the writer, a word for every occasion.

I was about to ask what for but checked myself from some sort of liberal politeness.

'What for?' he grinned again. When he grinned he wiped the side of his mouth with his hand, as if to wipe the grin away, like a wolf rubbing a paw across its muzzle.

'Murder,' he said. 'I've been in fifteen years.'

It's your solar plexus that fields the shock. That's where the blows come, where you suddenly feel sick. My natural reaction was to flee. But these were liberal days. Suppress your basic instincts. Surrender survival to an agenda of philanthropy. Smile at all you fear, welcome in all that threatens you. Who were the social engineers who had foisted that scenario on us, what was the programme behind those hypocrisies? These were the days when all the girls from the pub were visiting the prisons. They had given up on writers and artists and turned to armed robbers and arsonists and hired killers. Then they tried to turn the robbers and arsonists and killers into writers and artists. It was just one of the factors that added to the demise of the old bohemia, that turned the pub into a seething, treacherous sea of destruction. This was when bohemia was on the turn from innocence to evil; maybe its innocence was only our first perception of it and evil our embittered conclusion; maybe every generation had entered in in innocence and found it something other. Maybe. Maybe there always seemed to be a qualitative change.

And hadn't he begun in that innocent bohemia, wasn't that where he was hired for the killing, wasn't that the world of the person who hired him? Well, of course, he never did say who had hired him, just one day, maybe he had been drinking, one day he said something about that bastard down the pub, that same bastard who turned up in some other dubious episodes, who had got him into so much trouble.

These were the days when I had begun my programme of reading about the security agencies, after the coup, when the fantasies of popular fiction materialised as reality and what had been the materials of escapism were now refocussed as analyses of our political existence. These were my daily topics. These were the issues I had become interested in. Not through perversity, not through deliberate, conscious self-destruction. It was that day in 1975, November 11, when the government was removed by coup that had triggered the inquiries. It got a lot of people thinking. Until then the world of spy fiction and political coups had seemed the escapist fantasies of other hemispheres, the sensationalist consumer garbage of western decadence, cold war crap for the jaded imaginations of Europe and North America. And then it changed. What it was all about I still don't know. The volumes written about it have clarified little. But if no answers ever emerged, the questions that have been asked remain of interest. That was how I got interested. That was my interest at this point that he turned up.

Recruiting assassins from prison, hiring psychopaths for political dirty work, this was unremarkable in itself, there were endless novels and movies about this, I read and watched them interestedly, yes avidly, you never knew what truth you might see in schlock, it was all part of consciousness control, but at least the patterns, the models might be true, even if the specifics were not. Certainly I ended up asking him about this.

The society ladies who visit, he said, they come in as do-gooders, but they have connections, being society ladies, to captains of industry and captains of war and captains of intelligence and who knew what else, they could run the messages, vet the possibilities, get someone remission in return for, for what he didn't elaborate, perhaps he didn't know, or preferred not to, like when someone in the cell next to him was tunnelling out every night he preferred not to know, so many of the conversations we held drifted off, faded away, not just with him, this was the mode of those times, the mode of many times, the detail not revealed, the specifics not spelled out, but the drift, the tendency, you could see that, where it headed.

These were abstract researches I engaged in, or if not abstract then academic, conceptual, not things I ever thought to apply to my own situation. How did the security service recruit crims to do jobs? It was known, or at least I knew, friends from the demi-monde of the dope world and its allied areas had told me, that police from the armed robbery division would spring armed robbers from gaol to do a hold-up and then put them back in when the job was done, perfect alibi, sure a similar modus operandi but he's in maximum security, sprung out presumably on the promise, fulfilled or not, of earlier release, a share in the profits, a supply of smack, and maybe a hot shot in it to close the books. So if the armed robbery squad borrowed armed robbers, what would internal security not do? And asking these questions, did I imagine that would go unrewarded, did I think communication was a one way traffic, didn't I wonder why this transmitter was so conveniently placed to transmit information my way, did I never consider there might be a two way traffic? Yes, of course I did, eventually, in the end, in the fullness of time, too late, how else do you learn but by experience, book knowledge is about the other, for yourself you need the sensate, the tactile, the touch of fear.

Through the ensuing weeks he would drop into my room to talk. What else are contact hours for? How could I refuse? How could I confirm that fear of rejection I could see hovering around his eyes, how could I in effect say you are a pariah, you have the brand of Cain, I have no time?

There was never much talk about his thesis. He hadn't begun that yet. He was still completing his final undergraduate year. The thesis was for the following year. He expected to be inside still. 'I keep putting in for parole. But if I don't get it I need something to get me out on day release.'

Since the thesis was not under way we talked of other things. This was the inevitable pattern with many a thesis supervision.

One time we shared a joint and went off to get lunch.

'Don't ever do that again,' he said. 'It made me totally paranoid. I got all upset at you maligning the lily white security services, saying all those terrible things about conspiracies. I felt I should be defending them against you. St George against the evil dragon. That sort of thing. Don't ever do that to me again.'

At least he told me. It had never occurred to me that anyone would want to defend the security services. I had made that basic error of the times, I'd assumed that someone in gaol was an underdog and underdogs were against the system. But authoritarian systems are maintained by the underdogs' belief in the system, by their complicity. Underdogs want to be top dogs, they await rehabilitation and redemption. Gaols were no different from universities, they shared the same dominant ideology of conformity and hierarchy and authority.

I was overcome with the terror of it one evening. Maybe it was the same bad dope that had so affected him. The abyss opened up in my stomach. Sweat streamed down my arm pits, the sides of my ears, my feet. Don't ever do that to me again. St George and the evil dragon. What if he suddenly turned? What if he came after me? How did I know what he mightn't do? I hadn't seen any psychological reports. Why was he still in gaol? Why hadn't he been released by now? Who ever served a full sentence these days? There had to be some reason, some doubt, some uncertainty, or some purpose in hanging on to him until the right moment.

It was absolute terror. I sat on the steps of the house alone, rolling joint after joint considering it all. And whichever way I considered it, it was a nightmare. If I tried to escape, to disentangle myself, if I refused to supervise him, mightn't he be offended and revengeful? If I agreed to supervise him wasn't I locked into an ongoing connection? I kept coming back to the time he had served, why wasn't he out, surely he was due to be released after that length of time. And the socialite ladies. Was that something else he had told me? Not only never feed him drugs again. Had he been visited by the wife of a captain of something or other, you are due for parole, but there are still doubts about you, but you could demonstrate your loyal citizenship, all very simple, just attach yourself to this person, find out what he thinks, who his friends are, what he talks about, what he plans to do, he'll talk to you, he'll let you know because he'll think you're against the system, but you can prove to us you're not against it, prove that you're fully rehabilitated by just letting us know, just drop in and see him, and then we'll see, it should get you a good report for the parole board.

And who was it he had murdered before? Why had I never asked? I had assumed it was some sort of criminal contract, but what if it had been political?

What if he had been hired by the security services. Remove some dissident. Maybe remove more than one.

What if one morning after breakfast in gaol, just before setting out for day release, someone offered him a joint? Or what if they slipped some substance into his prison porridge? What if he went berserk and defended the security services by running a steak knife between my ribs in the university club, or throwing me out of the window of my office, nothing lost, he'd be inside for another fifteen years, or until they needed another job done, maybe he'd plead extenuating circumstances and just serve a couple of years more, and the world would have been freed of one more inconvenient person, thank you St George.

By now I'd withdrawn from the steps and barricaded all the doors, chairs against them, blinds all down, pretty well out of dope now, saturated with sweat, ought to have a bath but terrified of being drowned in it.

It required another corridor manœuvre. I was in there early. Prowling up and down from my room to the general office, hanging round the photocopier, until I could bump into the graduate programmeß co-ordinator, 'Oh, that thesis on my work, I've talked to him, happy to talk to him, but I don't think it's quite appropriate I supervise a thesis on myself, do you? Lack of critical distance. It might be best if someone else takes it on, anyway I'll be on leave next year, yes, only just applied, but I'm due for it, need to get away for a while.'

And if it meant he ended up leaving me out and writing the whole thesis on Joe and Sam Samson, and turned it into a book that brought them into critical focus and world acclaim, that was just the price I would have to pay. At least there was the chance I'd still be around for the dubious pleasure of reading it.

11

Some Dealers

Down at the Forth and Clyde where we drank at weekends and night after night in the week, Andy would come round with a big brown paper bag selling deals. Those were the early days when people came round offering it to you. You didn't have to go round looking for it. You didn't have to engage in a house to house search, an endless hanging out or desperate pilgrimage. It just came and you paid your thirty dollars and there you were. You didn't even have to go down to the pub to deal with Andy. He specialised in home deliveries. Saturday morning he would cruise round Balmain with his brown paper bag, dropping in for an hour, and then off again. He never stayed long, just that hour, just long enough to disrupt your morning's rhythm, and then off again, leaving you stoned and disoriented and disinclined to resume whatsoever it was you'd been doing. Not long enough for a social call. Not short enough just to see if you wanted a deal and then to leave you alone with it. Just an hour's chat. Who's doing what? What's up where? Where are you off to? What's new pussycat?

    You never knew why about any of it, where it came from, where the money went. Once in a while some dubious looking characters would turn up at Andy's. Preoccupied looking people. Not laid-back, stoned dope-freaks. More edgy and anxious than that. People you might have thought in those days could have done with a couple of joints to relax them. Impossible to place them. Of no obvious background, nothing that fitted in anywhere. Uncomfortable people. People who made you feel uncomfortable. They seemed to bring the supplies in bulk. They never wanted to hang around, get to know anybody, preferred to leave Andy's guests round the kitchen table and talk outside in the yard, away from the street-lights, dark nights with no moon. And then Andy would come back in and ask, 'Anybody need a deal?' and the plastic bags and the money would change hands.

And then there would be the times Andy wasn't holding stock and he'd pass you along to somebody else. You never knew why. It was all unexplained. And then you would be dealing with somebody like Buddha Bob. Back from Beirut, bald, he went around in army fatigues and a bare chest like a Middle Eastern militia man, a desperado's moustache and a remorselessly genial smile. He liked to ride shot-gun on your car if he saw you in the street, which would have been easier if you were driving a World War 2 Jeep with a running board, but since you weren't he'd just sit on the front wing and hold onto the door frame. Nothing low profile about Buddha Bob.

Rob and Deidre moved up from Melbourne. Again it was a literary connection. A junkie novelist put me on to them. At least everyone said he was a junkie. 'Is he still on heroin?' Sled, the suspected security man on the Literature Board would ask. Rob and Deidre had the aura, too. Hard drugs and massage parlours. Or was that just because visiting the novelist in Melbourne one time and being out of dope, it was to the massage parlour girls he went looking for some? Or maybe it was the aura of gaol Rob exuded. He'd done time in Europe. Dope smuggling. He didn't ever say whether he'd done time in Australia. But he had that air of eager charm and untrustworthiness, the beaten hound that you never knew when it might see its chance and turn and bite, all charm and co-operation, slavering tongue and wagging tail, but with that cold watchfulness in the eye or the corner of the eye or behind the eye, something that when you looked for it was never there to be seen, that would vanish in a flash, but that nonetheless could not keep itself from coming back, watching.

But they smoked marijuana. That was what it was about. Unless that was just the surface and it was about something else.

'My old mum works for ASIO,' said Rob one day. The Australian Security Intelligence Organisation. Rolling a number. Sitting round the wooden kitchen table, cups of tea. Always a social occasion buying dope from them, sit down and relax, have a cup of tea, what's been happening? Impeccable joints, seeds and stalks picked out with tweezers, papers meticulously rolled. Or was that someone else? Or was that all of them, always the same, that endless performance as the papers were lined up, the cardboard filter prepared, the dope measured out, the joint slowly rolled, what's been going on, mate, what's happening in the big world out there or the little world of man you inhabit, seen anybody interesting, tell us a yarn, make us laugh, make us cry, spill the beans, take a puff of this, clear your head, blow your mind, open your word horde.

'Yeah, my old mum, fancy that, she's a tea lady at ASIO. Just takes the tea round. Or so she says. Makes you wonder. Amazing what she knew about what I was up to. Quite embarrassing, really. Fancy your mum being a spook.'

He chuckled, took off his dark glasses, laid them on the table, rubbed his eyes with the back of his hand. There was a weariness, a strain.

'Yeah, they used to follow me for training exercises. Track me round the streets of Melbourne. That's before they moved to Canberra. Bit of a nerve really. Practice in shadowing. I could've done without that, I can tell you.'

It was Rob and Deidre who told me about how the police armed robbery squad sprung armed robbers out of gaol to do jobs for them. How there wasn't a straight barrister in all of New South Wales. How the police recycled the drugs they seized.

Or Rob would talk about his new job, working on a fishing trawler. Out all night. Cold. Wet. Dangerous. Somehow it seemed too much like hard work for the sort of world he inhabited. Later I began to wonder if maybe it was one of those trawlers that rendezvoused with Asian freighters and picked up a cargo of dope. Or retrieved it from the waves. Later still I began to wonder if it wasn't an undercover operation of the drug squad. Prior to recycling the haul.

He packed that in after a while. One day he drove past my place in a pick-up truck full of canisters of chemicals and plastic tubing. He pulled up for a chat, smiling beneath his steel-rimmed dark glasses.

'I'm an exterminator,' he said.

Deidre came round with a friend one evening, Anna. Rob was away somewhere. Gone fishing, maybe. People were always going away somewhere. We smoked a few joints and they talked about Melbourne. Nothing memorable at all; nothing, anyway, that I can remember. Anna was stuck for accommodation so stayed the night in the spare room. I probably would never have remembered the incident again except a couple of weeks later I bought the evening paper for the TV guide. The front page story was a list of Australia's ten most wanted criminals. Anna was one of them. Art robbery I think was the charge. It seemed rather a mild charge for such a high profile listing. They must have been valuable paintings.

This was when Tim showed me the manuscript of his novel about a drug experiment. He had been a scientist so presumably knew what he was writing about. About a drug that enabled consciousness to be tapped into. You took a drug and you could immediately merge with another consciousness. Or was it the other way round, you took a drug and whatever you thought and felt was immediately available to someone else. Everything sucked out. He never wrote very clearly anyway so the details were hard to disentangle. Maybe he had taken too much of the drug.

He would phone me up and proceed with a battery of questions, how are you? what're you writing? how's it going? what're you publishing? who're you seeing? how're you feeling? what's going on? sucking out answers like a vacuum cleaner. The camaraderie of the literary. Open door, open phone, open house to fellow writers.

Tim would smoke a joint and tell me how bad it was for you, for me.

'The THC doesn't dissolve. It lodges in fat tissues. The liver. The brain. Doesn't go away.'

It sounded good to me.

His wife would burst into tears over the wood-fired stove, Tim would propose a retreat to his study, put some atonal, abstract, avant-garde music on the record-player, and we would have a smoke to the background of this atrocious howling. Was this some further experiment, some weird programming or conditioning project on which he was still working? I never knew.

'It's bad for you,' he would tell me, 'you really shouldn't smoke it.'

Rolling another.

The awful electronic tones drilling through the air.

Well, yes, it did make you paranoid. But I wasn't sure that was necessarily bad for you. It gave you plots. Maybe not very well defined ones. But we were entering post-modern days, anyway. It gave you a sense of plots. Of conspiracies. Of menace and the marshalling of dark forces. And I'd always felt I'd not been into plots enough. I quite enjoyed reading them or watching them on movies or TV. But writing them, generally I thought they were rather silly. Not the serious part of a writer's business. So to be provided with the intimation of plots, with a penumbra of the suggestive, that seemed like a good thing, whether you ever got round to using them and writing them down or not.

And the plots were there. Round the kitchen table. Cargo planes full of drugs flying out of Vietnam to Pine Gap as the Americans evacuated their supplies when they lost the war. Container loads of dope being trans-shipped to America, trucked down to Adelaide. Plantations of dope growing in the Riverina, financed by a bank whose directors all seemed to be CIA or US military, including one who was found dead with a bullet in his head and another who was never found at all, just vanished. There were great plots there, municipal councils linked through their councillors to the drug trade, depositing their money with the bank. The rest and recreation bars and brothels set up by ex-CIA men to cater for American troops on leave from Vietnam, borrowing and lending, depositing and withdrawing through the bank, financing the drugs-for-arms trade with South East Asia and the Middle East. I remember the police presence round the morgue after they'd exhumed the one shot dead and were checking were they really his teeth they'd buried. Great stories but not ones you'd feel too confident writing. Even rolling another smoke and talking about them you'd wonder, was that radio on the window-sill playing or taping, was this dope supply all right or had it been doctored?

'It lodges in the brain,' said Tim. 'Drive you mad, turns you psycho.'

His wife howling downstairs, the record player howling around us.

Was that the real story, was that what it was all about, a campaign of mass poisoning, eradicate the radicals by feeding them bad dope?

And some of it was certainly bad. After the first heady days of good stuff the supply began to change.

It was a world full of stories. The container company. We passed the yard every day. And the story was they repaired containers, taking out the concealed heroin from wherever it had been welded in at the port of departure. Or the travel agency with a defrocked priest as one of the directors, and a few local crim identities the rest, municipal councillors and Labor party heavies. The story was that the travel agency arranged the flights for drug couriers. There emerged an amazing interface between drugs, the CIA and the Labor party. Was this a plot to penetrate and discredit Labor? Or had the CIA always run the Labor party? A safe Labor party. Americano-Socialist as they say in Greece. In which case why had the government been removed by the coup, if they already ran it? Was the waterfront heroin trade the CIA pay off to the crooks for keeping the Communists out, like in Marseilles? Or was that just another story, and the real point, the basic point, the drug trade anyway? Or was the Labor party's alleged involvement in the drug trade just a cover story, the real corruption coming from illegal immigration rackets? This was the beginning of the Asian immigration. It was billed as the liberalisation of Labor, the removal of the discredited White Australia policy. But in reality, if we could ever use such a word in these times, wasn't it Labor bowing to US pressure to let in the Vietnamese collaborators, gangsters, secret police, drug dealers and the rest of the anti-communists after the liberation of Saigon? And once you thought about that you wondered, was that why Labor was put into office in

1972 in the first place, the Americans knowing by then that they had lost the war and they had to start making provision for a mass exodus from Vietnam, which would also help continue the economic war, draining out capital and impoverishing the country when the war ended: and the old Australian coalition was too racist to move on this one, so why not put in Labor for a couple of years, get them to change the immigration policy, and then kick them out, the Labor government that is, not the Asians.

'Better roll another one,' Rob or Andy or Tim would say.

Heady stuff, heady days, lots of stories, lots more plots where that lot came from, let us know when you write them.

12

An Australian Christmas

That was the Christmas I chose Philip Agee's *Inside the Company*, as one of my Books of the Year. Its account of covert operations in Latin America cast interesting light on recent events in Australia. I think it was the last time I was asked to contribute to the Books of the Year feature for any newspaper.

I read it on holiday. Holidays were not something I knew much about. Living in Sydney was holiday enough: the sun, the beaches, the parties, the bars, the restaurants. Living in Sydney was what in England you would save up for a year to experience for a week. It was the perpetual Mediterranean, the eternal Pacific, the endless tropical escape. It had never been somewhere I felt the need to escape from.

But I was in love and open to persuasion. We drove north, up the Pacific Highway, its very name redolent of escape, adventure. The world up there merged into one continual holiday, the days on the beach, making love, swimming, smoking dope, eating hippy food at the hippy beach shop, teriyaki lentil burgers, fresh fruit. The endless summer of Byron Bay.

If Sydney was a holiday city it was also an active city. Busy isn't the right word. Productive sounds somewhat responsible. But we were productive. Years later Joe said to me, 'People say, "Your books are all about going to the pub, getting drunk, going to parties, having fun. You seem to have spent all your time in the pub and at parties." But we were productive too,' Joe said, in uncharacteristic need to justify himself in terms of his father's business ethic. 'We partied a lot but we wrote a lot.' And it was true, we did, all of it.

So out of town, lying on the beach, it took some getting used to, just to lie there, to absorb sun and sea and wind and sand, to be amongst the elements, in nature. I took up books and read them in no time. That was when I read the Agee.

And we were serious, I could have said to Joe. Even he was. For all the parties and drinking, for all the sex and drugs, for all the endless indulgence and enjoyment, we were serious in what we wrote and read. We didn't read thrillers or spy fiction. Graham Greene I had dipped into and turned away from. Le Carré I had once reviewed and not returned to. Eric Ambler, Ian Fleming, Len Deighton and so on I had never bothered with. Even reading Agee was something done rather guiltily, and it was probably only because I was on holiday, taking a break from the serious stuff, that I read it. It was not literature, it was not cultural commentary. The Vietnam war had certainly challenged that world of 'purely literary values'; but challenged it, for those of us in the literary business, in a literary sort of way. It put some rather more committed literary criticism into circulation. But it was still literary criticism. I hadn't found myself reading political commentary as a consequence. We still remained - or at least I did - narrowly specialised, professional, in our literary activities.

The Vietnam war had been our prime preoccupation. That had been politics enough. We were not ready for a new conspiracy. And if we read *The Quiet American* or *The Ambassador*, that was fiction set somewhere else. A coup in south-east Asia. Like South America. It did not apply to us, we assumed, and so we were unprepared. We had not been briefed. Or rather, the briefs were there but we had not bothered to read them, or if we had read them, not thought to learn and understand and apply their message.

In those days I used to read the weekend papers. I bought them for the book pages, and having bought them I would read them through. So I encountered the news at least once a week. Presumably that was when I came across the Agee book, unless someone mentioned it somewhere, or I saw it in a bookshop. I don't remember. And I go on rather laboriously about it because it was not the sort of book I normally read. For me, spy books, conspiracy books, revelations about the secret services, Cold War chronicles had all been in the category of the unserious. They were not literature. That, of course, was all to change. November 11, 1975 altered that.

They were beautiful, those summer days, the sky a clear blue, the sea sharp and salt and fresh, the surf a steady, rhythmic pounding like the contented purr of some powerful creature, peacefully relaxed. Overhead the ospreys and sea eagles would circle, a note of elegant menace. I would stretch out there reading Agee's catalogue of deception and destabilisation in Ecuador and Uruguay and Mexico. And it all had a familiar note. The press discrediting of left-wing ministers. The pressure on the political leaders to have leftists removed. The fabrications spread through the newspapers, forged documents, false innuendoes, printed as if true. The creation of a climate of suspicion and mistrust paralysing the working of government.

Even in the low-level details there were points of familiarity, like the way graffiti gangs had been hired to paint up slogans. There were graffiti in Sydney that had always puzzled me in their ingenious ambiguity, their self-cancelling contradictions. 'Australians are woolly-minded sheep' went up on the wall of the trotting track after Fraser was elected. Its purported leftism showed a disturbing contempt for the people. It wasn't saying the election was rigged. It wasn't even expressing the old Libertarian cynicism of 'Whoever you vote for a politician gets in.' It was opposing the right from a position of contempt for the populace. 'Fraser = Mussolini' was another slogan, in one of the Italian suburbs, that made me wonder too. Was this intended as for or against the Liberal party?

But that was pretty low-level stuff. Ingenious, perhaps. Or perhaps the ingenuity was all a matter of perception, smoking a joint there on the beach and pondering on it. More significant was the account of the way the CIA had journalists and columnists and editors on its payroll, whole newspapers, even. A story, a rumour, a lie could be fed through one of these connections and once in print it would be picked up and followed by other journalists, other papers round the world. And if the stories were later shown to be untrue, what did it matter, the damage had been done, no-one bothered with corrections or retractions, that was yesterday's news, now was the time of the next fabrication, more innuendo, more lies.

The parallels with the last year of the Australian Labor government were inescapable. There was the continuing media campaign discrediting left-wing ministers. It is hard now to see how we ever thought the Labor government was at all left-wing. The twenty-five per cent reduction on the protective tariffs and the consequent destruction of industrial production in no way helped keep the working class in work. But in the uneasy compromise of the different factions, there were some figures who could be called left. The deputy Prime Minister Cairns, for instance, had opposed American and Australian involvement in the Vietnam war in a way the Prime Minister Whitlam never had. Now Cairns was endlessly pilloried in the press. There were implications of some never defined sexual scandal, the suggestion of a powerful female hold over him, getting him to grow his hair longer, a Chinese woman whose husband represented Ethiopian Airlines in Australia: not one of the household names of international air-travel, and later alleged to be a CIA funded operation. And then there was the minerals and energy minister trying to raise a loan from Saudi Arabia in order to keep Australia's mineral and oil resources in Australian hands, something treated as a scandal in the press. There were suggestions, never spelled out, of corruption, never substantiated. Reading Agee, the whole scenario was familiar. It had all been done before, in Ecuador.

'We'll get some mushrooms,' said Lily.
   'Mushrooms?'
   'Magic mushrooms.'
   'Magic mushrooms?'
   'Haven't you ever had them?'
   'No.'
   'They're incredible.'
   'Really?'
   'They're much better than acid.'
   'Yes?'
   'Haven't you dropped acid?'
   'No.'
   'Oh well, mushrooms are much better. You never want acid when you've tried mushrooms.'
   'Really?'
   'You'll see.'

Except they weren't easy to find. Now that it was known that this was where they grew, hippies and freaks and farmers and public-spirited people had been combing the fields for them, hippies and freaks to ingest them, farmers and the public-spirited to eradicate them. The farmers didn't want hippies and freaks walking over their land: or public-spirited people for that matter. The public-spirited didn't want hippies and freaks having pleasure or having visions or having insight into how things are, didn't want hippies and freaks at all. And some of the hippies and freaks lacked, or shared, public spirit, depending how you interpret the concept, and ripped out the root system when they picked the mushrooms, and that helped eradicate them. The considerate thing to do was to break the mushroom off at the stalk, leaving the mycelium intact to produce more mushrooms. And breaking it off you could see the purple die that appeared on contact with the air. That way you knew they were psylocibin mushrooms. There were other gold-topped toadstools whose stem didn't turn purple at the break when they were picked, and they just made you feel ill.

But this for a while was in the future. After a morning on the beach we drove slowly through the country lanes, scouting for likely fields, Lily practising her extra-sensory divinatory skill for a likely spot, a magic glade. Then we would stop the car and walk to the fence and check out the proximity of farm houses. This had once been a district of small dairy farms, and there were cottages scattered everywhere. Then we would gaze across the green sea of grass looking for tell-tale pin-pricks of white and gold. And if our eyes lighted on dried cow-pats, that was good too, because cow dung or, even better, horse dung, was a great incentive to the production of magic mushrooms.

For hours we cruised the back lanes, but it kept us from getting burned on the beach. Occasionally we would meet other reconnaissance teams, parked beside the road, walking through likely looking fields, and share complaints about the iniquity of farmers ripping the mushrooms out or ploughing them in. And sometimes we would stop at a farm selling avocadoes or corn or tomatoes or zucchinis and buy food for the evening's meal, so we weren't totally empty-handed, and it also gave some legitimacy to our cruising these back roads, in case some public-spirited citizen apprehended us and made a citizen's arrest, you never knew what sort of craziness the public-spirited might get up to, now they'd ripped out all the mushrooms they might start on the mushroom eaters.

We found them on Christmas day. We had driven down to the Bay for a swim, it was a beautiful morning, and on the way back Lily insisted we stopped beside some paddock. And there they were, glistening golden in the morning sun.

'You really should eat them where you find them and trip there,' said Lily.

'We can't do that.'

'We can,' she said.

The only thing preventing her immediately doing so was the lack of honey or bananas or something to disguise the taste of them.

'Your brother and sister-in-law are coming for Christmas dinner.'

'That's not till tonight,' she said.

'We have to help cook it.'

'If we take them now we'll have come down before they arrive.'

'We might not. Then we won't be able to drive back.'
'We'll fly,' she said.
These were the days of the shaman and levitation, of becoming a crow and cutting through the silver ether.

We went back.
Lily put the mushrooms on the kitchen table.
'Aren't they beautiful?' she said.
We looked at them.
'We should take them now.'
'What about your brother and sister-in-law?'
'They'll never notice. It'll make it easier to deal with them.'
'We should help get the meal ready first.'
'We can't start cooking yet.'
'We can peel the vegetables.'
'We should take them now,' Lily insisted. 'They take about an hour to come on.'
She got out honey, bananas.
'If you're going to eat those,' said her father, 'I might have some too.'
'Of course,' said Lily.
'I don't want to be sitting on my own while you two sit there giggling. It will be too hard to explain.'
'They'll think we're all crazy,' I said.
'They already do,' said Lily.
We washed the mushrooms and shared them out, covered them with honey, forced them down despite the taste that made you gag. We made a pot of tea to help wash away the aftertaste. Then we set about crumbling bread crumbs and chopping up onions and herbs for stuffing. The tea must have potentiated the action. Or perhaps it was eating them freshly picked. Soon, anyway, in so far as the concept pertained any more, time began to elongate. Peeling a sweet potato took half way to eternity, the spiral of peel slowly lengthening, the necessity of not breaking it, of keeping an endless strip of deep red outer skin imperative. The bread crumbs fell one by one, grains of stellar matter in the endless interstellar space. The tears from the onions coursed down my cheeks in some hilarious cosmic grief, like a drop of dew inching its way down the impassive Sphinx in the first light of dawn. Each tear, each crumb, each sliver of peel demanded total attention, unique, immanent, their message poised at the full moment of comprehension, in the demi-second before delivery.

'We should have put the mushrooms in the stuffing,' Lily's father suggested.

'But then we wouldn't be able to have eaten them now. We'd have had to wait till dinner.'

'That's true.'

'We could have saved some,' I suggested. 'Or we could go and look for more.'

We considered it. The distance to the car seemed beyond human possibility. The keys themselves too heavy to lift. The atmosphere weighed on us, forcing us to stay in place, deterring us from moving from our seats round the table.

'Anyway,' said Lily, 'you should never do that. You should never slip people drugs without telling them.'

'That's what the CIA did,' said Lily's father.

'How do you know?' said Lily.

'It was in the papers.'

'I never read them.'

'There you are then, you should. They gave LSD to people without telling them. One of them thought he was going crazy and jumped out of a window and killed himself.'

We wondered whether they had experimented with mushrooms.

'That's probably why they're so hard to find,' I said. 'They've been harvesting them all for experiments.'

We thought that was quite amusing, at least Lily's father and I did, visions of white laboratory-coated scientists combing the fields at dawn like Israelites looking for manna.

Our swimmers and towels dried on the line in the sun. The sky was cloudless and clear, except no doubt for invisible surveillance satellites. We crumbled bread crumbs and peeled potatoes in accord with all established normalcies. The crumbling was getting slower, the peeling was somewhat more meticulous and painstaking than perhaps it had begun. But to the casual satellite lens, it would have appeared no other than a representative Christmas dinner preparation: unless they had sensors that could detect psylocibin ingestion, like they had infra-red sensors that could detect where dope crops were being grown. Did we register on their film with sudden sparks of intuition, blinding flashes of clarity cutting through the varnishes and coatings of the everyday?

'The CIA must have been involved in getting rid of Labor. All that loans affair. How did the newspapers get all the information on the borrowing attempts?

From America and the Middle East and Europe? The newspaper managements are so mean they hardly have any foreign staff any more. They don't have any investigative reporters. They must have been fed it. And who would have the world-wide intelligence network to get the information except the CIA?'

'I could never see what the fuss was,' said Lily's father. 'They were just trying to borrow money.'

'The fuss was what they wanted to borrow it for.'

'To keep control of oil and mineral resources.'

'Which meant keeping out American oil and mining corporations.'

'Plus who they were borrowing the money from.'

'The Arabs.'

'Which meant keeping out American and Jewish and European and British money-lenders.'

'Which meant keeping out IMF controls on the economy.'

'So no wonder they turned it into a scandal.'

'But there wasn't any scandal.'

'But the newspapers made it look like one.'

'No money was raised. No one was getting any kick-backs. There was no corruption. Nothing happened.'

'Except Cairns was sacked.'

'And Connor was sacked.'

'Because he was still asking about loan availability two days after he'd been told not to.'

'Even though he hadn't agreed to any loan or made any deals.'

'Oh you two,' said Lily, 'stop it. It's Christmas. Why do you have to talk about all this? It's a time of peace and love and all you talk about is -'

'Politics,' we said.

'Economics.'

'Conspiracies.'

'Reality.'

'It's not reality,' said Lily.

'Probably not,' we agreed.

'Probably a hallucination,' we agreed.

'Stop it,' she said.

We stopped it.

The bread crumbs looked up at us impassively. The spirals of peel wriggled in slight unease.

'Play some music,' suggested Lily's father.

'What sort of music?'
'Christmas music.'
'Carols.'
'*The Messiah.*'
She went across to the record collection, forcing her way through the jellied air that opened before her and closed behind her. She sat down before the records and engaged them in rapt concentration. They engaged readily in dialogue. This might be good. This might be more appropriate. There again this might have a more cheerful note. But is it cheerfulness or seriousness that would be more appropriate? They plunged into the deepest silence of concentration, Lily, the records, and the interstitial space.

'And then there was the Cairns business. That was all loans stuff too.'
'The letter he was supposed to have signed offering a commission.'
'Which he said he never signed.'
'It was probably a forgery. Agee describes the CIA forging documents and leaking them to the press all the time. And it always seemed to work.'
'The press creates such a climate of suspicion that when a minister says he never signed such a letter everyone assumes he's lying.'
'A fair assumption about a politician.'
'True. But an equally fair assumption about the press.'
'True.'
True, true, what had truth to do with it? Who lies more, politicians or the press? The intelligence agencies? A structure of lies and innuendoes and forgeries, our public life, played and manipulated by the CIA. Probably with the co-operation of their British and Australian counterparts. Was this what we argued over, voted for, protested about, campaigned for, believed in? Never again, belief had died. Innocence, that as a veil had shadowed them from knowing ill, was gone.

Lily burst into tears at the horror of it. Her tears coursed down into the bread crumbs.
We took the bowl away from her.
'It'll make the stuffing too salty,' we explained.
'I can't stand it,' she said. 'It's so horrible. It's Christmas, why don't you talk about beautiful things?'
We looked around for beautiful things to talk about. They curled and spun and metamorphosed in the air. The air had become viscous, palpable. The

hills in the distanced breathed in and out, gently, like a sleeping animal you watch carefully to make sure it is alive. They were alive, the trees quivering on them in slight frissons of movement, like fur on a cat's neck, or feathers on a fledgling bird. Everything partook of everything else. Trees were like feathers, feathers like clouds, clouds assembled like Jove and Poseidon, like eagles and spears and thunderbolts as the day heated up and the pressure bore down. The music separated into its component notes, each one hanging there, fading into silence as another and another came into play.

'Maybe we should have something to eat,' said Lily's father.

We agreed. But we could think of nothing that appealed, when it came to it. Chocolate. It was too manufactured. Bread. Too artificial. Bananas. They made us shudder with the memory of the first taste of the mushrooms.

'A drink.'

'Yes.'

But how to provide it? Making tea was too hard. Let alone squeezing oranges. Poor squeezed oranges. Poor scalded tea leaves. We didn't need it anyway. We needed nothing.

Lily dried her tears and poured water over her face from the tap. She gazed entranced at the globules of moisture on her hands.

'Water,' she said, 'is so amazing.'

We suppressed thoughts of how the military had considered lacing the reservoirs with LSD or psylocibin.

We would utter only happy thoughts.

We couldn't think what they were, but it made us giggle, suppressing the black thoughts.

We spent a lot of time giggling.

When it came to it we couldn't face the meat. The dead bird. Fowl or duck or turkey. The further horror of it. The Christmas slaughter. The killing of the living for gross celebration.

We did our best. Lily's father stuffed it, basted it, put it in the oven.

'I don't think I can eat it, though,' he said.

'We should cook more vegetables,' said Lily.

We peeled more potatoes, more sweet potatoes, more onions. We sat surrounded by mountains of peel, red and brown and white spirals reaching out of their bowls and snaking across the floor.

I began to feel tragic about the holocaust of vegetables.

'You have to live on something,' said Lily's father.

'Mushrooms,' said Lily.

I expressed grief at the consumption of mushrooms.

'They're eternal,' said Lily. 'Like everything. Their life force goes on. The psylocibin passes through your body alive.'

Christmas dinner was not a great success. We didn't burn it or undercook it or anything. It all came out all right. As far as I could tell. A bit belated. More than a bit belated. When Lily's brother and sister-in-law arrived we hadn't advanced very far beyond covering the floor with spirals of peel and breadcrumbs. We explained.

'We didn't want to start cooking until you were here,' we explained.

'We didn't want to have it ready too soon,' said Lily.

'Or too late,' I added, for balance.

'It already is too late.'

Did we say that or did they? Or did it just float around the room, its letters spelled out on a scroll of peel?

'We told you when we'd be here.'

'Ah, but we weren't sure. You might have been late.'

'We're never late,' said the sister-in-law.

'No, she's always on time,' said the brother.

'That's true,' said Lily's father. 'That's an excellent characteristic.'

Time, we thought. What is it exactly?

'It was we who lost track of time in fact,' said Lily's father.

'Not really,' said Lily. 'We knew what we were doing.'

'That's true too,' he agreed. 'You've always known what you were doing.'

'So does anyone know what they're doing now?' asked the sister-in law.

'More or less,' said Lily's father. 'We're about to start cooking.'

'Well?' said the sister-in-law.

'Well?' we echoed.

'So start,' she said.

'Good idea,' we agreed.

But it was hard to move. Moving seemed superfluous when your thoughts could move for you, could roam such vast distances dissolving space and time. We could have gone on like this for hours. We may well have done.

'We got caught up talking politics,' said Lily's father.

'Yes,' I agreed. 'We were talking about –'

'No,' Lily howled. 'Don't. Stop it.'

In the end the sister-in-law took charge, put the poor dead bird in the oven, organised the vegetables. Did we have traditional old cold world Christmas pudding? Or did we have fresh fruit? Or a fruit salad? It was all immaterial, really, because we had no desire to eat. Indeed, when the dead bird was brought out we had a positive revulsion from flesh. But that was emotional, moral, principled. Beyond that there was also the failure of appetite. The mushrooms required nothing else. They had taken over the body, themselves its only food that could be countenanced. We picked at a few things. For appearance's sake. Though by then that was pretty well a lost cause. Though there again, it was only what was expected. Lily they knew was a deviant, a hippy black sheep, and anyone she brought home would be in the same category. And her father was eccentric and subversive and political. The public-spirited had been known to throw rocks on his roof more than once. So it was nothing out of the ordinary. A bit strange, but we were a bit strange. They knew that. It wasn't a great success. But nor was it a great disaster. We got through. Which was more than the Labor government had managed. As Lily's father and I pointed out a few times.

13

Arts Doco

I was in England again. Cold winters. Parental visiting. The dutiful son. But duty and the cold, sometimes, often, so much of the time, were too much. I would visit elsewhere. Old friends, former colleagues. One was Grenville. We had worked together nearly twenty years before and kept in touch. At first sight an unlikely old friend. He was public school, scholarly, conservative. At least, conservative in manner, not given to making the wilder statements I had favoured over the years. But he was one of those conservatives increasingly at odds with the way the world was, and increasingly we found ourselves in agreement.

Scholarly I have said he was, but it was the sort of scholarship that led into obscure by-ways, fascinating enigmas, that increasingly departed from the mainstream and his career with it. This winter he had been working on musical codes.

'Like in *The Lady Vanishes*?' I said.

'Well, something like that.' He laughed. 'A bit more complex. But yes, that sort of thing.'

Secret agents whistling on a train. I had never been totally sure about Grenville. All that intelligence, all that knowledge, and yet he seemed to do so little with it. Was it because he got diverted into obscure byways, or was it because he was doing something else as well? Academics with some other life, putting in long hours at the computer and yet publishing almost nothing, were there other things they wrote, other missions they went on? Not that Grenville ever seemed to go anywhere, and when you came to look at it he had published quite a lot, obscure as it might be and in obscure places as it inevitably was.

He had been in touch with another enthusiast, a retired civil servant who wrote about literary mysteries, Shakespeare's lost plays, that sort of thing, and musical codes.

'What sort of civil servant?'

'Civil servant,' said Grenville. 'Quite high up I imagine. Used to hire people on the basis of whether they did crossword puzzles or not.'

I wasn't sure this was the sort of thing I wanted to know about. I had come to treat revisiting England for the winter chills as a kind of fumigation. The idea was that the frost killed off the sub-tropical bugs. The atmosphere of suspicion and mistrust, of suspect dealers and literary agents was intended to be left behind. And now this looked like more of the same.

'Do you know Dick Furness?'

'No,' I said.

'No, he doesn't know you either.'

'Should I?'

'He went to your school,' said Grenville. Here we were, back in England, forever locked into the school you went to.

'He's a television producer,' said Grenville. 'Something came up about the school he went to and I asked him if he'd read any of your stories. He hadn't, so I leant him one of your books. Gave him quite a turn.' He chuckled. 'Brought it all back. More than he cared for, I got the impression.'

'I can't remember the name,' I said.

'He said to ask you to give him a call,' said Grenville. 'I got the impression he was interested in making a programme, or something.'

'Really?'

The quickened pulse, the increased heart beat, the never failing lure, if not Hollywood at least British non-metropolitan television.

'Do you have his number?'

'They're in the book,' said Grenville. 'Their studio's in the middle of town. Just give him a call there.'

'How do you know him?' I asked. 'Are you making something with him?'

'Possibly,' said Grenville. 'This musical code idea. He's caught up in that. He'd been looking at Elgar.'

'*The Enigma Variations?*'

'In part. But Elgar was quite deeply into codes.'

'Really?'

Grenville chuckled. 'A murky business,' he said. 'Makes you wonder what they were all up to, doesn't it?'

'I suppose it does,' I agreed.

Outside a light drizzle falls. Inside Elgar's Cello Concerto on the CD player. The Midlands. The pastoral heart of England. But what I recall now, with the drizzle, with Elgar's evocation of the place, are Indian restaurants. These were the days before Sydney had many Indian restaurants. Or many Indians for that matter. And nothing it had compared with what the Midlands offered. I would have spent the day escaping from my parents I had come to visit, working in the university, away from the manifold distractions and temptations and diversions of Sydney, so I would be getting something written, something academic usually, some promised article or book review, then a few beers with Grenville in the Faculty Club, and then I would sit down in red-flocked isolation with another beer, and a biryani or a dhansak or a Madras curry. The drizzle stops, the cello touches some heartfelt anguish, the salivary glands contract.

I had never kept in touch with the school after leaving it. My parents used to ask why I didn't join the old boys' association. I tried to explain it represented all the things I hated about the school. But it's not the school, they would say, it's keeping in touch with the boys you were at school with. I had no wish to keep in touch with them. It was probably them and their values that I was in recoil from rather than what the school could offer. The one person I did keep in touch with was my old English master. It was he who had encouraged me to write, it was he who had organised the way to Oxford for me, it was he who had always encouraged me. I was always grateful. So in between visiting parents and visiting aunts on those winter returns, I would also visit him. And at some point he foisted some old boys' association magazines onto me. I dutifully took them away with me and my mother browsed through them evening after evening. 'You should join it,' she said. So for five pounds a year I broke all my solemn vows and joined it. Perhaps this was after my father had died. When the father dies the son's authority models change. Maybe I no longer felt the need to resist.

And then the president of the old boys wrote to me. What a Pandora's box I had opened up. Perhaps he would have written to me anyway. But I think it was through my membership, or some self-promoting item about a recent book I had sent to the magazine, that he found my address. He had been head boy when I was at the school. Standing outside the prefects' room bending his prefectorial cane in two hands. He was one of those head boys who used his privilege of office to cane young boys. I remember arguing with him on the playing fields about the British invasion of Egypt during the Suez fiasco. He naturally supported the Anglo-French-Israeli offensive. I no less naturally opposed it. Later he became president of the Conservative club at Oxford and was hired to write the memoirs of various Tory politicians. His most recent book had been written in collaboration with a specialist on the British secret service. It may even have been about the secret service, the magnificent achievements thereof.

So a letter from this bastard was not an unambiguous pleasure. What he wanted was some memorabilia of Adam Lindsay Gordon, the nineteenth-century poet who had attended the school and emigrated to Australia. He had been expelled from the school, in fact, and he shot himself in Australia, the day his latest book of poems appeared, unable to pay the printer.

I wrote back that I knew of no available memorabilia. Impoverished, unappreciated, unpurchased in his lifetime, every scrap of manuscript and old clothing of the poet's was now in the hands of wealthy collectors. However, I suggested, a stroke of genius I felt, how about planting a wattle tree in the school grounds from the seeds of the tree growing on his grave? It kept him embroiled with the cemetery officials, the departments of plants and wild life, the departments of agriculture and the customs authorities for many a month.

'Incidentally,' he wrote, 'it seems that you are doing well. The school had a visit from a graduate student writing a PhD on you, inquiring about your early days.'

It is the incidentals that chill the bone. After the first fond moment of flattery, its effects. What graduate student? What PhD? No one had written to me about writing a PhD on my work. The murderer on day release had abandoned me as a joint topic and turned to my erstwhile friends as subject, whether in pique at my sidestepping as supervisor or at the suggestion and encouragement of one of my colleagues who took over the task, I neither knew nor asked. Someone expressed a wish to work on my poems, the head of department told me with much mirth. That project had been scotched. Even the head of department knew I did not write poems. So who was this graduate researcher inquiring of my old school in the UK for details of my early life?

These were by now the paranoid years. By now I had begun to recognise the trace of the secret state. Though, as I realised, not that precisely. Much I no doubt missed. And much more, and this was the problem of the forensics of paranoia, I over-interpreted. The PhD student visiting the school seemed to me without doubt suspicious. But the suggestion to call the television producer, what was that? It was the hinterland of musical codes that worried me. Who else but intelligence operatives would be caught up with musical codes? Crossword puzzle enthusiasts, maybe. That offered little reassurance.

Yet it might all be peripheral, irrelevant. Perhaps Dick Furness really had enjoyed the stories, perhaps something good might come out of this. Perhaps this was the way it was done, through old boy networks, even from a provincial grammar school. But if there was the possibility of something good coming out of it – fame and fortune with a television series of course – then there was every reason to be paranoid. So many things that might have been good had been thwarted in the past, that recent past. Projects had been derailed and come to nothing. If anything was to come of this I had to proceed carefully. Like not phoning from my parents' house but using a public call box. A simple enough principle, but in practice such a major hassle, particularly trying to phone a television producer who was never in his office, always in the studios, in London, out on location, travelling overseas. The endless attempts to collect the right coins in sufficient quantity, the roar of traffic past the phone boxes, in the end it was impossible, in the end I had to use the phone in the house. A meeting was arranged.

'Remember me?' he asked.

He stood in his doorway, cardigan and carpet slippers, eyebrows angled upwards like some theatrical representation of the devil, a tentative smile of welcome hovering on the edge of a smirk. Of embarrassment, of unease, or of the expectation of recognition.

I didn't. Remember him.

'No,' I said. 'It's so long ago, anyway,' as if to ease the pain.

'I wondered if you might,' he said. 'I used to play the organ. At morning assembly.'

'I still have nightmares about that.'

'My organ playing?'

'No, the assembly. Having to read the lesson. Waiting in the prefects' room and then having to climb up that little staircase and out onto the stage. Like Julien Sorel going to execution.'

'I never read the lesson. I was never a prefect,' he said. 'I was one of those rejects who left school at fifteen.'

We could have stood there all evening, the still dark night, the illuminated doorway, locked in the eternal anxieties of status, failure, recrimination, the organ playing 'I vow to thee my country all earthly things above,' the morning's lesson eternally lost, was that the nightmare, standing at the lectern and finding no Bible in front of me, nothing to read from, the school ranked in front of me waiting for the organist to stop who would not stop and the lesson to begin that was without beginning.

'Come in,' he said at last.

It was a big house and I glimpsed some elegant rooms. But he took me through to a small room at the back which was where he presumably spent most of his time, television, sound system, shelves of videos and CDs, newspapers.

'I've got you some Foster's Lager,' he said.

I was not sure whether this was some British joke about Australia or an attempt to make me feel at ease. It was Britain and I could never tell. I would rather have drunk English beer, but it would have seemed churlish to have demanded that, wouldn't it?

'It brought it all back to me,' he said. 'Those dreadful cross-country runs. That master with the bullet hole in his chin. It was like I'd never left. It was terrible.'

He laughed.

'I mean they're very good. The writing. Don't get me wrong. It was just remembering it all again. I thought I'd put it all behind me.'

I thought I'd put it all behind me too. And here we were, going over it all again.

'If you look back at it now,' he said, 'you can see they were just a bunch of pederasts and philatelists and psychopaths. But at the time –' Words failed him. 'Do you ever see anybody who was there?'

'No,' I said.

'Do you remember Tarleton?' he said. 'Used to act in the school plays. I bumped into him. He's become a clergyman in some East End parish. Very fruity. Quite a line in altar boys. And Kemp, do you remember Kemp, always wore his coat like a cloak and sported a carnation. I often wonder what became of him.'

It was not my idea of an evening's entertainment, going through memories of the old school. I thought I'd left all that behind when I left the country at twenty-one, left a country that was locked into the past, so preoccupied with its schooldays, endlessly recurring to those sites of bonding and terror. And privilege. But if your schooldays had not been days of privilege, why recur to them? And Dick's certainly had not been. He made that clear. It had been a career through the C-stream and leaving at fifteen. That was the ultimate stigma. But no doubt it was that very stigma that had given him his drive, that had pushed him to whatever lofty and wealthy eminence he was at now.

'Have you ever been back?' he asked.

'No,' I shuddered. 'Have you?'

'I have, actually,' he said. 'They call me up. They found out I was in television. Never fails. The lure of glamour. Would I come and address careers' day? Almost on their hands and knees.'

'Did you?'

'I did, actually. Management likes us to do things like that. Community relations.'

There was a silence.

'And?'

'It was all rather pathetic,' he said.

If asked I would have said I hardly thought about the school once I left it. Yes, I had written a handful of stories about it, but those were very early stories, when I had little other experience to write about. It wasn't something I recurred to, after I'd left England, after I'd discovered another life. If asked again I would explain that they were by way of exorcism, those few stories. Externalising and confronting and rearranging uncomfortable memories. And that was it. Bye bye schooldays.

But the dreams I suppose belied that. I was still at school in those dreams. The morning prayers. Now Dick mentioned playing the organ at assembly, I remembered the nightmares about reading the lesson. Yet except for stage fright I rather enjoyed reading the lesson, standing up there declaiming from the Bible, enacting my role as mediator of the word, even if at that stage I refused belief in the word, that word. But yes, now he reminded me of the setting, I did remember the morning prayers, they did recur in nightmare. And how much else did I revisit at night? I rarely remembered dreams. But now the fringe of the curtain had been ruffled I became dimly aware, or not even aware, dimly apprehensive rather, that there were other memories, lost to the bright glare of the Australian sun, but hovering there, elicitable in the grey twilight of an English winter, ever ready to materialise in the long nights. What they were, these memories, these re-enactments, I had no idea. They were just the rustlings the other side of the curtain. I wasn't sure that I wanted to re-encounter them. I wasn't sure even that there was anything to re-encounter. But now a process had begun, prodded by Dick's recollections and resentments and traumas. Was this what the alleged PhD student had been seeking out and maybe even found? Was this why the English were so fixated on their schooldays? Did they believe there were clues to the personality to be discovered, formative incidents, imprinted models? I certainly had no wish to go back to that place I had left behind.

But Dick did. He came back to it the next time we met, and the time after. I had been hoping, ever hopeful, for great television extravaganzas. There was a nineteenth century novel about the city we had grown up in, it would make a marvellous television series. There was my first novel, what a potential for dramatisation there, with a sitcom run-on potential for all eternity. He side-stepped everything like that. It was of course all budgets now. What appealed to him was revisiting the school. 'I'd love to take the crew in there, stir up some of the ghosts.'

He had a transmission slot for that, a series of half-hour documentaries, the sort of programmes they could point to when the licence came up for renewal: local content, cultural content, the arts.

I wasn't terribly interested. Indeed, I wasn't at all interested. I could see little point in wasting time on a half-hour documentary. Who would ever see it? Would it sell any books? It would be one more distraction from writing, another in the endless series of traps and diversions of book reviewing and conferences and festivals and committees, all the time-wasting lures and flatteries and inauthenticities and embroilments that kept you from ever producing the real work. A major production, I could be tempted by that. But not piddling around at some old school revisited twenty-seven minute token arts production.

On the other hand there wasn't much else happening. I was getting into the on the other hand mode by this time. The old certainties were becoming less certain, the committed refusal to compromise, the sure sense of direction was faltering. Nothing much good seemed to be happening any more. And even if this wasn't something that seemed especially good, at least it seemed to be something happening.

Though even that soon became uncertain. This was the world of illusion and spells, creations of light and darkness, evanescent, immaterial, all so transient and never more so than when in concept, uncertain of realisation or delivery. In that context, and there was no other, to go along with it was no great commitment. Nothing might come of nothing. And even if it ever did it was so far down the track it was beyond the frame of planning. At least for me it was.

The next stage was to meet the director.

'Come and have dinner. There's two directors I could put on it. But I think Paul will be best. He's a bit arty. You'd never know he made soapies for a living. It must be a torture for his sensitive soul. So I think he'd be right for something like this. Give him a chance to express his art. But strictly within twenty-seven minutes. Never know how much art he's got bottled up inside there.'

This time it was one of the formal rooms. Paintings of ancestors on the wall. Somebody's ancestors. Maybe Dick had found them in some provincial antique shop while out on location. He'd found a girl-friend, too, to help with the dinner.

Drinks, dinner, drinks.

I don't remember that we discussed the documentary at all. The English way of doing things, eschew the vulgarity of ever mentioning the task in hand. So we talked about assassinations and political corruption and the financing of terrorism and how AIDS was a manufactured virus and how the SAS trained all over Herefordshire and how to fly a light aircraft across central England you had to get permission from the United States Air Force military commander and how the motorways were all monitored by video cameras.

'What I'd like you to do,' said Dick, 'is write a treatment.'

'A treatment?'

'Yes. So we have something to go on.'

Again I winced. Inwardly. But nonetheless painfully. So now I was going to be spending time writing the thing. I don't know what I'd envisaged. Someone asking me questions. Distinguished literary figures nodding wisely at my wisdom.

'Don't want all that talking heads stuff,' said Dick. 'Some nice locations. The old school. I think we should go back in there.'

It was yet another distraction from the novel I wasn't writing.

'It doesn't have to be a finished piece,' said Dick. 'Just some ideas we can work on.'

We sat in his little room at the back and he ran me a couple of videos. At least the series existed. Every so often I had wondered, was it all make believe, some elaborate inquisition?

'I don't want it to be like these,' he said. 'This is just to show you a couple of things we've done. Give you the idea.'

Maybe I could jot down some notes on the flight back.

I wouldn't be in England again for twelve months but that didn't seem to worry Dick. Such unconcern made me wonder whether there was any reality to the project. But maybe they worked at a different pace in the media, maybe it was yet another test of my patience.

I roughed out a treatment. It wasn't that different from any other writing. Always the basic issue of what to put in and what to leave out. And if the whole thing was an elaborate contrivance to get me to reveal early trauma, identify crucial sites, provide some minute map of my psychology, then I had obviously better be cautious. But assuming it might be real, then revealing your psyche for a million viewers, it was worth being cautious anyway. But how cautious could you be without being bland? It had to have some substance. And doing it yourself, doing your own profile, then you had all the taboos against self-promotion, the necessary English modesty. And no guidelines, no structure, not even the inkblots of a Rorschach. There you were, there I was, nothing but the blank page, the empty space, fill it in how you will, what a potential for self-incrimination.

Back in England a year later at least it gave me something to do. Beyond the filial duty, the family visit. Visiting Dick became part of the routine, all of a piece with working in the university library, drinking with Grenville in the bar, having a solitary meal in an Indian restaurant. And Dick seemed glad to have a visitor. These were the days of restructuring. The media were beginning their decade of destabilisation, the universities were already well into it. So we would sit in the snug at the back of the house sipping Fosters and muttering about job dissatisfactions. And satisfactions, too. He would be back from the States from planning some co-production, off to Moscow for some tentative project, across to Frankfurt, down to London all the time. And we talked about the programme. Not a lot. It never occupied a major part of the evening. But it was there. A bait, a lure, a thread.

'How's the television project?' Grenville asked.

'I don't know,' I said. 'Nothing ever seems to happen.'

'Much like universities,' said Grenville.

And then when things seemed to have lapsed altogether there would be a sudden flurry of activity. Paul had a couple of days free from his soapie and wanted to look at locations.

It is strange showing someone round the city you grew up in. Years of sardonic observation, all that pent up frustration and resentment, give you a critical perspective. But you don't appreciate an outsider's contempt. The local loyalties you never believed you had begin to flare up when the visitor is unimpressed by the bridge built by a friend of Dr Johnson's, by the house from which Queen Elizabeth addressed the citizens, by the plaque marking where some martyr was burned to death, by the car park on the site of the hall where Elgar conducted, by the ring road round the line of the city walls. This was provincial England, the wreckage of.

'It's so depressing,' said Paul. 'I've always found it a depressing little town. I really don't see anything here at all. What about the school?'

We walked down to it, looked through the gates at the headmaster's house.

'It's on the site of a medieval nunnery. There's supposed to be a tunnel that leads to the cathedral. Back in the fifties shops in the High Street used to collapse into it. A nun got locked up in it once and died. They say her ghost still haunts the place.'

'Ah, spookery,' said Paul. 'Now that might be something. But would we get it on camera?'

He moved as if to enter the grounds.

'I don't think we can just walk in,' I said, shocked at the effrontery of it, shocked again at my own shocked reaction.

He smiled. 'We'll get Dick to fix it. He's dying to get back in there. Haunt the places where his honour died. What about a pub? Isn't there a pub you drink at? Get a sandwich or something?'

The school had made me jittery enough. Was this next manœuvre a way of getting me to reveal my haunts, what haunts, what connections were left? Yet the friends at the pub had had a visit too, now it came back to me, someone had called in there, 'A friend of yours who'd cycled round France with you.'

'I've never cycled round France,' I said.

'That's odd,' they said, 'he seemed to know all about you. He spent a whole evening talking with us about you.'

Maybe I said there was nothing much in town, let's head out to the country. Or maybe that was some other time. Maybe we did go to the pub. Often it seemed I was capable of the extremest suspicions and yet incapable of acting on them.

The countryside received a more positive response. I had taken paragraphs out of stories, paragraphs that had some scenic potential, and put them into the treatment. Now we sought out these sites. Tracks along the river bank. Leafy lanes. Watermills. Churchyards. How important had these been to me? They had come to hand as images, but was that any more than because something was needed at that point in the story, some illustrative focus? The stone slabs of the tombs in the churchyard slipping out of alignment, gaps appearing out of which a skeletal hand might reach. Was this childhood trauma or fictional opportunism? We tramped along the towpath of the silted up canal and I wondered, am I revealing the deepest reaches of my consciousness, the tracks of my formative years, or is this passive fraud, walks of discovery along paths I have never trod before? And these so scenic, filmic locations, unknown till now, will they in time take on significance, recur in later fictions, take on their own role in the memory theatre of these haunted years?

They were always travelling. Dick was in Florida, Paul in Hong Kong, Bangkok, and then when he was back, off to Paris for the weekend. They earned fantastic salaries. Fantastic compared with mine. They didn't deny it. Paris for lunch was nothing. And they existed at a level of high anxiety. I thought I was restless enough. But these two were endlessly somewhere else. Dick was locked into committees and receptions night after night. Perhaps it was part of his work, keeping a watch on the cultural life of the region, ancient buildings, arts advisory panels, choral music, galleries. And day by day the company restructured and reviewed and shed staff and put people on contract and let them go altogether.

'You've seen the best,' said Paul.

We were sitting in the Farrier's Arms, my local pub in the middle of the city. We had despite everything ended up there.

'You might think it's all crap now but just you wait. The good years of television are all over. Now it's nothing but money. Money is the only value.'

'We might just get this made before they close us down,' said Dick. 'This year's schedule is all right but I still haven't got a budget for next year's productions. This could be the last thing we ever make.'

'So what will they make instead?' I asked.

'Who knows?' said Dick.

'Nobody knows,' said Paul.

'How do they decide?'

'They can't decide. Everything is so expensive they're paralysed about making a decision in case they make the wrong one,' said Dick.

'So how do things get made?'

They looked at each other.

'Generally they don't,' said Paul.

'The deadline comes up for next season's budget and whatever happens to be lying on the executive producer's desk or whoever he just had lunch with,' said Dick, 'is it.'

We gazed lugubriously into our beers and nodded.

And then Dick got us into the school.

'I'm amazed you managed it,' I said.

'The magic of television,' said Paul. 'Just say the word and anybody will do anything. It never fails.'

The haunted corridors, the dark stairwells, the old brown classrooms.

'That's where I was beaten,' said Dick. 'That's where I had to crawl on my hands and knees to the wastepaper bin with a dead rat between my teeth. That's where I fell down the stairs carrying a milk-crate.'

The proportions were all different. Yes, it was smaller, I had known it would be smaller but it still amazed me how much smaller it seemed.

The headmaster showed us the new buildings, the extensions. But it wasn't the new we wanted, we tried to block him out as he wittered on about careers days and computer terminals and entering Europe. It was the old we were looking for, the triggering glimpses of forgotten horror, the cloakrooms, the toilets, the gym, the prefects' room. He took us down to the playing fields and shouted at us when we nearly walked across the wicket. He was eloquent about the new pavilion club house they were going to build.

This should have been a gem, this should have glowed with a glorious light, but the stomach contracts again and the hand refuses to write.

We drove out to a country pub to cheer ourselves up. Dick was ashen. Whatever ghosts of mine had been stirred up, he had certainly failed to exorcise his.

They did it. They got the headmaster playing croquet on his lawn.

'People will do anything for television,' Paul said again.

They got the poor little first-formers running through mud and marl and puddles and rain on a cross-country run, cold and damp and wretched.

They got a literary figure to talk into the camera about how good I was but didn't use the sequence.

At the end of the last day's shooting Paul sat me down and asked me a battery of questions on camera. 'Just for the record, in case we need to use them.' This was the only time it started getting political. Anything else vaguely political had been excised from the script. But this last afternoon, with the butterflies and bees flitting around, he got into some more substantive questions.

I remember recognising the trap. Here you are being thrown questions and you're on camera and it's like being on the playing fields, you feel you have to answer, you can't just drop the catch, you're being filmed and you feel you can't just 'ah' and 'um' and say, 'I don't know,' your pride is involved in showing how you can respond, how you can reply immediately without having to stop to think, no incompetent silences, no fumbling the ball, you have to show how you can play the game, their game.

I don't remember what the questions were. They didn't use this sequence. Not for the programme that went to air. Well, they wouldn't, would they?

14

Nephew's Story

The bed sitting room, the afternoon light streaming through the window, the high-backed easy chair, the dark furniture around the walls, the mementoes, photographs, pot plants, dried flowers, little objects. The little objects I cannot immediately recall. They meant a lot to my aunt, they were the memory theatre of her life, all with their associations. They took her out of the room through space and time. To me they represented the fetishism of objects, they were just clutter. I could afford to reject all that, or thought I could. At the time I felt I had no choice but to reject it, the oppressive weight of the old world, old values, which I had travelled so far to escape. But every time I revisited the objects would all be in place, in still, silent repose.

Not that my aunt was necessarily silent.

'What about our poor boys in Aden being attacked like that?' she greeted me.

I muttered that I didn't see our boys had any justification for being in Aden.

But she would ride roughshod over my mutterings, hearing them yet refusing to hear them, so that every visit was a battle of Empire, a confrontation of politics, of faith, of aesthetics, of haircuts, the lot.

'Oh, I thought you were the man come to mend the boiler,' she greeted me in my denim phase. She didn't have a boiler, of course, whatever a boiler might have been. The denim looked like a boiler suit, or could be held to look like one, the uniform of the working class, that was the only point.

And so the photographs and objects around her room became the memory theatre for me of confrontation, mnemonic icons of the class war, of all the appalling oppression and exploitation and privilege that she was committed to supporting, benefiting from none of it herself. Lady Diana somebody or other in hunting gear, on horseback, a photograph from the 1920s, hung on the wall. I do not immediately remember if the horse was stationary, Lady Diana erect in silhouette; or if it was leaping over a hedge, Lady D. leaning forward along the horse's back. The detail did not matter to me; or, if it did, I refused it. For me it was a simple image of privilege and all the economic and political and social repression privilege bore with it. Here was Lady Diana, daughter of the family to which my aunt's father was head groom, still lording it over us from the wall. It embodied that inalienable distance between the privileged socialite and my aunt, and me too, of course. And yet here was my aunt commemorating that world, Lady Diana's sprawling country house, my aunt in a bed-sitting room.

The resentments were, of course, all mine. To my aunt there were our betters, the upper classes, the aristocracy, and then all the various gradations. For me such a vision was one of injustice and exploitation: to her it was the natural order. Those who advocated change of the order - Labour people, Communists - were wicked. I think that was her word, wicked. It sounds right. But writing this I find how much I can no longer remember. Whether forgotten or repressed, I am not investigating. Those conflicts were so painful I am happy so little remains.

Her bed-sitting room I suppose I saw as an imprisonment, the solitary cell. There were the people she admired, she adulated, living in spacious splendour, and she was reduced to the one small room. But I don't know that she felt that way about it. She never said so. But there again, she wouldn't have. She had all her things around her, few as they were. And looked at another way, this room of her own, this room to herself, must have been the triumph of her escape from childhood, where in the head groom's house on the estate there would have been inevitably a shared room for the five children. So that escape, that first position as a governess, would have been a marvellous one, that room to herself. The children she was governess to were still there, amongst the photographs on the chest of drawers. She still talked about them, about their achievements; the girl had married a doctor, the boy had gone to a public school and was now housemaster at another one. It sickened me. I knew their stories off by heart, so often was I told them. Now I can recall almost none of it.

When she was housekeeper to the local railway manager, again she had a room to herself. The manager was a genial old reactionary. He fulminated against Stalin, Archbishop Makairios, Aneurin Bevan. He enthused over Churchill, Beaverbrook, Anthony Eden. His daughter had married an

Olympic runner who became headmaster of the grammar school to which I won a scholarship. Endlessly my aunt would talk about the grandchildren, my headmaster's children, what amazing children, what promise, what achievements, what beauty, what brilliance, until I began to hate them with an implacable loathing. That made no difference. They were always there. At every visit, from my teens to my fifties, I had to hear about them: and there was always, as with everything in her conversation, the implied rebuke, why are you not like these impeccable children, these are the models for you to emulate, this is the social ladder for you to climb, to be like them. But you couldn't as far as I could see. This was England. The classes were castes. The gulf between manual labourers' children and the public i.e. private school educated offspring of the bourgeoisie was not to be bridged. I had no wish to acquire those strangulated accents. I had no wish to pretend to be other that what I was. What I was was hard enough to know. But to pretend to be something other, that would always be a pretence, always be detected. It was such a relief to get to Australia. And that, I suppose, was the final disgrace, the final mark of my not being like those splendid children. I had left England. I had deserted. In the First World War they had shot people like that, like me. Some three hundred and seven of their own troops they executed in World War I.

When the railway manager died my aunt had to find somewhere to live. I think she was left some money. And perhaps she had saved a bit. My father tried to persuade her to buy a house, to provide herself with some security. But she wouldn't. Perhaps she could not accept the indignity of it: here was my father, a working man, a manual worker, giving advice on property. Perhaps she was afraid of the responsibility. Whatever, she missed the opportunity.

So it was a succession of rooms. I think the first place was a couple of rooms and a kitchen. But it is the sitting room that I remember, with the afternoon light coming in. It was at the corner of Sunnyside Road, and because of the name I remember it as a sunny room. Not that she liked the sun. She made a point of keeping out of it, wore hats that shaded her face, kept a pale complexion. I think it was a mark of refinement for her not to be sunburned. Whereas my mother, who loved to potter around the garden in all winds and weathers, would develop the dark, suntanned, windburned complexion of a countrywoman, a gypsy even. But being a countrywoman was what my aunt was distancing herself from. It was a matter of separating herself from the soil, aiming for the alienation of privilege. So she would have had the lace curtains drawn across the window to filter out the intrusive light, and if the sun was shining in directly, she would have pulled the full, heavy curtains across too, to block it.

She had never married. She was the classic maiden aunt. Those were the years of that classic type. And I don't think it was with her, as perhaps it was with my father's two sisters, a matter of choice, a matter of preference. She was of the generation whose husbands who might have been were mown down in the first world war. The millions of them sacrificed to the nationalists, the arms-manufacturers, the politicians, the generals, the business interests. There was never any choice. Just a mass carnage that left a mass desolation, spinster aunts living in single rooms, sewing by the light of the window, but sewing not for children of their own but for nephews and nieces, writing letters in the fading light, but not to children of their own or their own absent partner. They were the unburied victims, the unslaughtered, the ones who survived to a life of incompletion, isolation, the loneliness of an independence they surely would never have chosen, if choice had been theirs.

'She hasn't had an easy life,' my mother would say. When she was housekeeper to the railway manager and his wife, when there were visitors, she always had to sit at the back of the room, on a hard chair, at the back of the room away from the fire, in that cold draughty house.

I could never quite visualise these occasions. Perhaps they were too painful. Perhaps the image told more of my mother's priorities. My mother loved to have a fire going, would sit beside it in her easy chair, prodding and poking away at it. 'Leave the damn fire alone,' my father would complain. The fire was my mother's delight, and to her those rooms my aunt lived in without open fireplaces were soulless, like their landladies who always at some point decided they needed the room for themselves or for a relative or they decided to sell up, and my aunt had to find somewhere else to move to.

Well, that happened twice: and every move is a major stress, a massive disruption. After the second time she moved to an old people's home with its self-contained units, its bed sitting room and kitchen. It was an indignity at first, of course, subsidised council accommodation, a provision of that socialist welfare state she so condemned and which is now being demolished. She kept herself in superior splendour, like most of the people there. 'That great big sitting room and no one uses it,' my mother would remark. The communal room was always empty. Everyone preferred to stay alone, each in his or her own cell, writing letters to absent relatives in the fading light, sewing beside the window, or looking out at the rooks nesting in the high cedars.

The last room was in the nursing home. The smallest room of all, only a few sticks of furniture remaining now, only the few that could be fitted in. Now she was in her nineties, no longer able to look after herself. There was the window, a few sparrows chirruping in the branches of a tree, the occasional sound of pigeons cooing. She could no longer manage to write letters, no longer maintain that determined connection with the family, with former charges, with friends. And indeed most of her correspondents had now died. She no longer bothered with television or radio. It was not just that she could not operate them. She was no longer interested. Slowly she was withdrawing from the constrictions of the world. She was back in conversation with her mother, she was living on some intermediate plane, wafting back in and out of the present to some other dimension.

The last time I saw her she asked, 'And where have you come from?'

'Sydney,' I said.

'Oh, really,' she said. 'How interesting. I have a nephew in Sydney.'

'That's me,' I said. 'I am your nephew.'

'Are you?' she said. 'Do you know him?'

The photographs still stood on the chest of drawers. Her older brother, one time butler, in his army uniform. Her youngest brother in air-force uniform, standing beside a palm tree in Egypt. A family photograph of my parents, my sister and me of nearly fifty years back. The children she had been governess to. Lady Diana on horseback, standing there, yes, definitely static. And the mementoes, the carved elephant from Egypt her brother had brought from the Middle East, the carved goanna I had brought from Australia, little boxes, a clock no longer going.

'How did you get here?' she asked.

'I hired a car.'

'You hired a pony and trap?' she said.

I hear it pass down the narrow, hedged lane, the clip clop of the hooves echoing in the still night, as the white flash of a barn owl rises up out of an overhanging elm.

15

Symposium

It was an international conference on Masques and Masquing, a way to claim an overseas trip, or part thereof, from research funds or against tax. Everyone had a role, everyone was listed on the conference programme, a stiff powder blue production with deckle edges, a wedding invitation crossed with a menu for a Chinese restaurant. Even the people reading grace before meals got a credit. Convenors and chairpersons and responders and panellists, the raw material of a hundred and fifty curricula vitae, the raw material of a hundred and fifty lives. At one point I'd backed out. I wrote and said I'd be quite happy to be a chairperson or panellist or something, I hadn't realised about reading grace, but I'd like to withdraw my paper. But they seemed to have sufficient chairpersons and panellists and suchlike so they wouldn't let me off the hook, ever so politely. So a hot summer writing a paper. And there I was in an undergraduate's room emptied for the vacation, it was like being a freshman again, a new room, knowing no one, nothing to do except look out of the window till the bell tolled for dinner. Then the exquisite hell of communality, the risk of who you might find yourself sitting next to, what silences or what terrors that might give rise to. It was palpable, the terrors were imprinted on the room, embedded in the ancient timbers, saturating the fabrics.

I stood in the sun in the corner of the quadrangle. My brain was fried. Finally I knew it. My eyes sizzled at the rims. The golden stone caught the evening light around me. I didn't think I could stand it. Not paper after paper. And souvenir mugs. Everybody who'd paid their registration fee was given one. I'd paid my fee and taken my mug back to my room and then I'd left that dark and gloomy cell to stand in the sun, waiting for the dinner bell, waiting for anything really except more papers, and I'd only been to one session. But that was three seventeen minute papers. People flying all round the world at the taxpayers' expense to talk for seventeen minutes. Not just people. Me too, I was one of the people in question.

"Snice in the sun,' said a smiling man.

'Sure is,' I said. Why was it I always seemed to speak in other peoples' idioms, and unidiomatically at that, when they spoke to me? Why this American 'sure is' except somehow to say the right thing for the smiling American?

'You're not carrying your souvenir mug,' said the American.

'I thought I'd save it for a special occasion.'

'That's very noble of you,' said the smiling man. 'I thought I'd give mine to my brother. He likes that sort of thing.'

'I'm not really sure about this,' said the smiling man. 'It reminds me all a bit too much of outings. Of the Sunday School variety.'

'It is a bit like that,' I agreed.

The coaches were lined up outside the college kitchens.

'I wonder what they say on the front,' said the smiling man.

We strolled down the length of the coaches. They didn't say anything on the front.

'I was hoping it might be Mystery Tour,' said the smiling man. 'Not even SPECIAL.'

There was an exhalation of air and the front doors opened.

'You can get in if you like,' said the driver.

'Might as well,' I conceded.

'The seats lay all before them, where to chose their place of rest and providence their guide,' said the smiling man.

We sat together, why not, I was going to have to sit with somebody. Later I wondered if I'd been easily manipulated, directed, monitored. But later. It was always but later. Later I remembered from some espionage thriller read on a plane that surveillance teams operated in threes. But that was later, too. And there didn't seem anything odd. Nothing that stood out in the context of two bus loads of academics hurtling through the English countryside. Later I tried to run the conversation through my head again but there didn't seem anything troublesome. I hadn't talked about politics, hadn't talked about drugs, hadn't espoused violent revolution, hadn't been soft on communism, hadn't discussed terrorism. Just talked at a bland superficial level. Or had I?

'Yes, it looks beautiful,' I could hear myself saying, remorselessly, irrevocably droning on, irremediably unsound, 'I was a milkman round these villages once, not for long, just a holiday job. You should have seen these cottages then. In the early sixties. No electricity. No mains water. A pump in the back yard. The pig sheds next door to them had running water and electric light. I couldn't believe it. Not then. Nor now. Livestock got better treatment than humans.'

'They look so charming,' said the smiling man.

'They are now. Now they're all middle-class commuter cottages, weekenders, business people. The people who can afford to renovate them. Know how to get the government grants. Totally gut them, put in central heating, new kitchens, bathrooms. Not new bathrooms in the sense of replacements. Bathrooms for the first time. When they were tied cottages belonging to the estate nothing was ever spent on them.'

'So what happened to the cottagers?'

'No need for them any more. Farming's all mechanised now. You never see anyone in the fields any more. Have you noticed, all the way along, all these fields, and no one in them? Maybe a lone tractor, that's all.'

The empty landscapes. Hedgers, ditchers, pruners all gone. No one weeding between the furrows, weed killers sorted that out. No one scaring off the pigeons. Just the detonations of automatic bird scarers. The great depopulation achieved, the final eviction from the land, the great removal, men eaten up by sheep, England's birthright lost.

'That's very interesting,' said the smiling man. 'You've really given me something to think about. It all looks so charming and you've totally undermined it. Toxic with pesticides and chemical additives and alienation.'

'I'm sorry,' I said.

And how. Why couldn't I just keep my sad thoughts to my breast? What was the point of wearing funny clothes if I had to babble on like this. If you're going to look straight, talk straight; and if straight talk means double talk, talk double talk, and remembering that the point of double talk is to make it sound single. But this was afterwards, thinking it through afterwards, that I worried about all that.

We walked round some ancient author's house.

'What are these extraordinary plants?' said the smiling man.

Along the edge of the wall, white, sheet-like, unfurled flowers the size of a small hand, each around a livid, upstanding phallic stamen.

'Lords and ladies.'

'Are those lords and ladies?' said the smiling man. 'Which shepherds call a grosser name?'

'That's them.'
'What's the grosser name?' said the female person behind us.
'I don't know,' I said.
'Or is that just politeness?'
'Not for ladies' ears,' said the smiling man.
'Sexist asshole,' she said.
'We just called them lords and ladies,' I said.

'I was interested in your talk,' she said.
'In my talk?'
'Of course I couldn't catch all of it. I was sitting just back of you.'
I hadn't given a talk, had I, yet? What talk was this? I would have said, but she bowled on down anyway, not waiting.
'On the coach,' she said. 'Talking about the dispossessed peasants.'
'Oh,' I said.
'I could just overhear snatches,' she said.
'Ah, right, yes.'
'Pretty radical, huh?'
'Oh well, not really, just observations,' I said. 'I think radicals and conservatives sort of agree about the country. All a bit sad, really.'
'Oh, I'm no conservative,' she said. 'You don't have to worry about me.'
I didn't know what to say. I tried smiling.
'It's hard to tell these days,' she said. 'The most radical people wear the least radical clothes. It's like everybody's in disguise. Well, I guess they are. My name's Rebecca.'
Somehow she seemed to take over. One moment I was with the smiling man discussing the flowers in Shakespeare's plays and the next I was hijacked by this person I didn't remember even seeing on the bus or anywhere else, talking to me about radicalism all the way back, over my shoulder.
'Of course they're compiling lists again now,' she said. 'They encourage the kids. Dossiers on subversives on campus. Communistic thinking in Renaissance studies. It's getting ugly, I can tell you.'
'I don't think it was ever very beautiful, candidly,' said the smiling man.

We sat down in my room. Jonah had a quart of whisky and he and Rebecca and I sipped away at it. Jonah was someone she thought I ought to meet.
'Ice?' asked Rebecca.
'I'm sure there isn't any,' I said.

'Don't they have ice?' said Rebecca. 'Well, what do you know? All this elegance and no ice.'

'What are the possibilities where you are?' said Jonah.

'For what?'

'For anything?'

'I don't see many,' I said.

'So now I wear a suit,' said Jonah. 'I conform, so if I have to wear a suit I wear these hideous ready made suits.'

'Is that your gesture?' said Rebecca.

'It embarrasses them.'

'These clothes,' said Rebecca. 'I had to buy these straight clothes so I could come to this conference. But they embarrass me.'

'Why do they embarrass you?' said Jonah.

'I'd hate people to think I look likes this,' she said. 'Even if I do.'

'Illusion and reality,' said Jonah.

'To name a classic of Marxist literary criticism,' she said.

I said nothing. I didn't feel in any position to. I could either look too casual in jeans or too formal in my suit. It was the sort of suit we used to call an interview suit at college. But these days I didn't even go for interviews. Interviews now represented the unsought and the unwelcome and the probably hostile. I could wear the suit jacket with the jeans for a more literary effect, late night readings at the Colosseum Cafe, as befitting that ambiguous world. It was all overfamiliar, these anxieties, I was a born again freshman and feeling hopelessly out of place, as lost as the first time round.

'The trouble is when you find out you've been investigated you start acting quite different,' said Jonah. 'I had all these friends, you know, who wrote away to get hold of their files under the freedom of information act.'

'And they were all censored,' said Rebecca.

'There was that, yes. Great paragraphs deleted. They say deleted, they don't say censored. Value free language they called it when I was in school. All it means is when anything's deleted now you just assume it's been censored.'

'Which is probably true enough,' she said.

'Probably. But that's the problem. Paranoia. These friends of mine, they started acting according to what was in the files. They started conforming to the files' portrayal of them. They started behaving like the way the FBI saw them. They became like caricatures of the projections of the files. Paranoia, for instance. They suddenly realised how much they'd been being observed. Well, if they'd thought about it they'd have know that was the case. But seeing it in print, in black and white and was it black, there wasn't much white, black and white and red all over, that's what it was. So they started acting like they were red revolutionaries. Real paranoid. They realised how they'd been observed so closely like we were told Eastern Europe was, and they figured there must have been a lot of people they knew who were not what they'd thought they were, who were just into the scene to report on it. So they got very paranoid, quite properly, that maybe these same people or at least their replacements were still into the scene. Still watching them. So they started acting like they were up to no good, very secretive, like they were up to violent revolution, and they just cut themselves off. I mean in many cases they probably did realise that some of their best friends as they'd thought had been hired to report on them. Spy on them. But when they cut them off then it sort of looked like they were indeed up to something they didn't want the FBI and CIA and the rest of them to know about. And of course they cut themselves off from authentic people, so their whole range of human contact was suddenly reduced, and so any chance of cooperative activity was immediately removed. It was a great trick, releasing those files.

'Then when they realised they were acting crazy and tried to do something about it and straighten up and wear suits and ties, no one believed them; then the people watching them were sure they were up to something, suddenly, eventually, going straight and sociable. So from then on they could never win, whether they acted paranoid or straight, whatever they did, someone was going to read it as evidence of some subversive intent.

'What you think is, when you grow up you'll be free from constant surveillance. That's your ambition as an adolescent. To evade the constant observation and indictment and retribution of the family. The adult world looks like marvellous freedom. What you don't realise is that the surveillance continues. There are always father figures and mother figures and big brothers and old aunts. You burst into adulthood thinking you can do what you like without being harassed, and all the time people are checking you out to see if you're stable enough for this job, discreet enough for something else. The one's who succeed in this society inevitably are the infantile ones, those fixed at a childhood stage of winsome charm and duplicity, baby fat smiles and uncomplicated selfishness. They are our rulers. The school sneaks and the school bullies. And nappy rash the endemic disease of the cultural apparatchiks.

'The horrible thing of being on a file,' he said, 'is that you're neutralised. Nothing ever happens to you. They don't kill you. It seems like they've decided against that. Too obvious. They just makes sure nothing ever happens to you. Everything is intercepted. They interpose their bodies. Between you and it, you and the other, you and yourself. Between the desire and the action falls the security service. They've got you cocooned up in their web, buster, and don't you ever forget it. Nothing'll ever happen to you again. You'll be like that character in the Henry James story. The man who waited for something special to happen and nothing ever happened and that was what was special. Well, they cloned the idea. They've fixed it so that's the way it is with anybody on file. No way at all. Nothing will ever happen. They're very literary people. Probably graduates of Yale.'

'Who's this they then?' asked Rebecca.

Jonah shrugged. I shrugged too.

'We're in such a fascist phase of late capitalism that to be a conservative is to be oppositional,' said Jonah. 'To have any other than nakedly cash values is to be oppositional in this society.'

'So you think we should all masquerade as conservatives to survive?' said Rebecca.

'It's not clear that the conservatives will survive any better than us,' said Jonah.

'It certainly doesn't see a time for radical initiatives,' I said.

'What are radical initiatives?' asked Rebecca.

'Like starting a magazine or a press or something.'

'She thought you meant starting a terrorist group or going underground,' said Jonah.

'Or are you thinking of literary criticism as a form of revolutionary activity?' she said.

'I'm not thinking of anything, certainly not that,' I said. 'It doesn't seem to be the time for anything vaguely radical, whatever you're thinking of.'

'Was it ever?' said Jonah.

'Probably not,' I agreed. 'It just seemed different.'

'It certainly was different,' said Rebecca. 'Things have certainly changed.'

'From the glorious sixties?' said Jonah. 'That was all based on false analogy. The assumption was that the academics were the oppressive capitalist and students the proletariat. But it was the staff who were the proletariat if the analogy had any sense. Or more correctly, the petty-bourgeois. The students were the jeunesse doré, the scions of the ruling class. All their rebellion did was strengthen ruling class control. Just what you'd expect from the dutiful beautiful children of the ruling class. They turned the university into a consumer oriented reader-response supermarket. Take a bit of this and a bit of that and an exotic line on special. The students are the enemy, that's what you've got to remember, just like their parents are the enemy.

'And it all had the effect of diverting attention from economic and social reform into university reform. Instead of that social energy being used in the streets and engaging in a political battle, it was diverted into looking at courses. Did the New Criticism serve as the ideology of the military-industrial complex? It made them feel good, that what they'd always felt was irrelevant now at last seemed meaningful. It could kill. So.'

'I remember when I used to wish I'd been alive in a political time like the thirties,' I said. 'As for the sixties, I can't say I really believed in them at the time. Not that they'd achieve anything.'

'Middle-class school kids thinking up naughty words to shout at their parents,' said Jonah.

'I don't buy that Oedipal politics line,' said Rebecca. 'That's just a way of depoliticising what went on.'

'It was depoliticised from the beginning,' said Jonah. 'It was charades. People going round with masks and body paint doing street theatre. Claiming to support their revolutionary comrades in North Vietnam.'

'I think it was just designed to turn people off,' I said.

'What was?' asked Rebecca.

'Most of it. Just so that reasonable people would have nothing to do with the movement. It was a way of discrediting it from inside. Clowns and jugglers and all that shit. Apart from all the sex and drugs.'

'It was all individual liberation,' said Rebecca.

'That was the best part,' I agreed. 'When you come to think of it. The sex and drugs. I could never get off on the demonstrations and marches. Too much like school games. Having to turn up and support your team. My team. Their team. Only now the prefects were getting you to march and be beaten up by the police. Write your name down here, sign it, not even a thank you, and there you are, on a list, a self confessed opponent of government policy in regard to foreign war, peace, conscription, nuclear weapons. There's your address. Perfect. I don't believe any of it any more.'

'Not even the sex and the drugs?' said Rebecca.

We talked about losing tenure and the left being squeezed out, shed. The thrown away generation of our contemporaries, of us. Rebecca produced some marijuana. Jonah refused. I accepted.

'What do you reckon?' she said.

'Nice stuff,' I said, always polite when I could remember to be, and anyway it generally was, especially when you'd been straight as a die for a few days.

'No, what do you reckon about surviving?'

'Oh, surviving. I hadn't seen it quite as bad as that. But maybe you're right. Maybe it will get tougher. I guess it will. I guess you can keep your head down and avoid publicity and just keep on saying the things you believe in, only quietly, hoping the wrong people won't hear them. And gradually you see your courses taken away from you under various pretexts, you go on leave and they're abolished in your absence, or they're "given a rest" because they've been running too long, or because it's time to give new blood a chance; and you mutter a bit but not too loudly and gradually you've got a sinecure, no teaching, lots of time. That's the way to look at it. Think positive.'

'Then they say you're dispensable, they don't need you any more.'

'There is that problem.'

'Have you got tenure?' Rebecca asked.

'Tenure's meaningless in the face of economic arguments. They just say we don't have the money to pay you. That's the bottom line and you can't argue against it,' said Jonah.

'Yes, I've got tenure,' I said, 'but I agree, it's meaningless, like most things.'

'Not when you don't have it it isn't,' said Rebecca. 'It would seem very meaningful to me.'

'Well, I wasn't planning to surrender it.'

'You look after it and hang onto it,' she said.

'Don't ever let it out of your sight,' said Jonah.

'So you're burying your past, is that it?' said Jonah.

'I wish I could bury some of mine,' said Rebecca.

'You can't bury it selectively,' said Jonah. 'Not without amputation or surgery.'

'I've had that,' she said. 'I've been amputated. I've been cut.'

'The trouble is that as soon as you try to suppress something you draw attention to it,' I said.

'I don't see why,' said Rebecca. 'You could just silently leave something out of the record. Each year my CV gets shorter as I decide some things are best not mentioned. Most things.'

'That's playing it on their terms,' said Jonah, 'cancelling your own life. Publishers remainder books they want to suppress. Or pulp them. That's even more effective. If you pulp them you make sure no one gets to read them. You start suppressing your publications yourself, you're just doing the same.'

'Anyway, the computers are programmed to pick out discrepancies,' I said, 'They notice every time you leave something out.'

'You've sure gone into this,' said Rebecca.

I couldn't deny it.

There was a knocking at the door and we all sat suddenly silent, this is the call you have been waiting for, your fatal curiosity has led you to invoke.

It was the smiling man, lodged in the room next door, hearing voices, needing company, hoping they weren't fatal fires of will o' the wisps, the impulse to community driving him to our door, my door. And we looked at him with that uncertain suspicion, the doubt of what each other was thinking of him before the individual intuitive response could be allowed to float past.

'How-dee,' he said.

Outside the clocks chimed the quarter hours, footsteps could be heard on the gravel paths.

'There's a lot of things I've written I wish I hadn't,' said Rebecca. 'It would be nice just to be able to erase from the record, don't you think?'

'Never explain, never complain,' said Jonah.

'Yeah, but some of those things explained all too clearly,' she said.

'Just leave them off your CV,' said the smiling man.

'Doesn't leave much on it if you take out all that,' said Rebecca.

'Ah well,' said the smiling man, 'you'll just have to write more.'

'More of not the same,' said Jonah.

'But how do you do it?' said Rebecca. 'You find all the things you start to write can't be written; all the things that are worth writing, that is.'

'Write them under a pseudonym,' said Jonah. 'You ever thought of that?'

'Hands up who ever thought of that?' said the smiling man. 'I must confess I certainly never had.'

'I find it hard enough writing anything under one name,' said Rebecca.

They turned to me.

'Well, I guess the point of writing under a pseudonym is that people aren't supposed to know what you write, so presumably you wouldn't admit to it even if you did,' I said.

More tortuously poised ambiguities of the stoned aesthetic of make it pregnant, complex and possibly ironic. Wanton creativity of the dilettantism of the cold wars. Inviting the tired and impatient decoder just to crush it with one simple hammer blow. Which maybe wouldn't necessarily be the best way to elicit meaning but certainly would render it all into crushed fragments. It all, me all.

In the end she was the only one left. Jonah and the smiling man had slipped off, and here she still was. It was the Circean principle, Comus' orient cup. As long as she kept rolling joints and sharing them, I would let her sit there talking. Or just sit there. I knew it was a bad idea.

'What dope does,' she said, 'is psychically open you up. It makes you more aware of other people. Vibrations. You are more responsive to their consciousnesses.'

And did I need that? Instant empathy. The disorderly orderly. I am not I, pity the tale of me.

'Of course the catch is, it opens you up to them. You're totally susceptible. They can suck out your thoughts. It's like a psychic vacuum cleaner.'

'What is?' I asked.

'What they do.'

Those dark steady eyes, that impassive high-cheeked face.

'They're welcome,' I said. Cavalierly. 'As long as they put them back again.' The thoughts. But I couldn't pretend I very much liked the idea. Take this and don't call us, we'll be listening to you.

'I'm going to have to throw you out,' I said, 'and crash.'

I'd been formulating ways of saying it for a long time but she seemed not to have picked up on them. It caught her a little bit by surprise.

'Sorry, I'm keeping you up, I should have gone, I was forgetting myself.'

'That's all right,' I said.

'Feeling so at ease, like I've always know you or something.'

'Just an old cliché,' I said.

She looked startled.

'My familiarity,' I explained, 'not what you were saying.'

Though saying it like that only seemed to make it worse.

I shepherded her to the door, got her onto the staircase.

'Goodnight,' I said.

'Good night,' she said. 'I love you.'

It took me rather by surprise. A frisson of terror ran through my veins. Or whatever frissons run through.

'Me too,' I said, though I wasn't sure that came out quite as I'd intended either. 'Take care,' I added. And I certainly meant that, and for myself, too.

'You know last night,' she said.

'Yes.'

'I nearly came back hammering on your door to let me in.'

I smiled, frozen, pondering the polite 'you should have,' but wouldn't that be taken as an invitation for the next night, tonight?

'I created escalating chaos,' she said.

'What happened?' I asked.

'Well, first of all I was locked in the college so I had to wake a porter up to let me out.'

'Oh no,' I said. Why hadn't she just climbed over the wall like undergraduates used to?

'Then I couldn't get into the college where I'm staying. I couldn't raise anybody at all.'

'So what happened?'

'So I walked back here and considered getting them to let me back in. But I figured that might be tricky.'

'Yes,' I said. I could feel the anxiety pounding in my solar plexus.

'So I went back to my own college and threw stones at a window and finally someone let me in,' she said. 'I just hope I didn't wake too many people throwing stones. At least I didn't break a window.'

'What a nightmare,' I said.

'I got into a phone-box and I was going to call you up, but then I realised the rooms don't have phones, amazing isn't it, all this elegance and no phones.'

'Amazing,' I said.

16

Somewhere Else

You never make a fresh start. You are always carrying the lumber of the preceding into every new beginning. There is always the hangover of the past evening blighting the freshness of the new morning. So that you start already feeling sick. You have imported a continuity. Even when you don't remember what it is. Just the dull ache. The consciousness of past bruising, the consciousness of past consciousness. So that waiting for the light plane to take us up and away, fresh seas, over fresh seas to the separation of an island, all that salt water in between, purifying, sterilising and yet also preserving, waiting there I felt the dull throb of the accumulated past. Even if I couldn't specify it. Trying to focus on it I couldn't define it, whatever it was, generating that unease.

The things you carry are also the things you find there when you get there. You try not to recognise this, of course. You are somewhere else, afresh, anew. Carrying your baggage helps obscure this. The blinkers of change of place are in place to protect your vision. No, that wasn't a peripheral perception: you don't even tell yourself that, you don't even recognise the possibilities that there could be a peripheral perception, not with the blinkers on, no everything is ascribed to the baggage you carry, the pain in the neck, the ache in the arm, the strain in the shoulder, the fluttering fear in the heart. But you feel it even when you have the baggage on wheels and you draw it along behind you like a compliant poodle.

Still the flutter in the heart, the ache between the shoulders, the strain at the neck. These are the pains and fears of perception.

'So where have youse two blown in from?'

Not the usual restaurateur's greeting. But then we were away from the usual, this was somewhere to get away to, somewhere to escape to and write in, somewhere away from the world that had lost its charm, away from the destabilising doubts and suspicions and blacklists, somewhere else.

I was too tired to know, it was a matter of being here a while to find out why we were here, it had been somewhere to keep going towards, at least things will be different when we get away.

Too abstract, all this? Too wordy. Sated with words, I was too. You would prefer, as I preferred, or felt I preferred, or wanted to prefer, the reed-thatched roof at the edge of the beach, the wooden chairs with their wicker seats, the sea gently lapping just across the sand there, the boats drawn up on the sand, the restaurant just across the road, the road running between it and this thatched extension, to eat out there on the edge of the beach, the gentle night air, the long stone jetty, the ferries moored to one side, the headland to the other, across the sea the just twinkling lights of the mainland, three, four restaurants in a row, maybe one was a bar, a café, this row of reed-thatched awnings between the road and the sand, chequered table cloths no doubt, nobody there yet, too early to eat, but we had our alien habits, alien hungers, wanting to eat before the music began, before everyone came out and strolled up and down the road or wove in and out on their motorbikes.

'So where have youse two blown in from?'

'England,' I said.

'Australia,' Lily said.

'Don't youse know?' she said, 'can't you get your story right?'

Oh, if it were so easy to get a story right.

'Him, England,' Lily said, ' me, Australia. He was at a conference in England and we met up in Athens.'

'How romantic,' she said.

Lily smiled a romantic smile. I ruffled my hair in imitation of an Englishman.

'I keep saying to my hubby, why don't we go to Athens for a weekend? Have some romance again.'

'Yes,' said Lily, 'you should.'

'You know what he says, who's going to cook, what do we do, close up the business now the tourists are coming?'

'You could go for a weekend,' said Lily.

'That's what I say to him. Just a weekend. What's life without romance?'

'Nothing,' said Lily.

'What's life without food?' I said.

'Was that a hint? You want to eat? Is that what you're telling me?'
'Well, yes.'
' "Well yes," isn't he a hoot? He reminds me of someone I used to know in Oz, an Englishman, he used to say things like that. Is he English?'
'Well, yes,' I conceded.
'There he goes, what a hoot, I thought you said you'd come from Oz.'
'I did. I do.'
'An Ozzie Englishman, is that what he is, just like this fellow I used to know, a real good looking guy, I thought he was amazing, I still think about him. Anyway, enough of that, what do you want?'
'A menu?' I said tentatively.
'There isn't one. Or there is but most of it we don't have and what we do have isn't on it. I'll tell you what we have, how about that?'
'We don't eat meat.'
'You don't eat meat.'
'Not really.'
'Not really.'
'Not if we can help.'
'That makes it hard. Let me think. No meat at all? How about fish?'
'Not really.'
'Not fish. What do you eat?'
'Moussaka?' I said, tentatively.
'That's got meat in it.'
'But not much.'
'Ah, you don't mind a bit of meat.'
'Not in moussaka. Or pastitsio.'
'What about stuffed tomatoes?'
'Beautiful,' said Lily.
'They've got a bit of meat. Or peppers. Or melitzanes. Stuffed egg plant.'
'Sounds delicious.'
'Pastitsio?'
'The pastitsio all went at lunch.'
Lists of foods. Mouths watering. Even with meat.
'And a beer.'
'A beer.'
'A beer to start with.'
'You mean you want it now?'
I nodded, weakly.

Was it always going to be such a hassle just to order, a dialogue, a catechism, even before I could get a drink, did I have so much relaxing to learn, yes I did, I knew that anyway, that was why I'd come here, probably, one reason, anyway, wasn't it, so many words to unravel, so much relaxing to learn, so many further words to endure. Beer, harbour-lights, stuffed tomatoes, the gentle lapping of the sea, warm air, twilight, moonlight, lamplight, romance.

I heard the bang and it merged into a dream but then I heard Lily call out, and I dragged myself up out of sleep.
'Wake up,' she said, 'wake up, quick, what was that?'
I lay there, unable to speak for a while, vocal powers still lost in the dream.
'What was that explosion?' Lily said.
'I don't know.'
'Didn't you hear it?'
'I heard a bang.'
'It wasn't just a bang. It was an explosion.'
'I don't know,' I said.
'I could hear people outside.'
'When?'
'Before. Before it went off.'
'Maybe it was a gun. Shooting rabbits or something. Or a trip wire.'
What did I mean, a trip wire, where did I think I was?
'There were lights flashing outside.'
'Lights?'
'Yes. It was like they were shining a flashlight into the windows. And there was whispering. And then suddenly there was this explosion.'
'Maybe it was the hot water system.'
I checked the fuse box. We'd had to switch on the various power circuits when we arrived so for once I knew where it was. Maybe I'd switched on the heater switch and forgotten to turn on the water. Nothing seemed to have burned out. I went outside, we went out together, Lily wouldn't stay there alone, she was terrified, whispering, afraid to raise her voice. The bathroom was still there, nothing had blown up. I felt a relief that it hadn't been reduced to a pile of rubble.
'I was terrified,' she said.
'I was asleep.'

'I'd woken up before. And I went outside to the toilet. And I suddenly got terrified there. I suddenly got terrified of people breaking in. And then when I got back into bed I heard this whispering.'

'What were they saying?'

'I don't know. It was just whispering.'

We stood outside the house. Dogs started to bark, hearing us there, barking across the village. It was dark, we couldn't see signs of anybody, anything, and while we stood there the sky began to lighten with the approach of dawn. We stood there indecisive, went back in, sat in the kitchen.

'There were people creeping around I'm sure,' she said.

We couldn't get further than that. It didn't make sense, whatever it was, a loud noise, the middle of the night.

'I didn't dream it,' she said.

'No, I heard it too,' I said. 'You might have dreamed the voices. You might have heard the bang and then dreamed the voices.'

'I wasn't asleep,' she said. 'I was lying there terrified. I was terrified by the flashing lights and I was lying there awake.'

'Did they wake you up?'

'No, I didn't get back to sleep after I'd been outside. I got that sudden sense of people being around and I couldn't sleep.'

'You might have slept and thought you couldn't.'

'I didn't,' she said.

In the morning I got up and went outside. So peaceful. Calm sun. Calm day. I tried an experiment, slamming the door to the kitchen shut.

'What was that? That was the noise,' Lily called out.

'The back door slamming.'

'That's what it was.'

'That's why I did it,' I said. Proud of my deductions. Super sleuth. 'I didn't want to say I was going to do it because that would condition you to expect it. I wanted to see if that's how it sounded without warning you.'

'That was it.'

'Maybe you didn't shut it after you'd been out and it just slammed in the wind.'

'Of course I shut it.'

'It mightn't have caught.'

'I'm careful about that. I'm used to doors that don't catch shut.'

I shrugged. Maybe. Maybe not.

'I was terrified out there,' she said. 'Of course I made sure the door was shut. I told you, I was terrified there were people around going to break in.'

I sat in the kitchen, the door open, waiting to see if a breeze would slam it shut.

'There wasn't any wind last night,' she said. 'Anyway, it didn't slam shut by itself. They must have been in here, that's the whispering I heard, they must have had flashlights.'

'Who?'

'It must have been more than one because there was whispering. You wouldn't whisper to yourself.'

'But who would break in?'

Nothing missing; passports, tickets, money, travellers' cheques, credit cards still there.

It was hard to believe, could it be, I hadn't heard whispers, hadn't seen lights, but I had heard the bang, and why would the door slam in the middle of the night, unless someone was going through it and the only way to close it was to slam it shut, it opened with a key, closed by slamming it shut, and unless you were in the house you wouldn't realise what a resonating echo round the bare walls, the tiled floors, it would make.

'Who would come in knowing we were in there? Isn't that a risk? The place has been shut up for months, why come in when there's someone in there when they could have come in before?'

'Maybe they didn't know we were in there. Maybe they didn't care.'

'Why would they come in anyway?'

Burglars, bandits, security police. This quiet village. This quiet island.

Then we began the walks to the beach, the days on the beach, the long slow days, the numbed surrender of consciousness. Just lying there. The shade of the beach umbrella. The cool of the sea. The sleep of exhaustion and a few beers with lunch. Well, I would get tired of it. There were beaches in Australia. Why travel across the world for beaches when you had beaches? Why travel across the world anyway? But Lily seemed to enjoy it. And for now, for a while, it was welcome enough, it was what was needed, doing nothing. Occasionally a lift to or from the beach, saving us the walk, that was especially welcome.

That was how we met the microvia. Microvia was what we heard one little girl calling another. Microbe, pest, bug, germ. Microvia. It was what we came to call the Australian tourist. A family gave us a lift up from the beach one afternoon and she was walking along the road too and they stopped for her. She was very limp, that limp manner, though apparently tough, had been walking miles, arrived on the ferry the night before, walked up to the village, was going to walk to the market the next day. The family told her what time the bus went.

'I'll walk,' she said. But still that limp manner, we didn't take to her.

And then the next day she was down at the beach, it was a windy day and she'd sheltered in the sheltered spot in one corner and that was annoying, since we thought of it as our spot, so maybe we felt ill disposed to her, and then she was in the restaurant when we went for a beer late in the afternoon, we smiled, took another table, she seemed to be talking to a couple of people, we didn't take a lot of notice, but then she came over and talked; and then the next day she was in that corner of the beach again, doing some sort of exercises, not swimming, but sitting up, stretching, posturing, reaching her arms out and above her, and it was hard to tell if she was naked or half naked or in flesh coloured swimmers, pale flesh coloured. And it was as if she were signalling there, I am here. Nobody else on the beach was drawing equivalent attention. The lone girl.

She came up and joined us in the restaurant again. She didn't seem to have any reason to be there. Someone had said she could stay with them. But she didn't want to outstay her welcome. She was just travelling around. Maybe it would make her boyfriend come and join her. She was aimless, pointless, hopeless. She was an intrusion, an alien insertion into this otherwise unobtruded on beach, enough room not to have to notice anyone, and now there was this creature, and not to respond to her, not to talk, not to communicate, was hard to do without being rude.

There she was, alone there, pacing around, standing at the sea's edge, walking up the beach, we had to pretend to be asleep, myopic, preoccupied. There was nothing to pin down, but the beach had qualitatively changed with the arrival of this creature. And she didn't even seem to swim. But she walked. She walked miles. 'They always give you lifts,' she said. 'I just flick my blond pony tail.' She gave a hideous leer of manipulation. The hairy heel beneath the limp cloak.

So we tried the other beaches, down by the ferry port.

'Youse two again, where you been hiding out, what you been up to?'

'Nothing much. Just swimming.'

We sat at one of the tables beneath the reed roof, out of the blazing sun. A beer, I would have loved a beer, but she had us pinned down there, conversation, dialogue, instruction, inquisition, anything but the simple drink.

'Well don't swim here,' she said. 'I shouldn't say that. They'd kill me if they heard me. But it's filthy. Last year the kids were getting really sick. The sewers run straight into the sea, you know how it is. If you want to swim, go up the other end where there aren't all these houses, you know. Where there are shops and houses it just runs into the sea. But up there it's safe enough. There's a couple of lovely beaches. Suit yourself. But you wouldn't catch me swimming here.'

Children were running along the sand, jumping into the water, German tourists lying there turning from pink to brown, topless French and Italian girls glistened in their basting oil, and the sea gently lapped onto the beach.

'I don't say you'd necessarily get sick, but I wouldn't take the risk. You need a hat in this sun too.'

'Where can I get one?' Lily asked.

'Where can you get one? What, here? You can't get anything here, you know that. What size are you, let's have a look at you, I'll bring you one down.'

'No, no.'

'Yes, yes.'

'No, I can buy one.'

'I doubt it,' she said, 'nothing you'd want to be seen dead in. Don't be ridiculous. I've got one, my hubby gave it me and I never wear it, when do I get the time to go to the beach, I'm in there cooking all day and serving and cleaning up, when would I wear a beach hat, it's only wasted, you come by later and I'll see if I can find it.'

'There's no need.'

'Yes there is,' she said, 'there's every need. We don't want you getting sunstroke.'

'You're too kind.'

'Too kind. You should see the people I have to deal with. If everyone was like you I'd be in heaven. You don't fuss, you don't demand. Most of the people who come here they're barbarians. They demand this, they demand that, warm up the baby's food, bring those drinks now, I feel like throwing the food at them, some days I just refuse, Dimitri, I say, you deal with the bastards, excuse my French, I won't be responsible for what I might do if I go out there again, but you two, now you're different, it makes such a difference you serve people you like, people you can talk to, dealing with the public, you know what I mean, it can do terrible things to you. Now what you going to have?'

How could we ask, without meat, how could we be demanding, how, how, how?

'Moussaka, no, I tell you what, you come down one day and I'll make a special moussaka, you just name the day.'

'Is there anything without meat?'

'Moussaka's got meat.'

'I know, but –.'

'Oh, I see, he likes his meat but he pretends he doesn't, is that it?'

'No –.'

'Give a man meat, that's what they say, isn't it, why don't they say give a woman, makes you wonder, doesn't it, excuse me, I tell you what, how about stuffed tomatoes, there's only a little bit of meat, you know.'

'That would be perfect.'

'Two stuffed, well, you're easy to please, that's what I like about you two, easy to please, no arguments, makes life so much easier, doesn't it?'

So to avoid the microvia we went down to the beaches by the ferry port. But we still ended up talking about her, there was no escaping her intrusive presence.

'Are you sure you don't know her?' asked Lily.

'No.'

'She's not a student of yours ?'

'No.'

'Not some former discarded lover who has followed you round the globe?'

'Not at all.'

'Not a secret admirer who has nursed an inextinguishable passion? Some literary groupie?'

'I hope not.'

'You hope not, but you're not sure.'

'I'm sure.'

'She certainly seems to be determined.'

'Well, she's only going down to the beach each day which is all that we're doing.'

'Are we emanating come hither vibes?'

'Do you think that's what she's doing?'

'Don't pretend you haven't noticed.'
'She's not my sort of person. I don't find her at all attractive,' I said.
'Maybe,' said Lily, 'but that's not answering the question.'
'The question?'
'You haven't noticed the come hither vibes?'
'I hadn't thought about it,' I said. 'I hadn't seen her in that category.'
'Now you have,' she said.
'I don't know. I suppose it's possible. She's certainly very present.'
'Obtrusive,' said Lily.
'Yes, I suppose obtrusive is the word.'
'So why is that?'
'I don't know,' I said. 'Maybe she's just like that. Desperate. Weird. Lonely. I don't know.'
'You don't feel you might be the subject of these attentions?'
'I don't,' I said. 'How about you?'
'I think we'd do better to go somewhere where she isn't,' said Lily.
So we kept to the beaches by the ferry port which was a longer walk but we felt less intruded upon.

There were three or four restaurants down there but since Anna had been so effusive it seemed hard to go to any of the others. To do so would look like a deliberate rejection, a slight rather than the exercise of freedom of choice. So we went to hers. It didn't always involve an immense amount of talking. Sometimes she was busy, 'I got to rush, rush, rush,' and she would take our order and hurry back into the kitchen. But then in these flurried times she would be too busy to calculate the bill, or too busy to work out the change.
'Come back later, I trust you, you won't be suddenly sneaking off on the ferry, besides it doesn't come today, come back later when it's cool and I've got some change, we can have a coffee, I'll fix it up then, don't have any change now.'
But this easy going casualness had its own problems, now it meant we had to go back, we couldn't just leave for the house early when we saw a taxi or when there was the chance of a lift or when we felt like walking. We couldn't just go to the café by the quay and try something different when we saw some interesting things being served; or we could but we still had to go back to Anna's and sort out the bill and sit there over a coffee.
'Why don't I make you something special?' she said. 'You like moussaka, I'll make you a special moussaka, not much meat, specially for you, what day, you

say when, tell you what, why not Thursday, you come along Thursday and I'll make you something special.'

So we said yes, Thursday, why not Thursday, we were down there every day, now we were avoiding the microvia, so what did it matter which day? It hemmed us in, in theory, and I hated making arrangements in advance, but the odds were we'd be down there Thursday anyway, where else would we be? But it meant that arrangements hung there, inhibiting, circumscribing, this was supposed to be a holiday, free from these commitments and obligations and arrangements.

She was flurried when we arrived, flustered, hair tied back in notation of frenzied busyness.

'What will you have?' she said.

'Moussaka.'

She struck her brow with the palm of her hand. 'I knew it,' she said, 'I knew he'd ask for that, I said Dimitri, he's going to ask for moussaka, but Dimitri, he's got his fixed ideas, one day this, one day that, and you can't budge him, that's the way he is, why did I ever marry him, I ask him, I say, why did I ever marry you, you're so rigid, nothing can shift him. So if he's set his mind on what he's cooking, there's no shifting him. Tell you what, I've got this special egg-plant dish, I made it specially for you, no meat, all vegetables, why don't I get you that?'

Lily demurred.

'You have it.'

'Two egg plants?' asked Anna.

I nodded, ever one to agree.

'No,' said Lily, 'no, not for me.'

'I made it specially,' said Anna, 'no meat.'

'No, he'll have it,' said Lily, 'I'll have, I don't know, what else do you have?'

'You don't like egg-plant?'

I could feel myself wincing, the pressure to accept, not to resist, anyway I liked it myself.

'No,' said Lily. 'No, not really, not much. I'll have stuffed tomatoes.'

'She seemed peeved, Anna.'

'Why should she be?' said Lily. 'She promises us some special dish, she makes us promise to come here, then she doesn't have it, why should she be peeved?'

'No reason, I just remarked that she seemed to be.'
'She's got no reason to be,' said Lily.
'Maybe she's embarrassed having promised us and not delivering.'
'I don't see any sign of embarrassment,' said Lily.
And that was incontrovertible.

It was what I always felt about fixed arrangements, they were inconvenient, they were a pressure, and they never delivered what was promised.

'Still, we'd have eaten here anyway, whether there was something special or not.'

'Maybe,' said Lily.

We sat waiting for lunch which seemed an interminable while coming even for Anna's erratic procedures. Maybe it was a day she was refusing to serve. She didn't emerge from the kitchen again. Her sister-in-law took the other orders and we stopped her to order two more drinks while we waited, the tables filling up around us. There was no hurry anyway, we would only have got scorched in the midday sun, why be preoccupied with time, this was Greek time, we were not in America.

'I still wouldn't mind eating,' said Lily, 'and then going on to Greek time after lunch. I wouldn't mind something ordinary. To hell with this special dish nonsense, just anything.'

We were talking about compromising photographs. How being photographed with the wrong company or in the wrong place could cost you a political career. Or how a head from a photograph could be superimposed on a body holding a rifle. The classic dirty tricks conversation of our times. And then by an extraordinary synchronicity, or perhaps an ordinary synchronicity since aren't all synchronicities by definition extraordinary, I looked round towards the kitchen across the road in the hope of an emergent meal, to see a man with a camera about to take a photograph, maybe already had taken a photograph, the camera pointing in our direction.

'Talking of which,' I said to Lily, who looked round too.

The man turned away, talked to another man beside him and they moved on with a woman, a child in a stroller, and a boy with Down's syndrome.

They stopped again a metre or so along.

'Is this the background you want?' the man said, in English, as they stood for a holiday shot, click, and on they went.

I watched them go along the road. It was the unease that was odd. Not the tourist group, the family outing, but the unease of the man with the camera when I turned round and saw him. Or was it just an unease transferred from the conversation, the conspiracies and assassinations and suchlike, old memories of modern times transposed onto a perfectly ordinary group. Two men with short hair, shaved back and sides, trimmed moustaches, a bit too clean shaven for tourists, a bit Rest and Recreational, military on leave, not the shaggy haired tourist style.

'Why photograph here? There's no view. You can't even see the sea through the tables and chairs.'

'No taste,' said Lily.

'It's funny,' I said, 'we were just talking about dodgy photographs and there they are. And the guy looked so uneasy.'

'He saw the paranoid glint in your eye,' said Lily.

And then lunch arrived.

'Enjoy your meal,' said the sister-in-law.

As we were leaving Anna called out to us.

'When you've had your swim come by and we'll have a coffee.'

I nodded amiably.

'We'll probably be there all afternoon,' said Lily.

'Of course you will,' said Anna. 'But when you've had enough come by and we'll have a coffee. Maybe I'll make a cake. I've been meaning to make some cakes.'

She waved away our attempts to pay the bill.

'Fix it up later,' she said. 'You won't be running off with it. I can't do it now, that kitchen, it's like a madhouse, I got the whole family, husband, mother-in-law, sister-in-law, sister-in-law's kids, it's like a jungle, I can't think to add up, give it me later when it's cooled off, when I've cooled off.'

We wandered back around five. The place was deserted, nobody eats at five, most people are still at their siesta, hanging on to another hour's rest. Dimitri emerged from the recesses of the restaurant.

'Anna? No, she's not here. She'll be here later.'

'She said to call by.'

'Call by?' he said. 'Ah well, she'll be here later.'

We stood there aimlessly. Why had we dragged ourselves up from the beach? Now it was a no man's land, no point going back, and nowhere to go on to.

'You want to see her?' he asked.

'Just to fix up the bill,' said Lily.

'Fix up the bill?'

He took out his pack of cigarettes, shook one out, lit it.

'What do we owe?'

'You'll have to ask Anna,' he said. 'She does all that.'

He blew a column of smoke into the air, the picture of non-involvement.

'You want a beer or something?' he asked.

'Might as well,' I said.

'I'll bring it out to you.'

We sat looking at the late afternoon beach. The water lapping, nothing else moving. Dimitri came out with the beers and stood with his back to the view. He started a story about working in New York, drugs and guns, it was all drugs and guns, that's how you make your money, but once you're in it you're in it for life, or death, you can never get out, you can't make your million and retire, no one ever retires from that, they've got you locked in. It was abstract, conceptual. No good stories, no vivid reminiscences. More like a business administration manual, lacking the literary specificity of fiction. Anna drew up, took over, Dimitri went back to his cavern, she made coffee and came and sat with us.

'No, he can do it all, that's what he's there for, I don't have to start yet, life's too short, that's what I say, they can wait for their dinners for once, if it's not ready it's not ready, anyway it is ready, it's all prepared.'

She sat there, rabbiting on aimlessly.

It was too early to eat, a few people were moving along the street, the lights went on outside the bar next to the restaurant, some people came into the reed-covered bar extension next to where we were sitting, and there was a flash.

'What's that?' said Lily.

Anna carried on talking, Dimitri this, mother-in-law that, the public something else again.

'Just someone taking a photograph,' I said.

Across in the bar area next door were three tourist looking types, designer sunglasses, chains, bangles, rings, one of them with her back to the beach holding a camera up to her eye, wavering around, uncertainly, but in our direction. And then the lights came on in the bar extension and they left.

'Let's settle the bill,' said Lily.

'Oh the bill, forget it,' said Anna.

'No, don't be ridiculous.'

'It's nothing.'

'It was a beautiful lunch.'
'Don't worry about it.'
'No, we've got to pay,' said Lily.
'It's too hard.'
'We had salad, egg plant, stuffed tomatoes, two beers, two orange juices.'
'Make it a thousand,' said Anna.
'That's not enough.'
'That's plenty,' she said.

There were no taxis to be seen. We walked back to the village, up the uneven unsurfaced winding road from the coast, as the brief twilight rapidly faded to evening and the hills took on a dark menace of indecipherable blackness, trees, boulders, ravines, bushes, gullies.
'This is madness,' said Lily.
'Think of it as keeping fit.'
'We could be set upon by brigands and no one would ever know.'
'The brigands are all entertaining the tourists down on the coast.'
'Like Dimitri.'
'Like Dimitri. Or Anna. It sounded to me like he's in some racket or other.'
'Why won't she take our money?'
'Maybe she's already been paid.'
'What do you mean?'
'I don't know,' I said, 'just a thought.'
'What sort of thought?'
'One that just popped out,' I said.
'Well pop it back in and find out what it means.'
'I suppose,' I said, 'I don't know, the only reason you don't take payment is because someone's already settled the bill. You know, like someone's already shouted the round.'
'I don't know.'
'Nor me.'
'Don't close off,' she said. 'Damn, my shoes are ruined on these rocks.'
'Sit down a bit, get your breath.'
'It's not my breath, it's stubbing my toes on these boulders.'
We sat down at the roadside, looking across at the sea, at lights shimmering hazily across the strait.
'She's certainly acting oddly. What was all that about, she asks us to turn up for coffee then forgets all about it?'

'And leaves hubby to hold the fort,' said Lily.

'He was holding the fort too. He's never bothered to talk to us before. So why does he come out and talk to us tonight?'

'So we don't go away.'

'But what did he want to keep us for?'

'So we'd pay the bill.'

'But Anna didn't want us to pay the bill.'

The light glimmered, the crickets sang, the owls screeched as they criss-crossed the scrub. Suddenly there was a flash of light across us.

'What's that?' said Lily.

'A car coming down the road.'

We looked round, the lights spraying across the trees as the car wound its way past.

'That flashlight,' I said. 'Maybe that's what it was. Keeping us there till those people took a photograph.'

'Were they photographing us?'

'I don't know. When I looked up they seemed to be pointing the camera in our direction. I don't know where they were pointing it when the flash went off.'

'Why would they want to photograph us?' said Lily.

'I don't know. But it was the same as at lunch, remember? The special lunch that never materialised. And then that great delay till we got served. And then those tourists with the camera.'

'With a child with Down's syndrome.'

'And the military haircuts.'

We slept on it. Not especially well. We waited to hear whispers, explosions, slamming doors, clicking shutters. In the morning it was all calm and banal. We sat outside the house and looked across the village as we drank our coffee.

'Whatever it is, she's a hassle.'

'Maybe,' said Lily, 'she's just lonely.'

'Maybe she is. Maybe she's crazy. She's certainly erratic. It's such a nightmare even to pay the bill, come back for change, come back when I work it out.'

'It needn't be anything personal,' said Lily. 'They probably do this to everybody, check them out, find out where they've come from, who they are.'

'They might. But I don't see her carrying on like this to anyone else.'

'We probably wouldn't notice.'

'It's the coincidence of the cameras. That's what seems odd to me. That first lot, I turned round before they took a picture, I think I threw them just by turning round at that moment and looking at them. Maybe he didn't get a shot so they had to send a second team in.'

'And that child?'

'What about him?'

'Are you trying to tell me they are using agents with family groups and children with Down's syndrome?'

'The very fact of your scepticism shows what excellent cover it would be.'

'I suppose it would,' she said.

'Though it does seem a bit unlikely,' I conceded.

'It certainly does.'

'But why should it be any different here? Once you're on a list you're on a list. Why would it stop just because you go somewhere else? There isn't anywhere else. It's all one world.'

Whatever, we went down to the other beach, the original beach. There was no sign of the microvia. Quiet day, calm sea. There was only one restaurant and there was only fish, the fish were still in season, so there were no other dishes.

'Later in summer,' explained the German holidaymaker, 'then they have other things. But now this is early and there are not many tourists yet so they don't prepare other dishes.'

He arrived dusty and plaster splattered on his motor bike, his girlfriend on the pillion. He carried in his camera case when he parked the bike. He was helping a friend restore a house, he said.

But he kept to himself. He talked to us about the fish but then he and his girlfriend sat the other end of the terrace.

The owner took our order and his wife brought us fish and salad and beers and left us alone.

'It's different,' said Lily.

'For a while.'

17

The Black Rocks

In the middle of the night I announced that this was the last holiday I would ever go on. It was unbearable, I said, intolerable.

I had said it before, on most previous attempts at holidays. The snoring, the plumbing, the noises of pissing, drinking, singing, talking, fucking, farting, fighting in the neighbouring rooms. It was all unendurable, the sounds of human life.

It was Lily's bursting into tears over the pigs that upset me now. I could not disagree with her emotions in this case. I would have felt the same if I had been willing to feel them, but I did not want to feel them. The lady at the *chambre d'hôtes* had come out when we were sitting in the evening heat drinking from a bottle of *côtes du Rhône*. She was off to see her little pigs. Did we want to see her little pigs ? Of course Lily said yes. I, like I generally did these days, declined.

She came back shattered. It was the worst thing she had ever seen in her life. They were all inside the piggery, in their narrow stalls, tied up, eating, shitting, eating, until the time came to take them to the slaughterhouse. They were never let out, never went into the fields, never saw the light, never had the chance to walk.

She scrubbed the pig shit off her shoes in the shower and burst into tears in bed. The acrid smell of pig shit kept us awake all night, hung in the corners of the room, came in on the hot air through the open windows, so that we choked on every breath.

We left after the one night. The lady was disappointed, we had said we would stay for two, maybe three. We left so hurriedly we forgot the wine and lettuce and tomatoes and fruit we had put in the fridge.

The next day we had onion tart and Lily picked out all the bits of ham.

I did not point out the eggs used were probably from battery hens, the worst thing we had ever seen on a previous holiday, the hens kept in row upon row of boxes, their beaks pared, no chance to move, never let out, no chance to ever see the light. Nor did I remark that the pig had lived and died in vain if the scraps of ham were simply thrown away. I did not want to remark on any of it. I did not want to know it, all this that was already known too well.

Why was it when travelling that these dreadful encounters occurred? Doubtless because in my daily routines I knew where to turn away, where to cross to the other side. We ate no meat, no fish, but that was only for ourselves. We knew the slaughter went on, the forced feeding, the factory farming.

Even without factory farming it was bad enough. And again it was while travelling, in a Thai village, visiting my compassionate writer friend, that it made itself inescapable. The sound of the tractor going at funeral pace along the village street. And five minutes later, the awful death cry of the animal as it was slaughtered.

'Every night,' said Pira, 'every night they kill one cow.'

We couldn't bear it. We opened another bottle of wine to obliterate it.

We were both compassionate writers. I had become so compassionate I could hardly write any more. 'What is the greatest injustice in your country?' Frankie asked. Frankie wrote movingly about social injustices in the Philippines.

I could not answer. I was spending my life fleeing the horror. Being compassionate to myself. Maybe it had begun with the bad years, the blacklistings and harassment, when I had had to learn situations to avoid, false friends, last suppers, poisoned chalices, sirens, seductresses, bad drugs. Bit by bit I had had to pull myself away to survive. And now it was all avoidance.

Along the Breton coast the tide fell and the black rocks emerged, the terrible black rocks of lament, breaking through the emerald surface of the enchanting waters, the savage black rocks on which ships foundered, the irreducible black rocks.

'Holidays are always difficult,' said Lily. 'The best ones have always been when we were escaping.'

Running away from my sister and family when my mother had her stroke. Running away from the harassments and driving north, not even knowing ourselves where we were going.

Nor did we know now. But now, I reflected in the middle of the night, I have run away from everything. From life, from love, from art, from death, now everything difficult I have tried to avoid. Now I no longer write about sex or drugs or politics, all too difficult, too unacceptable. And as for writing about writing, fun for once or twice, now that was the final impossibility of all, the full futility and emptiness of that avoidance emptier even than the emptiest sea.

And when the tide went down and the black rocks were exposed, there were still further depths to go, as the water receded from the massive bay of mud and the oyster leases were exposed.

That was why everywhere sold oysters and mussels. The little fishing port we ran away to from the pig farm lived on the production of oysters and mussels. Every restaurant, every bar, every café had huîtres et moules as nos specialités. Great trailers of mussels in wire sacks were towed by tractor along the quay. The smell of emptied oyster shells greeted us in odd corners of the fields back from the coast.

It is not just the killing, it is the mass slaughter. Until refrigeration was developed there was no huge commercial meat trade. And even then the cattle roamed free until they were slaughtered. Before refrigeration not much meat could be eaten since it would not keep. The rich lived on slaughter as they ever do. But the rest of the us ate beans and once a week, maybe, maybe once a month, there was meat.

'Beans!' said my mother, 'we were never so poor we had to eat beans.'

And then intensive food production was developed, the brutality of capital's next stage, piggeries, battery hens, fish farms. The fish are grey with sickness and despair and have to be fed red dye. The hens are fed yellow die to colour the pallid yokes of their eggs.

The hawk hovering at the cliff's edge tells us there was always slaughter. But this cultivated slaughter, the farms of geese force-fed to produce pâté de foie gras, was something else again.

I felt better after indicting capitalism. Probably it would have been sensible to have fled in avoidance of doing that. But once the tide began to turn it was not long before the black rocks revealed themselves.

We drank a lot of wine and ate tomatoes and bread and cheese for lunch and tried not to think of the rennet used to curdle it. Even that was not necessary, it could be done with herbs. Then we walked round the shops and Lily persuaded me to buy a fisherman's hat.

When we had first moved to the island I used to meet this old sea captain on the ferry who had a grizzled sea-dog's beard and wore a fisherman's hat. We began talking one day and it turned out he wasn't an old sea captain but an old actor. He played the part to perfection. Another part, that of teaching drama, he hadn't played so happily.

'I found there came a point one day when I had nothing more to tell them,' he said.

It struck a chord with me.

One morning there was a notice on the ferry wharf giving the time of old Tom's funeral. It shook me. No more sardonic exchanges about the destructive effect of the arts councils, the futility of cultural festivals, the collapse of theatre and music and literature, the domination of it all by the entertainment industry and the consequent destruction of value.

'It was a bit of a horror at the end,' said Joey from the bottle shop. 'He had this heart attack and he managed to phone someone up, but the tide was out and the water police couldn't get to the jetty, so we had to carry him on a stretcher all along the tide line to the ferry wharf. It must have been pretty painful. He was semi-conscious and groaning every so often. There was some big-time heart surgeon at the hospital and they operated for hours, but it was no good.'

That bit I couldn't bring myself to tell Lily, that was something else too painful, something else I would have preferred to flee from.

I put on my fisherman's hat, le capitain, and drove down to buy a notebook and write it all down, or some of it, sitting overlooking the bay, Mont St Michel massive on the horizon. The tide was full, the black rocks hidden beneath the emerald sea. But it would turn.

18

Not the Last of the Long Hot Summers

I had stopped writing apocalyptic fictions. They had begun to seem passé. How many end of the world scenarios could you produce? But that summer we went to Mont St Michel. There were warning signs about the quicksands in the bay, but our feet sank into the melted tar of the car park, it was so hot. We had come from Rabelais's birthplace and the heat in the Loire valley had reduced that small stone home to silence. There were illustrations in the display case of Gargantua pissing, but outside our sweat evaporated before it even reached the surface of our skin. We slaked our thirst on supermarket wines, with that ineffable flavour imparted by the petrochemical refineries and cellulose plants along the Rhône valley.

Mont St Michel and St Malo had just been rocks in a salt marsh before a tsunami had swept out all the bay back in 790. And now the Himalayan ice was melting and flooding Bangladesh, raising the sea level that way, while the monsoons failed to deliver their rains over the rest of the country. People used to say it was the nuclear tests that were changing the weather patterns when the Americans and then the French held their nuclear tests. Then they said it was holes in the ozone layer that was doing it,

Now there were other bombings. Government buildings, metro systems, public utilities, hotels, embassies. It was surprising really that in the heat anyone could get themselves together to make and plant bombs. Unless they had air conditioned laboratories to work in. We rather suspected they did. The myth of terrorists was surely pretty well exploded by now. Everyone knew that at some level these were all inside jobs. You would need to know so much to make the bombs and know where to place them. It all seemed palpably the work of the state security organizations. But why? To keep us in a state of fear and terror? Weren't we already deeply enough in that? Apparently not.

The subways used to be billed as places of retreat in the event of nuclear war. Now they were the site of gas attacks, explosions, serial killers and random gun attacks. Something was going on. Or was it in fact that nothing was going on and all these events were simply staged to give the illusion that something was? This was the postmodern confusion about image and reality for which the philosophers and literary theorists had been trying to soften us up for decades.

We went back to our antipodean island to the coldest winter in a century. But compared with other winters we had been in it was mild. We stopped buying the newspapers and stopped watching television. We knew what the news was. Another former political leader indicted for corruption. More public funds siphoned off into family trusts. Why did they keep telling us this? It was obvious the current political rulers were equally corrupt yet they always survived, until their time came. Why did they expect us to believe of care about any of it? Maybe that was it. They wanted us to stop caring. Well, we did.

These were the ominous times in which the only positives left were negatives, refusal the only remaining choice. It was the only satisfaction available. But what a satisfaction. The newspapers were there, the magazines, we did not even open them, we glimpsed them from the corner of our eye at the street corner stands or through the open doorways of newsagents we no longer entered. Every day they exuded lies and poison, and our delight was in refusing to purchase them. Their posters became daily more strident as they tried to solicit a readership. But the mass refusal had begun, outside the shops the papers lay bailed up in yellowing stacks of returns, pallid simulacra of the autumnal leaves the trees felled to provide the wood pulp might in a better life have produced.

The weekend ones were the first to go. They were the most blatant, their endless provision of items promoting envy and dissatisfaction, between the blocks of advertisements for pseudo-satisfactions, cars, watches, drinks, revealed their strategy so nakedly. Resent the wealth of the billionaire in this story and buy a stupid overpriced watch or pen or other piece of junk so you can pretend you have the disposable wealth to waste as if you were a billionaire, though the billionaires would all have used the wealth to invest in some further exploitative project to suck more labour and resources and wealth out of the impoverished working poor and the despoiled and degraded nature.

Once we'd given up the weekend papers peace was restored to us. The sun shone, the cicadas hummed, there was no shroud of newsprint encasing our days. After then it was but a moment's decision to refuse the dailies. The weekly reviews had all died anyway. Occasionally a new 'independent' appeared, but 'independent' was one of those examples of the great semantic shift of our last days, like peace-keeping forces, freedom, choice, flexibility, education.

Next we refused television. Television news had never made much sense anyway, you needed to read the newspapers to find out what the flow of images purported to represent. Without the newspapers they represented nothing much at all, just distraction and sensation. The sitcoms had become increasingly distasteful, the movies we had either seen time and time again before, or were remakes and reshufflings of what we had seen time and time again before. It had all become increasingly stylized and insignificant. Yes, there were one or two things that still diverted us. But denying them gave a force to the pleasure of refusal. Without them to refuse, it would not have been of any satisfaction, just a matter of not switching on. Whereas to switch off decisively and refuse to switch on, that restored a sense of volition to us. And we needed that.

From then on it was a straightforward process. The details do not need to be inventoried. The joy was the joy of refusal and the consequent obliteration from our lives of the refused. There would be no return of the repressed. Whatever it was, once we had got started, had never been worth our attention anyway: cheapjack fashions, tawdry games, processed foods. Our consciousnesses were freed from brand names and petrol prices. Now we had a space in which to grow.

It became idyllic again. At dawn the crows and currawongs and magpies and kookaburras sang to us, taking over from the owl that had grunted all night. There were mysterious aircraft movements in the curfew hours but we had never believed the curfew was observed anyway. At night we would sit on the deck and look at the stars in a clear sky, watching the satellites track past as they watched us.

We used to complain about the old fashioned stories. All that structure of beginning, middle and end. Times have changed, we would say, we need new forms for new times. We need to reflect current social reality. Well, now we had it. Now we could dispense with the beginning and the middle. Now it was just stories of the end. And now we had stopped writing them.

19

Fabled Cities

The fabled cities of fiction were always spy worlds, spy cities, it seems, sites of surveillance and betrayal, red-baiting and blacklisting, informing and disinforming and deforming. Seems, of course, because in such a context how could certainty be expressed? How could you ever know? I can see now why so many writers were in the business, the great game, the company. It must have seemed like a splendid source of inner knowledge, privileged information, plots. Though being sworn to secrecy presented a problem; unless part of the business was to tell some licensed tales. And that would have presented its problems, too, recounting official lies rather than revealing the hidden truth. Perhaps not. Perhaps some of them enjoyed that, the feeling of doing their bit. In those early days none of this was an issue, we didn't concern ourselves with the secret world, the invisible government. We took ourselves seriously, we were not commercial genre writers, and all that area seemed the make-believe of sensation. But then sensation entered our lives. The government was dismissed by the governor-general. November 11, 1975. One of those significant days. The day they hanged Ned Kelly. Armistice day. Another myth, another great defeat to commemorate, another anniversary. No blood, no slaughter for this one, but it was in its own way a massacre. This time our innocence was destroyed, our naivety. Some of it, anyway, the outer layer of our delusions. And in the unfolding of events, in the retrospective surveys of the incidents leading up to the coup, so rapturously reported by the media, the hand of secret government, of foreign agencies, of the dirty tricks of the spy world were splendidly revealed. And nothing ever looked the same again. Now the themes of Berlin and Alexandria, Geneva and Saigon, Tangier and Vienna were our themes too. I am amazed that we have not welcomed this more than we did. Now we could look at the world around us, our immediate world, and see the signs of deceit and treachery, inauthenticity and subterfuge permeating everything, everywhere, everyone. Now every barman could be an informer, every restaurant a listening post, every journalist on a second payroll, every writer, every reader something else again. And once you thought the wrong thoughts, and expressed them, you were forever on a list.

It was not a transformation without its problems. How would you, could you, write about political realities unless you were in them? I thought about it, more than once. What a theme for a novel. But how could you handle it? And how would you know you'd got it right? And if you couldn't get it right, why do it? Would you have the trusted senior political figure, anonymous bureaucrat, department head, whatever, referred to in the press but unnamed, would you have him saying to the governor-general, 'Sir John, our American friends – or would it be our American cousins, second cousins, maybe – anyway, them, our leaders, are worried about what's happening, naming CIA personnel, threatening not to renew the American secret base leases, yes, the American-Australian joint-facilities as they are properly called, though tightly controlled by the Americans alone, they're up for renewal next month, got to give a year's notice, so, Sir John, we've got to get rid of them, the government, by then, could you oblige? Sir.'

What sort of dialogue would there have been? A polite request? A peremptory order? A threat? Blackmail, bribery, flattery? What do they normally do? Well, we know what they do, the record shows what they do, but how they do it, at the dialoguic level, isn't recorded. Over a round of golf? A summons to the US embassy? A clandestine coffee? A whispered exchange in a church? A society hostess bringing two figures together at a salon? A secret service briefing?

Not knowing the intimate detail of how it is done makes it less persuasive, of course. No doubt that is why the way these things are done is not much revealed. The canister on the pigeon's leg. The invisible ink. The pillow talk.

And this removal of a political leader was a bloodless one. No trained assassins lurking in book depositories or on grassy knolls. No besieged presidential palace being strafed by air force jet fighters, no tanks bursting their way through the parliamentary doors, no psychological operations specialists playing bad American music through loudspeakers, no months of well publicised build-up followed by massive bombardment with bombs and missiles and full-scale physical invasion.

Two pompous old men. Lawyers. Well, there have been law dramas. The cut and thrust of legal opinion. Isn't that one of the more dubious genres?

Don't we assume now that it's all fixed out of court with plain envelopes and used banknotes and the barristers' theatre is simply that, a theatre of distraction. So we could have barristers and their bagmen, the advisers, their hot lines. The governor-general supervising the sound-proofing of his office. Spending the weekend at the secret signals installation. DSD. Acronyms are always good for a frisson of knowingness.

Car chases. The mysterious money broker Khemlami met at the airport and spirited away with his bags of telexes to a secret motel by secret service men, followed by newsmen. The telexes that will tell all. All the administration's money raising schemes now displayed as corruption. In the end the telexes tell nothing. Nothing ever emerges. Still, at the time it gave an action shot. Speeding cars. Foreign money-lender, sinister per se. That it comes to nothing is unimportant, the suspicions discredit the government and that is enough. Unfulfilled narrative, the notation of our post-modern times.

And there is some continuity of image. Another speeding car. The prime-minister-to-be speeding to the governor-general's lodge, palace. Squealing brakes. Scattered gravel. The usual fx. Not the clip-clop of horses from Regency romance.

And then the huddled conversations. Shot through a long lens in the absence of dialogue. The top-hatted GG in his morning coat, the prime-minister-to-be in his country gent gear, riding coat, jodhpurs, the squatter touch. A man is sent out. Speaks to the driver. The car is moved on round the back, parked out of sight. Maybe the gravel is raked over to remove signs of the arrival.

Yet another speeding car. Another patrician figure. The prime-minister alights to see the governor-general.

A two-up shot makes the point. 'Shall I park round the back?' the driver asks. 'No, no, no just leave it here,' says some aide. Inauthentic but it makes the point. The point that it's not going to take long; and the other point that the soon to be-ex-prime minister doesn't know his replacement is already there, shut away in a back room, sipping a sherry maybe, or a scotch, waiting for the soon to be ex-prime minister to be dismissed, ready on hand to take the reins of office. Giddy-up.

The problem is not in the dramatic potential. Big men in suits. Black cars. Gravel. 'You're fired.' Doors opening and shutting. Car doors, residence doors, office doors, secret signals intelligence bunker doors. That has the iconography of it all. The problem is the motivation. Who would do it and why? A government already tottering. Likely to be out of office anyway within six months. A government that has already betrayed whatever socialist commitment the Labor movement ever had, no threat to international capital, no threat to anyone except itself.

I remember talking about it all to Phelan. 'We should make a movie about the coup,' I said. 'Why don't we write a script?'

He gave his usual, edgy shuffle. 'Yeah?' he said. He'd been talking about it, how it was planned in Queensland, he seemed to know. The University of Queensland had been taken over as Macarthur's headquarters in World War II: maybe they had just kept a base there, the OSS and its successors and some tame academics. There were always people around in those days who seemed to know things. I never thought to ask how.

The troops were on grey alert. It sounded so – what did it sound? – so knowing. Those coterie terms, those technical designations. Released to the public, we leapt on them, as if there was a secret language of the secret state, and knowing it we could share their intimacy with secrets. Grey alert, extreme prejudice, safe houses, wet jobs. They gave an authenticity, no doubt spurious, to any cold war spy novel, any journalistic investigation. Deep throat. Once you knew that, the secret phrase, the code name, you knew all the news. And we fell for it. Grey alert.

So there it was. Phelan, who lived alone with his German shepherd dog, or two German shepherd dogs, ferocious beasts, barking when anyone approached the door. And knew all about these things. And didn't want to collaborate on any film treatment of them.

Mel was another one who knew things. He leafed through my copy of one of the books on the coup that appeared

'Look at this Trotskyite idiocy,' he said, '"the phones to trade union headquarters were jammed with indignant workers demanding militant action?" What bullshit. What militant workers? The phones weren't jammed, they were cut off, the plug was pulled.'

Books and pamphlets appeared alleging CIA involvement in the coup. But the logic of conspiracy theory is unstoppable. Maybe, it inevitably had to be considered, these very books were part of the conspiracy. Certainly they were internally inconsistent. Their analysis of the government's reformist betrayal of the workers was a persuasive indictment. But if true, why then would there be any need to remove such a government that had just brought down an anti-worker budget and initiated such pro-business policies?

The conspiracy theories stressed the governor-general's connections with wartime security and the CIA's Congress for Cultural Freedom and

Asia Foundation. The liberal nationalists focussed on his being governor-general and ascribed the blame to Britain and the royalty, fuelling a republican movement and helping launch another splendid diversionary politics. The Prince of Wales' chance of becoming next governor-general was scuppered. The contradictions in the theories were striking. But contradictions are the very stuff of conspiracy. As we have come to expect now, the best conspiracies build them into their structure so the truth is never apparent, everything is arguable, everything refutable, nothing conclusive: except the fact of the contradictions.

So if there was a conspiracy, instead of trying to cover it up the strategy would be to let it surface, but let it surface in ultra-leftist publications that have no credibility, and that are probably permeated if not controlled by intelligence operatives anyway. By having the theories surface in such tainted sources they will fail to gain acceptance in so-called respectable, conventional discourse; but if they had been totally suppressed, inevitably they would at some point begin to surface, and so gain credence. Best to raise them and discredit them immediately.

Conspiracy replaced fiction in our preoccupations. It had all the plots that fiction had come to lack. It became a new mode of discourse, endlessly deconstructable. It irretrievably altered our world view, as drugs had done. Indeed, drugs, we were soon to deduce, came from the same source that brought you coups and conspiracies.

And the more we read of intelligence organisations, combing through accounts of them to try to understand our recent politics, the more it became clear that the gathering of information, the spying component, was not the significant part of their operation. Foreign enemies were one thing. But the control of domestic affairs, it slowly became apparent, was far more important. The real story, if anything can be so described with any conviction in such a context, was about the suppression of internal dissent. More than that, the suppression of questioning so that dissent never reached subversion, and questioning never reached dissent. Which implied that all around you people were watching and listening and informing and reporting back. And more than that; informing employers and thwarting ambitions, ruining careers and blocking publications, discrediting and demoralising and disabling anyone who asked the wrong questions, let along anyone who came up with the appropriate answers.

It had been written about before, but not in our societies. The good soldier Schweik knew that every café had its resident informer. Joseph Conrad knew that every intellectual was observed and every dissident group penetrated. Stendhal and Balzac and Dumas and Hugo knew that police spies and political surveillance were basic to the society that was their subject. But that was something lacking in our own literary tradition. A significant absence indeed. And moving from the tradition to the contemporary, it needed only a cursory look at our own literary environment to see the suggestions that all was not a cosy and sympathetic as once it had seemed. How could it have been? Why would it have been? In the end books began to appear that reported how our writers and intellectuals and movie stars had been subject to security surveillance, but they were never very interesting books. The reported files were very boring. The real story, which was not reported, was in the use made of the information for blacklisting, career destruction, domestic disruption, psychological destabilisation, tax auditing, police targeting, disruptive break-ins, spreading of gossip and scuttlebutt, discrediting, harassing, destabilising, not on the macro scale of coups and presidential assassinations, but in the immediate, everyday little world of man and woman. Simple character assassination.

The coup had focused attention on secret manœuvres, which in turn revealed how they were all around and probably had been for ages. And that in itself was a revelation that helped the secret state, creating fear, suspicion, isolation, paranoia. The point about secret police societies is that they let people know they operate that way and so instill a climate of fear and paralysis and doubt, that achieves far more than other police operations ever could.

To attempt to combat it by writing about it helped, paradoxically, to reinforce the fear and paralysis and doubt. Here it was, all around us, if only we chose to see. Many chose not to, and who can blame them? It was never that easy to see. Here it was, but always ambiguously, so that we never really could see clearly. Nothing could ever really be certain, and everything would always be contaminated with suspicion and unease. And here we were, amidst it all. Our eyes how opened and our minds how darkened. We viewed it all in wild amazement.